FRESH. CURRENT. AND TRUE TO YOU.

Dear Reader,

What you're holding is very special. Something fresh, new and true to your unique experience as a young African-American! We are proud to introduce a new fiction imprint—Kimani TRU. You'll find Kimani TRU speaks to the triumphs, problems and concerns of today's black teens with candor, wit and realism. The stories are told from your perspective and in your own voice, and will spotlight young, emerging literary talent.

Kimani TRU will feature stories that are down-to-earth, yet empowering. Feel like an outsider? Afraid you'll never fit in, find your true love or have a boyfriend who accepts you for who you really are? Maybe you feel that your life is a disaster and your future is going nowhere? In Kimani TRU novels, discover the emotional issues that young blacks face every day. In one story, a young man struggles to get out of a neighborhood that holds little promise by attending a historically black college. In another, a young woman's life drastically changes when she goes to live with the father she has never known and his middle-class family in the suburbs.

With Kimani TRU, we are committed to providing a strong and unique voice that will appeal to *all* young readers! Our goal is to touch your heart, mind and soul, and give you a literary voice that reflects your creativity and your world.

Spread the word…Kimani TRU. True to you!

Linda Gill
General Manager
Kimani Press

 KIMANI PRESS™

JDGuilford

The Edification of
Sonya CRANE

KIMANI
TRU
™

THE EDIFICATION OF SONYA CRANE

ISBN-13: 978-0-373-83077-0
ISBN-10:   0-373-83077-7

www.kimanipress.com

Printed in U.S.A.

To Ronica, Lin, and Momma aka Big Mo

and

To all my shining scholars, wherever you are.

Acknowledgments

In the fall of 2003, I moved to New York City with twelve dollars and a dream. I was going to write books. I was going to change minds. Had someone told me that I would move five times in three years, that I would subsist on pizza and Twinkies, or that the machine of New York would crank me through its cogs and then cough me out like a fur ball, I would have scoffed. But it did. Oh, it did.

And yet, here I am, tapping out my New York retrospective in the acknowledgments section of my debut novel. For this first opportunity to change minds, I have many people to thank. I will begin by thanking those who provided the chance for publication. To my glorious editor, Evette Porter; thanks for your time, your hard work and your sense of humor. To Linda Gill and Kimani TRU/Harlequin Books; I truly appreciate this opportunity.

I would like to give a special thanks to the woman behind the mask, überagent and literary mastermind Mondella Jones (*holler*). Who'd've thunk it? Who would have guessed that ranting over muffins at nine in the morning would lead to this? We've come a long way, baby. (Shhh. It's still too early to tell the full story). And, of course, I have to holler at Tracy Grant, the man who models the tenacity of a true writer. Thanks for the couch, the groceries and the real-world advice.

For their unconditional support, I thank Carolyn Ball (aka Mrs. Bell), William Ball and Pamela Upchurch. Without them, I would surely have died of scurvy. For providing the wind beneath my wings and serving as my Sunday study buddy, I send love to fashionista and longtime friend, Ngozi Odita. Ngozi, I promise I'll learn to share. For reading every page and giving honest, critical feedback, I thank Randolph and Iris Jacobs and Joanne Jacobs.

For sharing the horror and wonders of "this subfusc conurbation," I thank Ain "A. A." Grooms. Watch out, 'cause she's taking Vandy by storm. For answering the bat call whenever I needed pictures, thanks to April Jean, fellow writer and photographer to the stars (but what do I know). For the never-ending salads, cervezas and burgers at the pool, I send my undying gratitude to Gisele Litalien. Gisele, thanks for the shoulder. For a song that I am still singing, I sing my praises to Keesha White. And, for proving I'm not the only idiot who'll jump headfirst, I will continue to laugh and cry with Ayanna Williams. (Do it yourself!)

To Lamar Bryant, Jr., Adia Rasheema Johnson, Cary Jordan and Arteria Stephens, I type these two words: *Your turn.* Get out there and do it (well, I guess that's eight words). To the incomparable Farae: I feel the love. And I promise to pick up a pen and scribble something to you soon. To Erica Ash, see you on the silver screen.

Peace Queen and all that jazz to Derrin Moore. Derrin, thanks for going through it with me on Wrenwood, for sharing red wine and boiled eggs, for lining up those thangs and for being that regular black girl. I send my heart.

William Michael Smith, we have single-handedly kept money wire transfers alive and running. From the banana-chocolate-chip muffin behind the stairwell to the cabbie working off the brown-paper-bag rule, you've always been there.

To Walter Felton: you betta step! I'll see you in Brazil. And Akilah, you know you got on my last nerve with your "hundred times more" mantra, but you were write (get it). Now, it's your turn. To LaToya Denise Seal, I'm happy to see you've finally given in to your inner beauty. Keep shining.

Y, por mi amigo, Alexis Rivera, *gracias por su ayudan con mi español. Mira, necissito mas practicar.*

Lastly, thanks to all of my students everywhere. Your stories, your lives, your insight and your triumphs continue to inspire me.

THE EDIFICATION of
SONYA CRANE

part one

01

Hi, man…

Sonya hated Tuesdays. She hated doing what she had to do.

As usual, she heard her mother as she clacked through the hallway in her stiletto heels and crisp black business suit. Her mother would straighten things that are already straight and hum her anxious Tuesday hum. Today the sunlight streamed through the bare fifteen-foot windows, the harsh light cutting across the glossy cement floors. Sonya sat on the couch with her arms folded across her chest, staring straight ahead—staring at nothing. Sonya's mother shuffled across the room awkwardly in her high heels and sat next to Sonya. Her mother scratched her arm and smiled tightly, looking up at Sonya pleading like a puppy.

"Damnit! What?" Sonya said without turning to look at Doris Crane. She bit off the *t* in "what" making the sound scissor sharp. The shelf that held the crystal vase was now empty. Each week Sonya came home to find something missing, something sold or, more likely, traded by her mother. Last week it was the plasma television. The week before, it was the painting above the living room mantel.

"I'm...I'm..." Her mother reaches to stroke Sonya's hair, but she pulled away.

"Doris, stop," Sonya barked. "And don't apologize. I'm sick of this."

Her mother's voice became thin and plaintive. "I thought we agreed you wouldn't call me that?"

"It's your name isn't it?" Sonya said. "Let's get this over with." She threw her book bag over her shoulder and marched toward the door. The tartan skirt of her Crestman School uniform gathered under her bag. Doris stays seated.

"Mother!" Sonya eyes blazed hate. "Aren't you coming?"

"I have a meeting." Doris sucked her teeth and scrunched her face into an apologetic grimace.

"You'll have to..." her mother began.

"Take the fucking train again," Sonya said. "Whatever, Doris. Whatever."

The previous year, Sonya's teachers at Crestman agreed she needed therapy. "Despondent," her progress reports read. "Aloof." "Barely speaks above a whisper in class." A week or so after this second round of freshman progress reports, Doris found Sonya in tepid bathwater with her wrists gurgling blood. Doris rushed Sonya to Northside Medical where a friend of Doris's patched her up and agreed to keep Sonya's suicide attempt under wraps.

Doris asked her friend to recommend a therapist. She wanted someone discreet, someone far away from Buckhead, someone her clients would never run into. As one of the top realtors in Atlanta, selling million-dollar homes to neurologists and rock stars alike, Doris had an image to maintain. She chose Dr. Hillman mostly because his office was located in East Atlanta, in an all-black neighborhood. Surely, Doris thought, it was a place none of her clients frequented.

When Doris announced Sonya's Tuesday appointments with Dr. Hillman, Sonya shrugged her shoulders and kneaded the bandages on her wrists. "Whatever Doris," she said. "What-the-fuck-ever."

In the beginning, Dr. Hillman attempted to do his job. He asked Sonya questions he thought would draw her out. Sonya sat in the oversized leather chair and stared at Hillman with the same blank look she reserved for Doris.

Dr. Hillman pointed to Sonya's wrists. "How did that happen?"

"I clapped too hard," Sonya said. "How the fuck do you think? I slit my wrists."

"Why?" Dr. Hillman's eyes grew wide with concern.

Sonya smiled a quick, mean smile. "I don't know. Love for life."

"Sonya," Hillman sighed, "I'm here to help you. But I can only work with what you give me. And, right now, you're not giving me much."

Looking into Dr. Hillman's pale, seventy-year-old face, Sonya shrugged. "I'm ugly and unpopular. My life sucks. I tried to kill myself. The end."

Still, Hillman wanted to know. So Sonya told him about the father she never knew, about her only memory of him: the cuff of a bright shirt rearing back to slap her three-year-old face. Sonya told Hillman about the deceased grandparents. No aunts or uncles, her mother being an only child. Sonya told him about Samantha Klieg, the only person at the Crestman School Sonya could call a friend. How at first, Sami had been cruel, sliding fat jokes under Sonya's locker door and then giggling from a distance with the other pretty girls as they watched Sonya read the notes. Sonya was aware that she wasn't fat, not by a long shot, she told Dr. Hillman. She just wasn't skinny, or pretty, or popular like Samantha Klieg.

She told Hillman how one evening she went back into the gymnasium after school to search for her missing Algebra binder. She spied Sami behind the bleachers sucking off Mr. Stemma, the drama teacher. Mr. Stemma had his back to Sonya, but Samantha saw Sonya. Their eyes met. After that, an unspoken truce sprung between the two. Samantha left no more notes and she stopped the other pretty girls from laughing at Sonya. She even spoke to Sonya in the hallway. In exchange, Sonya told Hillman, she kept Sami's secret about Mr. Stemma. Mr. Stemma quit a week later, no doubt fearing lawsuit and scandal.

Sonya answered Dr. Hillman's questions unwaveringly. Her voice issued from her mouth monotone and indifferent, crisp as paper. She left some things out, of course: her mother's drug habit, Madison's "favors," and the black girls on the train. Sonya left out the way she coiled up the humiliation she suffered during the day and used it, like a whip of spite, to punish her mother.

Dr. Hillman prescribed Vicodin. He also gave her samples of another drug. "My private stash," he said with a wink. After each hourly session with Dr. Hillman, Sonya tucked the pills into her pocket and left.

One morning while Sonya was at school, Doris found the pills. There were vials and vials of them, four months' worth, stashed in the back of Sonya's underwear drawer. This was before Doris had begun to sell their possessions away. Things hadn't gotten that bad. Each morning, after Sonya left for school Doris slipped into her room and pilfered Sonya's medication. The pills helped get Doris through the days when she could not score any coke or when she had important meetings and needed a little kick, a little boost. One pill became two, then five and then entire vials until Sonya opened her underwear drawer one day and noticed they were all gone.

Sonya pronounced an end to her visits to Dr. Hillman.

"You can't stop going," Doris said. "I forbid it."

"Forbid it?" Sonya exclaimed. "Oh please!"

The standoff lasted two weeks. Doris broke first.

"Mommy needs them," she said. "Just to keep me going. Just to get through this slump. The market's dead right now. Nobody's buying property. I have five houses I need to move."

Doris whined into Sonya's ears. She pouted and frowned. Her voice warbled like a warped record. Listening to her mother talk like this was like looking down at her from the lip of a deep pit. It was like watching a brain-damaged version of her mother, some drooling and helpless woman, braying like a donkey and shitting on herself. It was pitiful. It was sickening.

"Please baby," Doris crooned. "Please, for Mommy."

"Alright, alright, alright," Sonya said. "Just shut the fuck up."

She held herself stiff when her mother kissed her in thanks.

Six months later and Sonya continues to visit Dr. Hillman. Dr.

Hillman has given up his probing since Sonya told him to save his psychobabble bullshit for someone who gave a rat's ass.

"Let's face it doc, I'm a loser," Sonya said in one of her sessions. She looked into Dr. Hillman's face and thought she saw something that resembled agreement. "You get paid to give a fuck. Otherwise, you wouldn't be here. Just give me my happy pills and I promise I won't go for my wrists anymore." Dr. Hillman sighed and slid her pills across the table. He may have even smiled.

Nowadays, Hillman sits across from Sonya and doodles in his steno pad while Sonya plays with the ring tones on her Nokia. Sometimes he nods off. Sometimes he tells amusing anecdotes about his days as a frat boy at Georgia State. Sometimes Dr. Hillman's wife shows up in lieu of his absence. She brings homemade cookies and sips gin mixed with grape Fanta. At the end of each hour, Dr. Hillman slides the pills across the table. Sonya helps herself when Mrs. Hillman is there, taking a vile from Dr. Hillman's top drawer.

Today Sonya leans in to admire Mrs. Hillman's knitting. It is a hideously knotted orange and purple scarf. "That's kind of pretty," Sonya says.

"Really," Mrs. Hillman says. "I could get more yarn. Knit you a sweater."

"Naw, that's okay." Sonya slips her hand into the desk and takes a vile. "Not my style. But it's pretty." She even manages a smile.

"Here," Mrs. Hillman presses another bottle of pills into Sonya's palm. "This one's on me."

Exiting the storefront office, Sonya looks back at the dingy painted window. "DR. H I - - M A N," it reads. Some neighborhood kid, as a joke, has scraped off the L's. How ironic, Sonya thinks. She walks two blocks to the subway station. At least she can look forward to the train ride home.

02

Losing everything

Each time the black girls get on the train, Sonya's heart flutters and dives. She revels in their smell, fruity bubble gum and what she will later learn to be the scent of newly relaxed hair—a sweet, rich chemically aroma. She loves the way they cut their eyes and purse their lips, chiding each other, egging each other on. Leaving Dr. Hillman's office, Sonya usually sees the same group as she and they go to and from their separate schools. Today the black girls board the train laughing loudly and knocking into each other. Their glee disturbs the hush of the car. An elderly black woman wearing a purple dress and flaring hat slaps her purse down in her lap and *tsks,* making a show of her annoyance. The girls continue guffawing. Their merriment is both a performance and a challenge.

A nervous excitement wells inside of Sonya. At that moment, she decides she will say something to the black girls. She will introduce herself. She will tell them she thinks they are beautiful, that black is beautiful. She will find a way to befriend them.

Sonya looks up and then quickly down. She cannot will her mouth to speak.

Though she can no longer read for the thick pounding in her chest, Sonya keeps her eyes focused on the book in her lap. She sneaks looks at the black girls. In quick glances, Sonya studies their round hips, bowed legs and deep brown skin, pulled tight over the hard high bones of their faces. To Sonya, the leader of the group is the most beautiful. Tandy, her name is. Sonya had heard someone call her that before.

Tandy sits on a four-seat row, under the arm of a lank Puerto Rican boy, and sucks a Blow Pop.

"Excuse me," the woman in the hat says. She looks down at Tandy's leg, which is spread across two seats.

"You excused." Tandy rolls her eyes at the woman. She wears a puffy pink jacket and matching sneakers.

"The *train* is crowded," the woman says. "People want to sit."

"Well," Tandy says, "get up and let them have your seat."

The woman *tsks* once more and turns away in a huff.

"Tandy," one of the other girls says. "Yo, Tandy. Why you dissin' us, all up under that niggah like that?"

Tandy pulls her lollipop from her mouth with a smack and rolls her eyes. "Whatever." As she exits the train with the Puerto Rican boy, Tandy pinches her hands to her lips, imitating smoking a joint. "I got to go get my head straight."

"Alright," one of the girls yells.

Another girl chimes in. "Save me a splif."

"I got y'all," Tandy says. "You know I'm always looking out."

For days Sonya replays the scene in her head, even acts it out while her mother is away.

Whatever.

Save me a splif.

I'm always looking out.

Sonya hates her anorexic life—sleepwalking through her classes at Crestman, feeding off Sami's dry crumbs of friendliness. She hates coming home to her mother who is either zonked out of her mind on heroin or curled over files, trying desperately, hopelessly, to move overpriced houses in lackluster neighborhoods. Sonya spends weekends alone in her high, hollow room while Sami necks with Zach Nelson, Crestman's student-body president who also models print ads for Banana Republic. She spends weekends watching *M*A*S*H* reruns while Tandy and the other black girls from the train smoke weed and sneak into clubs with fake IDs.

Sonya wants a life as full and exciting as the lives of the black girls. Sonya wants to have a cheating boyfriend, "no-good ass niggah," the stoutest black girls calls her boyfriend. Of course, Sonya would never say that. She would never use the n-word. But still. Sonya wants to be their friend. Sonya wants to belong.

Two days later, Sonya's mother sits her down in the kitchen of their Buckhead loft to tell Sonya the firm has folded, she has had to sell everything, and, unfortunately, they will be moving. Sonya's face is flush with anticipation, which her mother mistakes for disappointment.

"I've already bought a place." Her mother grimaces with the bad news. It is as if she sees a vase teetering on a faraway shelf, high-up. "It's in East Atlanta." Her mother bares her teeth and winces.

"East Atlanta?" Sonya's heart jumps. Tandy and the other black girls live in East Atlanta!

"I'm sorry, hon." Doris stretches her track-marked arm to stroke Sonya's hair, but Sonya bats her hand away. She hates her mother for being so weak and second-rate. What happened to the woman who made front page of the *Atlanta Journal*? What happened to the person they called The House Hunter?

"What school?" Sonya asks. She prays it is the same school as the black girls, though she is sure it won't be.

"The houses are dirt cheap there," her mother says. "And huge."

"Doris?" Sonya crossed her fingers and shuts her eyes tight. "What school will I attend?"

For years Sonya has had to put up with her mother's drug habit, her teacher's prying and, of course, Madison. The universe should grant her this one wish. She deserves this much.

"Your room is three times the size of—"

"Doris?" Sonya says. All she wants is the bottom line.

Sonya looks into her mother's sorrowful face. She hates her

mother for the same reasons she hates herself: for being puny, for her inability to stand up for anything.

Her mother squeezes her hands together then places them before her on the counter. Doris's once flaxen hair has gone wiry and brittle. Her skin is flat, matte colored. Dull. Her eyes have yellowed along with her teeth. Her hands are the only part of her that remain beautiful. They are long, slender, and a deep milky beige. Sonya looks down at her mother's still-beautiful hands with their elegant pianist fingers. She notices her mother's rings are gone.

"We're so deep in debt. We can't afford the private schools, even if we—"

"Mother," Sonya's voice grows slow and stiff. She balls her fists. "What school?"

Doris sighs. "Paul Lawrence Dunbar."

The name flutters through Sonya's head like a ballerina.

Paul Lawrence Dunbar.

Paul Lawrence Dunbar. In East Atlanta.

Sonya recalls the black girls on the train. Their sweatshirts, when they wore them, read *PLD.* Paul Lawrence Dunbar!

It is almost too much to handle. It is almost too good too be true, like the ending to an after-school special where everyone, even the dumb bully jock, says nope to dope. Sonya uncurls her fists. She feels smiled upon by the universe. East Atlanta. PLD. Finally, her prayers are answered. Finally, she will have a place to belong. Finally, she can become friends with the black girls.

03

A buffalo soldier with teen spirit

A week or so later, they are moved into their new house, a statuesque five-bedroom, newly refurbished with shellacked floors and large, glinting windows. On her first day of school, Sonya wakes up two hours early and paces the floor. Her stomach hops and jiggles. Her heart trembles in her chest.

A question, like a bubble in a bog, floats to the surface of her brain and then pops. "What will I wear?"

First Sonya tries on her distressed jeans and faded Kurt Cobain shirt, going for an I-just-threw-this-shit-on look. But it seems wrong, contrived. It seems exactly what it is: a rich white girl's version of poverty. Of course, they aren't rich anymore. Not by a long shot. But still. Sonya tears off the pants, puts on stretched denim, and changes the Kurt Cobain shirt for a fitted long-sleeve tee with a smiling Bob Marley on the front. This makes her feel even whiter. She thinks better of it and changes back into the Kurt Cobain shirt. But it doesn't go with the new jeans. A tank top, she thinks. After rumpling through her clothes hamper, she finds her favorite—solid black with lace around the hem. She slides into it.

Great. But it is mid-January and forty degrees outside. She'll look like a complete idiot. A sweater, then. She files through stacks of clothes on her closet shelf. All her sweaters are either dark wools or pastel cashmeres. Definitely not right. So, her choice is either Kurt or Bob.

She goes back and forth between the two, trying on each shirt with her jacket and book bag, trying on each shirt as she walks to and from the full-length mirror. The strip of carpet between the bed and the mirror serves as an imaginary school hallway. She tries on the various shirts and practices introducing herself to Tandy and the other black girls.

She extends her hand to her Kurt-shirted self. "Hi, I'm—" No, not Hi. It sounds too pushy. Too exuberant and needy. Too much like someone named *Cathy*, with a *K*.

Sonya switches shirts.

"Hey, y'all," she says to her Bob Marley self.

Hey y'all? What was she, a cowgirl?

She changes shirts again and tries a different greeting. "What's up guys?"

Even worse.

Sonya razzles her hands through her hair. Idiot! What has she gotten herself into? She should have insisted on Northside High. She should have made her mother drive her the twenty-seven miles every morning. But now, it is too late. She will be the only white girl at PLD—an all-black school in East Atlanta! Neither Kurt Cobain nor Bob Marley can save her. She is doomed.

04

Mix-up

Principal Carlton, a banana-colored black man, walks Sonya to her homeroom on the second floor. Paul Lawrence Dunbar looks much different than Crestman. The walls are colored a dull green, nothing like the fresh pastels and whites of Crestman halls. And the ceilings hang low and sag in some places as if bloated with water. The halls are empty mostly, except for an occasionally straggling student. Sonya notices the lockers, dented and multicolored. Some of them lay open exposing textbooks so old the corners are rounded and gnawed.

At the door of her homeroom, Mrs. Larsen Two Two Three, Sonya sits in the back corner (she is still unsure about her final decision: Bob Marley, jeans and suede boots) and watches as other students file into the room. The boys rustle about in their oversized jeans, multicolored jerseys and matching caps tilted at slick, whimsical angles. The girls stand in clumps, smacking and giggling, with their hands tucked into the back pockets of their pants.

Sonya sits stiffly. She feels hyperaware of herself. Like a burglar caught between laser beams, she doesn't move for fear of setting off an invisible alarm. She stares down at her hands which are large and long, translucent as jellyfish, nothing like her mother's elegant fingers. Definitely nothing like the deep browns and rust-colored reds of her new classmates.

"Honey please," a voice echoes from the hallway. "I spent ten minutes on that assignment."

Sonya's insides pirouette. It's Tandy.

Tandy walks into the room with two girls trailing behind her. She holds a stack of notebooks limply in her arms and pops gum on her back teeth. Instinctively, Sonya's hands fly to the side of her head to tuck the hair behind her ears. Then, remembering their hideousness, Sonya slides her hands under the desk. In her head, she practices her introduction. "Hey, what's up," she decided on this morning.

Tandy says goodbye to the other girls, walks down the aisle, and slams her notebooks on the desk next to Sonya's. She sits down with a huff. She crosses her legs, leans back and looks over at Sonya with her head cocked exaggeratedly to the left. Sonya's insides spin double time. She feels a line of sweat tremble down her back. "Hey, what's up," Sonya says, but in the face of Tandy's sharp eyes and glorious, pouting lips, Sonya's little preamble shrivels in her throat.

Sonya thinks perhaps Tandy will recognize her from the train. But she doesn't.

"You're new," Tandy says. "Aren't you?"

This is the moment Sonya has been waiting for. But awe paralyzes her. It is as if she is standing before God, muted by his grace, with a single, fiery question banging against the cage of her soul. This is her one chance, Sonya knows.

She wills her mouth to open.

"I'm Sonya," she says, extending her hand like a foreign diplomat. Tandy looks down at it and scoffs.

"Excuse you, but what's wrong with this picture?" Tandy asks.

Before Sonya can answer, Tandy says, "You're in my seat."

"Oh," Sonya says, withdrawing her hand slowly. "Oh, I—" Sonya stands up to change seats and topples her pencil case in the process. "I'm…" Kneeling, Sonya gathers her supplies. "I'm sorry," she says to Tandy's pink sneakers. She is on all fours frantically snatching up her gewgaws. "I didn't know." Her highlighter rolls behind her and under the radiator. "The guy who brought me—" dust from the floor grays the knees of her pants "—the teacher," she says, pricking her finger on her protractor, "I mean Principal Carlton, he didn't say where I should sit." Sonya grabs up a pink Kim Possible gel pen rolling toward the seat in front of her then reaches for the Wonder Woman eraser wedged just under Tandy's other foot. She finds the base of her mechanical pen, which lay miles away from its stem. Lead filaments are strewn across the floor like a plane crash.

"I'm really really sorry," Sonya says. Her hair loosens from its scrunchee and flies into her mouth. "I didn't know there were assigned seats."

Blood rushes to Sonya's ears. This is terrible. This is worse than anything she could have ever imagined. Sonya feels dizzy and nauseous. She feels idiotic and incompetent and blaringly white. At any moment she will burst into tears.

"Just kidding, girl," Tandy says. She crouches now to help Sonya with the pencils. "That ain't my seat."

Sonya's eyes water in relief. She quickly wipes a tear away.

"I'm Tandy." This time, Tandy extends her hand. Sonya shakes.

"Mrs. Larsen's going to be late," Tandy says. They both rise and take their seats. "She's always late on Mondays."

"Thanks." Sonya sucks the blood from the tip of her finger. The dust from the floor crunches against her front teeth. Tandy is so close Sonya can see the part in her hair and the dark scalp gleaming from beneath.

"You nervous as hell," Tandy observes.

"A little," Sonya says fumbling Kim Possible and Wonder Woman back into their case.

"It's cool." Tandy gives Sonya the pencils she has gathered. "I got your back as long as you don't say anything stupid or try to play me and my girls."

From behind her pricked finger, Sonya's mouth parts in a smile. She can hardly believe her luck. Her first day at PLD and she is talking to Tandy, the friend of her dreams. The first hour of the first day and her dream friend has got her back. She feels excited and ambushed, like a one-millionth customer, greeted with confetti and horns. If she can make it through homeroom without saying anything corny, she stands a chance at being Tandy's friend forever.

"I was new here last year. So, you know," Tandy says. "Just two pieces of advice. One: Don't sit on the toilet after Tunisia Sikes. She's the fat one," Tandy says. "Over there." Sonya spots the girl three rows over. "Heard she got crabs."

"Okay," Sonya says.

"Two: Watch out for Maurice Maitland." Tandy points to a tall, beige boy leaning against a window ledge. He waggles his tongue in their direction and winks. "He can't control himself around mixed girls."

Sonya agrees to this also, to watch out for Maurice Maitland, though she does not know exactly what Tandy means. The word *mixed* throws Sonya off. Tandy smiles wide at Sonya. Whatever it is, mixed is not an insult. Sonya can tell this much.

"You probably hate folks asking," Tandy says, "but which one?"

Sonya's finger no longer bleeds, but she continues to suck it. The nervousness of a pop quiz wriggles in her stomach. She doesn't know how to answer Tandy's question.

"Your father?" Tandy asks. "Is he the black one?"

"Oh," Sonya says. "That?" Then it comes to her. *Mixed. Biracial.* Tandy thinks she is biracial.

Sonya forces a smile. "My father left when I was three," Sonya says, which is true. She will not tell the other part. Not just yet. She will revel, for a few moments, in her newfound belonging.

One word, *mixed,* and Sonya notices the olive tone of her skin, its muted brownness. And her hair, a mass of stringy locks, no longer seems so different from Tandy's or the other girls. But *biracial?* This is a stretch to her, though obviously she could be. At Crestman, Lydia Grant, who looked as white as Sonya, had been biracial.

Everyone had thought Lydia the prettiest freshmen girl. Her creamy face, with its pink lips and gray eyes, was crowned with a poof of curly brown hair. In the span of three months, Lydia made co-captain of the cheerleading squad, queen of the Mini Peach Bowl and assistant editor of the school paper. By second semester Lydia was a shoo-in for homecoming court. But when Lydia's parents visited—a slim Nigerian woman and an angular man from Holland—a buzz ran through the school. Lydia Grant was biracial. Sonya remembers being aghast, not by the fact of Lydia's black mother and white father, which was common enough, but by the fact of her not disclosing it. Instantly, all the things that made Lydia beautiful—her green eyes, her wavy hair and her perfectly tanned skin—became faux, a hoax. "I knew it," Samantha Klieg, second runner up to Lydia for Miss Mini Peach bowl said to Sonya as she lipsticked herself in the girls' bathroom. "I knew that little cunt was up to something." Sonya remembers thinking the same thing, thinking Lydia Grant had cheated.

"I'm sorry," Tandy says now. "I shouldn't have asked about your...your parents. I'm so damn nosy."

"That's okay," Sonya says.

Of course Sonya will have to tell Tandy she is not mixed. But how should she say it? To say, "I'm not black," will sound racist, as if she is denying something, as if she is taking offense. If, on the other hand, Sonya says, "I'm white," then what would that be? A social suicide? A boast?

No matter how she chooses to say it, Sonya knows she has to correct Tandy.

"I'm good though." Tandy smiles wide. "I told Celesta you wasn't white." Then, pointing at the top of Sonya's head, Tandy yells across the room. "Celesta. Celesta! I told you."

A stout, wide-faced girl responds from the other side of the classroom. "She ain't white?" Sonya recognizes her as one of the black girls from the train. Celesta, it must be. "For real?"

"Yep." Tandy smiles proudly. "She ain't white."

A voice booms over the others. "Who's white?" This comes from Maurice Maitland.

Sonya's hands tremble. She hides them under her desk. Celesta walks from one side of the room and Maurice from the other. They are closing in on her.

"Nobody, fool," Tandy says. "Mind your own business."

"You're white?" Maurice Maitland asks Sonya. Other students turn their attention on Sonya.

Sonya hears the accusation in Maurice's question. Her heart thunders in her chest. No words form in her mouth.

Tandy sucks her teeth in annoyance. "Why you got to blow her spot like that?"

"I'm just trying to get the four-one-one on the neo."

"Didn't I just say she is mixed?"

"No," Maurice says.

"Well she is," Tandy says. "What white folks you know would send their kids to PLD?"

"You right," Maurice says.

"White folks don't just roll up in East Atlanta like that," Tandy says.

"Unless they trying to arrest somebody," Celesta says.

"Or get some black thang thang," Maurice says. He and Celesta slap hands.

"Yep," Tandy says, "or buy up our houses and kick us to the curb or some shit."

"Girl," Celesta says, "that gentrification is a motherfucker. Soon East Atlanta will be whiter than Buckhead."

"They only come here 'cause it's cheap," Maurice says.

"Everything's cheaper when you're white," Celesta says. "Cheaper than being black."

"We can't complain," Tandy says. "We let them do it. We let them buy up our property."

Immediately, Sonya's room rolls out before her, bright and humongous and sickeningly pink, her four-post bed sitting in the middle of it all like the lounge of some slave missus.

"Ain't that the truth," Celesta says. "White folks want everything that's ours. First Eminem, then Justin Timber-fake. Now Mariah Carey's claiming black."

"Actually, she says she's biracial," Tandy says. "And that's not the same thing. I mean—" she looks apologetically to Sonya "—it is but…"

"But it isn't," Maurice says. "It's different with Mariah 'cause she wasn't trying to claim that shit before. Now she's a niggah through and through."

"Naw," Celesta says. "She ain't no niggah. She's a wigger. Just like Justin and Elvis and all the other motherfuckers who've been biting black folk's rhymes for years."

"Wiggers, wiggers here and there," Maurice says.

"Wiggers, wiggers everywhere," Celesta finishes. She and Maurice slap five again.

Sonya cannot decide how to fashion her face. Guilt drops an anchor in her belly. It is *her* mother, Sonya realizes, who has sent her white child to PLD. It is *her* mother who is rolling up in East Atlanta *buying up houses*. She and her mother are the people Tandy, Celesta and Maurice are complaining about.

Wigger.

Unlike *mixed,* Sonya needed no help deciphering the meaning of this word.

"So neo," Maurice has made his way to the side of Sonya's desk. He crouches down so that their faces meet and smiles like an evil cat. "What's up? Are you going to let me hit that? Give Maitland some of that yellow splah-dow?"

"Leave her alone," says a dark, thin girl seated behind Tandy. Her voice is wiry, frail almost.

"Shut up, blacky."

"Look who's talking," the girl says.

"Niggahs can't mind their own business," Maurice says. "Coffee-dipped ass. Looking like half-past midnight."

The students around Maurice snicker. The girl with the wiry voice folds her arms and slinks in her chair. Her bottom lip trembles. Sonya becomes afraid. The girl has been hurt trying to defend Sonya from Maurice Maitland, who Tandy told her to look out for. Sonya feels as if she should stand up for the girl. She should say something mean to Maurice Maitland. But she can tell by the glint in Maurice's eyes that no matter what she says, he will be sure to have the last word.

"So," Maurice continues with Sonya, "how about it?"

Tandy pulls Maurice away by the collar of his shirt. "Go to the office and find out about Mrs. Larsen," she says.

To Sonya's surprise, Maurice obeys.

I should tell them, Sonya thinks to herself. *I should tell them now.*

"Don't mind him, Meeka," Tandy says to the wiry girl.

"Don't you just hate ignorant niggahs?" Celesta says.

Sonya knows she cannot answer this question, which is not a question at all. She can't sit here and participate. She can't just sit here as if.

"Stupid-ass niggah," Tandy says.

Sonya smiles tightly, tries not to betray her brain swelling under her skull. How did she ever get herself into this? One minute she is trying on shirts at home and the next minute, she is pretending to be black. She has to say something now before things get out of hand. But Sonya's desire to belong overwhelms her sense of moral obligation.

Tandy glances at her watch. "Mrs. Larsen needs to come on. We're going to the High Museum this week. You ever been?"

"No," Sonya says. Sonya has gone with her mother to nearly every opening last year, but she thinks no is the right answer. "Who goes to museums?" Sonya adds for emphasis. As a new black girl, Sonya has to display the appropriate tastes. Surely, she thinks, black girls don't like museums.

"Tandy goes to museums," Meeka sings.

"Yeah," Celesta says. "She likes boring shit like that. That Discovery Channel shit. Wild Kingdom." Celesta nudges Tandy playfully. "Ain't that your shit girl?"

"Wild Kingdom?" Sonya chuckles her surprise.

Tandy looks directly at Sonya. Her eyes flare angrily.

"Whatever." Tandy opens her notebook and shuffles papers around. She stops and looks at Sonya, then shakes her head. Her lips twist to a mean pout. "Hmmph."

Distress rises like soup under Sonya's skin. Her ears warm and prickle. She has suddenly fallen out of cahoots with Tandy. Sonya sees herself shrinking in Tandy's eyes. She sees herself as Tandy must see her now: a olive-colored girl with stringy hair and gawky hands; a girl who lives in a neighborhood where houses are being bought up by white folks; a girl who listens to Justin Timberlake *and* Mariah Carey; a girl who Maurice Maitland wants to fuck and probably will.

Celesta and Meeka giggle with each other. Tandy continues to shuffle her papers about. Every now and again she cuts her eyes at Sonya and huffs.

"My mom," Sonya says, finally.

Tandy stops mid-shuffle. "What?"

"My mother," Sonya says. "She's the black one."

05

911...

Sonya approaches her new home feeling relieved, anxious and moderately guilty. She went the entire day, eight hours, allowing everyone to think she was black. The freshly cleaned windows wink at her as if they know her secret. Madison opens the door before Sonya puts in her key.

"Hey, babe," he says from behind his sunglasses. He stands in the door's opening in a leather jacket and boxer shorts, nothing else. His smile is deceivingly friendly. Over the years Sonya has learned not to trust it.

"Madison," Sonya says. "Oh."

"It's early," he says. "We weren't expecting you for another couple of hours." Madison leans just inside the door with his arms and ankles crossed.

"I'm tired," Sonya says. Only after she says this does she realize she is. "Could you please just—"

"Whoa." Madison pushes against her chest and cups Sonya's right breast.

His touch sends a dry heave through her body.

"What's wrong?" he smiles.

"It's cold out here," she says. Already, she hears the plea entering her voice. Already, she feels herself caving in under his eyes, which, she knows, are staring at her from behind his motorcycle shades.

"What time does school let out these days anyway?"

"Three-thirty," Sonya answers absently. She wants to get past him, to her mother. She wants to know her mother is okay.

"I'm hungry," she says, as if he would care.

"Whelp." Madison rears his head, lifts his shades, and squints at his watch. "Got a couple of hours before dinnertime. What's a girl to do?"

Sonya trembles, though not from the cold. She is caught in limbo. She cannot enter until Madison gives his permission, yet she has nowhere else to go.

Madison reaches his hand under Sonya's armpit and cups her breast firmly. His touch is rough, more punishing than sexual. This time he wants her to know it isn't a mistake. "You know," he sighs, "while little cunts like you snivel for hamburgers, there are kids starving in Cambodia."

Sonya feels the tears rush up to her eyes. They push hard to get free.

"Where's my mom?" She tries to say this sternly, issue it as a threat. But under the quiver of her tears, it comes out weak and cry-babyish.

Madison takes off his shades and pinches the bridge of his nose. "I've taken care of Doris."

The tears come full-fledged now, running rivers down Sonya's face. Her throat floods with salt. She can barely speak. "Where is she?" Sonya tries to look over Madison's shoulder into the living room. She can see her mother's bare leg peeking out from the sofa. Nothing more.

"Doris is in heaven babe." Madison's eyes glisten in his face. He pats the top pocket of his jacket. "Want to join her?"

Sonya turns and runs down the street. Her tears burn in the cold January wind.

There is nowhere to go.
There is nowhere to go.

Walking past the triangular houses, with their candy-colored siding and shimmering windows, Sonya stuffs her hands deeper into her pockets and considers where to go. Her tears have stopped. Still, her insides slosh and shiver. Unlike their neighborhood in Buckhead, there are no restaurants or coffee shops within walking distance. There are only square lots of triangular houses, large and blank and impersonal, built for white folks to buy up. Either that or freshly paved refurbished neighborhoods like hers peppered here and there by native residents, wrinkled brown women in faded house dresses with that hanging-on look in their eyes. Beyond the gates of these communities is a four-lane parkway, dotted with gas stations and fast food restaurants.

Sonya considers going back home. That would mean facing Madison's leering eyes and greedy hands. It would mean walking past her mother who would be nodding on the couch, spaced out on heroin. Sonya knew this day would come, when her mother became a slave to her drug habit. For years Doris maintained a balance, was actually fueled by her drug use.

In the beginning, cocaine elated Doris. It made her more alert and productive. As a child, Sonya had watched her mother come home from a difficult day of prospecting, shoulders slumped, eyes glazed with tears. She would go into the bathroom, clear a line or two and emerge sprite and spry and full of life. She would zip through her files, clapping and cheering all the while. Business prospered, which allowed her mother to buy more coke, which, in turn, increased her productivity ten-fold.

As a child, Sonya only heard sniffs from the bathroom. She thought her mother was crying. When she grew older and stumbled upon the dusty mirrors and little baggies floating, unflushed, in the toilet, Sonya put the pieces together. It seemed harmless, the powder sitting in dram vials in her mother's purse, behind her printer or in toes of her pumps on the far top shelf. It seemed more like an indulgence than an addiction. "Some people drink coffee," her mother responded when Sonya asked, once and only once, why. This answer was easier to accept while business boomed, while the cleaning lady arrived every day and the bills continued to clear months in advanced.

Thing changed when Madison arrived.

Crestman's game had been cancelled due to inclement weather. Instead of calling her mom, Sonya caught a ride with Samantha Klieg who, by then, had secured her spot from Lydia Grant in the homecoming court. Samantha had long since ceased the fat notes. "Nice car," Sami said as they pulled up to Sonya's house. And it was a nice car: a slick black Porsche convertible with fire red stripes streaking the hood. "Yeah," Sonya said, confused. Her mother hadn't mentioned guests and Sonya couldn't place the car as belonging to her mother's few friends who came by. Clients rarely visited the house and most were too conservative to drive such a flashy vehicle. There were no living relatives, no cousins or uncles as far as Sonya knew, who could be in from out of town. The car was a mystery.

"Tell your mom to take me for a spin one day," Samantha said, chewing her gum like a cow. "Bye."

Sonya closed Samantha's car door absentmindedly. The Porsche pulled all of her attention. Something about it sent waves of panic up her spine. Heat radiated from the car's hood. Sonya felt it as she passed. The Porsche seemed wicked, demonized, like an evil cat, hunched and prowling.

She noticed his jacket first, a heavy black leather worn gray. Then she saw his hair from behind. It jutted out from his scalp in chunky black spikes. A tattoo on the back of his neck, blue lettering across a bleeding red heart, read *Tommy*. Sonya assumed that to be the stranger's name. It took Sonya a second to realize that Tommy's head was buried between her mother's thighs.

The door's slam echoed in the otherwise quiet foyer. No one noticed but Sonya. Madison continued his work between Sonya's mother's legs, moaning and slurping, oblivious to Sonya's presence.

"Hi," was the first thing out of Sonya's mouth. Her eyes captured the scene before her: her mother's head thrown back, her beige skirt looped over the couch's arm, her black panties tangled around her right ankle, and this stranger, with his wide shoulder, his spiky hair and hairy neck, performing oral sex on her mother in the middle of their foyer. Sonya understood what she saw, yet her brain did not process the information. Shock immobilized Sonya. She could neither walk out nor dart past to her bedroom. So she stood there—"Hi," she had said—and greeted the stranger as if he were a guest walking in through the front door.

When he turned around, Sonya expected some bit of residue on his face. But there was none. His skin shone, clear and pink.

"You must be Sonya." He raised himself with a grunt. He stood in the center of the foyer rocking back and forth on the heels of his shoes. He smiled wide at Sonya, displaying a row of perfectly white teeth. He looked at Sonya briefly and then around the foyer, like a deliveryman waiting for a signature and a tip.

"I'm Madison," he said. His tone was so casual as to make Sonya doubt the fact of her mother's gaping legs and exposed vagina. "A friend of your Mom's."

Her mother lay on the couch, unmoving, except for an occasional loll of her head.

"Sonya," she said. Her name escaped her mouth like smoke.

"As you can see," Madison sighed as he walked over and stood behind Sonya, "Doris is indisposed at the moment." Sonya could smell her mother's rosy perfume on Madison's skin and her oceany vagina on his mouth. He leaned into Sonya, his hot breath irritating the nape of her neck. She felt his erect penis pressed against her back. "You should probably go to your room." He coaxed her forward with a little shove as if she were some shy three year old being sent to sit on Santa's lap. His voice was flat, uncaring. In it, Sonya heard danger and threat.

As she walked to her room, Sonya looked back, disbelieving.

"Go on." Madison smiled and clicked his tongue as if talking to a pesky cat. "Doris is fine. Believe me. I'll clean all of this up."

In her room, Sonya sat on the bed and stared into the mirror. She looked exactly the same as she did this morning when she left the school. Her frizzy brown hair, naturally curly, but not in any fashionable way, her olive skin, her thin shoulders and round hips, her blunt nose (Pug, Sami and friends had called it before the truce. That was one of the other things they had laughed at, Sonya's nose. Not directly of course. Samantha had slipped a picture of a pug under her locker door, circled the nose and wrote, *Yours)*. Everything seemed the same. Sonya's room was still pink and, in the kitchen, the oversized clock still chimed the half hour. Everything remained exactly as it was before Sonya left for school, except everything had changed completely.

Was she in danger? Sonya couldn't tell. Her mother didn't seem well but Madison assured Sonya that her mother would be fine. Who was this guy anyway? Obviously he was connected in some way to drugs. Obviously, her mother was stoned. No sirens rang in Sonya's head and Sonya's heart did not pound ferociously, yet she recognized this moment as pivotal and dangerous.

I should go back out there, Sonya thought. I should go out there and tell him to leave. Demand it. But her legs would not move. She was numb.

Every fall in grade school, a policeman the teachers and students called Officer Friendly came to visit. Officer Friendly gave a speech about dangerous situations, situations kids were supposed to avoid. "When you feel uncomfortable about a person or situation," Officer Friendly had said, "run and tell another adult." During his visits, Officer Friendly talked about bad men in slow moving vehicles offering lollipops to unsuspecting kids. He talked about uncomfortable touches and words that hurt. He never mentioned Porsches and leather jackets. He never mentioned your mother, high as a hummingbird, being molested by a six-foot-two drug pusher.

Either way, telling another adult was out of the question. There were no other adults Sonya knew well enough to tell. And even if there were, what would be the use? What could they do besides ask Madison to leave?

Sonya remembered another part to Officer Friendly's message. "If there is not an adult around," he used to say with a waggle of his finger, "call nine-one-one."

Sonya did not dial nine-one-one. Instead, she used her cell and dialed the non-emergency number to the police station. She did not want the attention blaring sirens would bring. She did not want the neighbors gawking and whispering. Sonya didn't say much to the dispatcher on the other end, only that there was a possible dangerous situation, that it was not immediate, but sending an officer over would help. Moments after Sonya snapped her cell phone shut and waited for the cops to arrive, Madison knocked once and then let himself in.

Madison sat beside Sonya on the edge her bed and stared down into his clasped hands. "This is really strange to you, I know." He spoke in the voice of a father preparing to apologize.

Sonya nodded.

"See this?" He pulled a black device from his pocket. "This is a CB device. Police frequency." Sonya's heart dropped. "On it, I can hear all dispatch calls. And in my line of business, it's very important for me to know what the police are up to."

Sonya's veil of numbness broke and in rushed a flood of fear. The sirens rang in her head and her heart pounded in her chest. Her face grew hot. Run, she thought, run! But she couldn't move. It was as if Madison's deep gaze and monotone voice had hypnotized her. Surely, if there were a time to scream this was it.

"Now I'll take care of the police this once," he said. "Alls you have to do is stay put right here in your room." He shook his head and sighed. "Sonya," he said. "You know why I'm here don't you? You know your mother needs me."

Sonya nodded.

Madison's hand came hard across Sonya's face. Before she could cringe against the slap, he grabbed her cheeks in a vice grip between his fingers and thumb. His eyes were serene with anger. "Don't fuck with me you little cunt."

Fear quaked through Sonya's body. Her eyes flooded with tears.

"Shhh." Madison wiped the tears from her cheeks with his hard thumb. "There's more where that came from," he said. "Believe me. I am nobody to fuck with. Do you understand that?"

He squeezed hard. Sonya felt her teeth cutting the inside of her cheek. She tasted her own blood. "I need an answer."

"Yes," Sonya managed to say through her salty tears.

"If you ever attempt to call the cops on me," he sighed, "I'll slit both your throats and be out of the door before the first drop of blood hits the carpet."

Madison got up, wiped his hand on his pants and smiled. "Now, stay put while I clear up this misunderstanding with the cops."

That had been over two years ago when Sonya first met Madison. Since then, his visits had been sparse. Mostly, he'd come to drop off packages and fuck Doris into oblivion. Every once in a while, he asked Sonya for a favor.

Now, suddenly, Madison is back. And it looks as if he is here to stay. But why? Surely Sonya's mother has nothing to offer him. She is attractive, but not strikingly so. Not anymore. By the looks of Madison, Sonya can tell there are other women. Is he back for money? As far as Sonya knows, her mother no longer has any. In fact, she may even owe Madison. Sonya is almost sure she does. She has heard her mother on the phone some nights begging for a loan, "a couple of spots to get me through the week," her mother said. So no, Madison is not back for money. What then?

No matter what Madison's reason for showing up, the fact of the matter is he *is* back. Sonya cannot go home until late tonight, when she can be sure he is gone. Otherwise, she'll have to listen while he fucks Doris like an animal and pumps her veins full of dope. Afterwards, of course, Madison will call Sonya into the room. He will ask for a favor. His razor blade will be drawn and ready.

As Sonya walks down the long empty street with no place to go, she recalls the sinister chill of Madison's voice. "Come over here little girl," he would say. "Come do me a favor."

06
....

"I'm not racist!"

It is walking distance: four blocks down, three over, a right and there it is, two houses from the corner. That's how Tandy gives the directions when Sonya calls from her cell phone. She tells Tandy she is bored, that she doesn't want to go home because her mom is tripping—though, with Tandy, Sonya does not mean literally. When Sonya tells Tandy where she lives, Tandy says, "Girl come to my house. You're practically right around the corner."

Sonya is excited at the prospect of visiting Tandy until she remembers her white lie. Nervousness kneads a knot in Sonya's belly. Hopefully, Tandy will be alone. Hopefully, Sonya won't have to explain herself, again.

When Sonya reaches the address Tandy gave her, she is stunned by what she finds. Sonya had prepared herself for a modest house with a leaning porch, perhaps and a junk car in the driveway. She even prepared herself for housing projects with trash blowing in the street and clumps of black men smoking and slapping five on the corners. Sonya had prepared herself for the titillation of walking past these men, for the loud music, the booze and marijuana. For the danger. But nothing could have prepared her for this.

Never had Sonya thought Tandy would have a house like hers.

And Tandy doesn't. Tandy's house is larger. Much much larger. Tandy's house boasts crests and columns. It is huge and stately and grandiose—out of place among the prefab cottages surrounding it.

"You're the infamous mulatto girl." The door opens and behind it stands a rotund woman with a shinning face, a gleaming smile and a mound of dreadlocked hair twisted in a complicated knot on the top of her head.

"Well don't just stand there glass-eyed," the woman says—this is exactly what Sonya was doing.

Sonya steps into a foyer of magnificent brightness. It has an orange glow, which, she realizes, is caused by the reflection of the sun from high-up windows on the painted walls. Contrasted with the tree-shaded walkway leading up to the house, the foyer is so bright Sonya squints against the sudden flood of light. As her eyes adjust, she finds herself in a long hallway, the back wall of which is covered from end to end with a mural of intricate, twisted shapes.

"Tandy was right," the woman says. She takes Sonya by the shoulders and twists her around, inspecting her. "You do look white, white as the dead. But I can see the black in you. It's all in those hips and that ass," she says slapping Sonya on the butt. "Only a black girl can have an ass that round."

Sonya feels the red rise in her cheeks. She is both flattered and embarrassed.

A voice rings from somewhere in the house, "Momma!" Tandy marches down the hallway.

"Your friend's here," Tandy's mother says.

"What did you say to her?" Tandy asked. And then, to Sonya, "What did she say to you?"

"I told her she looks white," Tandy's mother says with a pat of defiance. Tandy rolls her eyes. "Well she does," the mother says. "She knows she looks white. Don't you girl?"

"Yes," Sonya says, and nothing more.

Sonya stands in the grand foyer shuffling her feet awkwardly.

At Crestman, no one ever discussed race. Even after the Lydia Grant incident, no one dared to say directly to Lydia, "Oh, why didn't you just say your mother is black."

Sonya had grown up with the understanding that race is a touchy issue. The word *black,* in the few times Sonya has had to use it to describe someone, feels crass coming out of her mouth. In spite of her liberal attitude, the word feels like an insult. Something she is spitting. *African-American* is no better, one, because not all black people are American; and two, because when she says it, or when she hears other white people use the term, their voice reeks of a rehearsed respect. It screams, "I'm not racist! I'm not racist!"

African-American was the catchall phrase at Crestman, a pseudonym for anyone brown. Once, a guidance counselor at a school assembly, when describing a student who was obviously Latino, said, "He is a young, intelligent, African-American male." The counselor was not even aware enough to be embarrassed.

Now, as Sonya stands under the obvious inspection of Tandy's mother, she thinks of Lydia Grant. She thinks how, for Lydia, it might have been a relief if someone had said, "Why didn't you just say your mother is black?"

"I'm Nzinga," Tandy's mother says. "Most people call me Zing."

"Nzinga Herman?" The name hops up from the recesses of Sonya's brain and out of her mouth. Sonya has read the name before, at Crestman, in her art class. There had been an entire page in the "Magic Modernist" chapter of her art book dedicated to Nzinga Herman's biography. "One of the premier African-American painters of the last thirty years," the passage had read.

"Oh god," Tandy says. "Another fan."

"You're a painter," Sonya says, mesmerized.

"On my good days," Zing says.

Tandy hooks Sonya's arm. "We're not going through this again. She's *my* friend," Tandy says, steering Sonya by the arm. "She came to see *me.*" Then to Sonya, "Mother has a habit of stealing my friends."

"What friends," Zing says. "You ain't brought anyone by the house in umpteen years. Not even them little ghetto chicks you hang out with."

"They're not ghetto."

"Tandy's embarrassed 'cause we're rich."

"We're not rich, Mother," Tandy says.

"Yeah baby, we're rich," Nzinga says. "We better be or else we'll have to move out of this house."

The brightness of the foyer quickly gives way to the dim, cavernous rooms within. Tandy guides Sonya through the large rooms quickly, which gives Sonya the sense that they're running away from something.

After several turns and two flights of stairs they come to Tandy's room, which is at least twice as large as Sonya's. Books fill the shelves and sit in stacks on the floor. Posters of Bjork, Sheryl Crow and Kurt Cobain are plastered on the wall. Sonya stares at the posters and then at Tandy. They don't match.

"I know," Tandy says. "White folks' music."

That's exactly what Tandy's music choice is: it was the type of music Sonya would expect a white girl to listen to. It certainly seems out of place with Tandy's tough black-girl-from-the-streets demeanor. Then again, so does her house, her room and her famous mother.

"You better not tell anyone in school. My reputation would be ruined." Tandy pinches Sonya playfully. But there is a edge to her voice.

"I like Kurt Cobain too."

"Yeah, well, you're half white so that's acceptable. But at PLD you better keep that to yourself. If it's not R&B or rap, then forget it."

"I'm serious about not telling," Tandy says. Suddenly her eyes grow conspiratorial and fierce. "I don't want folks knowing who my mother is. I had to live in her shadow all through elementary and middle school. I was always the rich black girl, Zing Herman's daughter. I've gone through a lot of trouble to be sure that doesn't happen at PLD. Don't blow up my spot, Sonya."

Tandy straddles Sonya and tickles her. "You have to promise."

"Okay, okay." Sonya giggles and slaps away Tandy's hands.

Tandy's catches Sonya between the armpits. A wave of giggles rises in Sonya's stomach.

"Promise," Tandy says. "Say, 'I won't blow up Tandy's spot.'"

....

"I won't...I...I can't," Sonya gaffaws. "The tickles."

"Alright." Tandy let's up. "Alright, now say it."

"I won't blow up Tandy's spot."

"Again."

"I won't blow up Tandy's spot."

"Once more for good measure."

"Tandy," Sonya huffs. "For Christ's sakes."

"Three's a charm."

"Okay, okay. I won't blow up Tandy's spot."

"Thank you kindly, Madam," Tandy stands and bows dramatically.

Sonya settles into a corner of the bed and pulls a pillow to her chest. Tandy's pinch burns on her skin, itchy as a tattoo. She can still feel the red-hot tickling fingers under her armpit. Tandy, Sonya thinks. Tandy Tandy Tandy. She is at Tandy's house, the black girl from the train, the leader of the group! Sonya snuggles into the pillow and prepares herself for something luscious. Perhaps Tandy will pull out a packet of marijuana and roll a joint. Perhaps she will share gossip or tell Sonya stories about the Puerto Rican boy she sat with on the train that day, the boy she went with to get her head straight. Sonya waits, like a child at a fireworks show, neck craned, glaring up at the sky. Her eyes shine on Tandy as she waits for that first, bright, whistling, magical explosion.

07

...at first sight

"Choose your weapon," Tandy says, holding out a cup of perfectly sharpened pencils.

Tandy tears through the Biology homework labeling diagrams at lightening speed. On the Geography homework, she skips the reading and goes directly to the questions, composing paragraph-long responses. Tandy devours Advanced Calculus, zipping through the equations, composing the formulas on her paper in typewriter-neat font. Sonya can barely keep up.

"Are you still on number seventeen?" Tandy says. "Here." She snatches the paper and scribbles out the lines of the equations.

After three hours of intense and silent study (Tandy shushes Sonya several times when Sonya tries to initiate conversation), Tandy looks up with a fresh, chipper glow on her face. "Break time," she says, hopping off the bed. Sonya's legs prickle and creak when she unfolds them. They have fallen asleep. Her eyes are heavy and her brain feels as if it has shriveled inside her skull. She grumbles off the bed.

"Finally," Sonya says, "you come up for air."

"We have to save my favorite for last," Tandy says downstairs, during their ten-minute milk and cake break for which Tandy sets a timer.

"What's your favorite?" Sonya asks, expecting the standard answer of English or Social Studies. Some part of her still hopes against hope for the magical explosion.

"Spelling Bee," Tandy says. "It's something I made up. I turn to a page in the dictionary, read the words aloud and write down their spelling and a one-word definition."

"Oh," Sonya says, attempting to hide the perplexed surprise in her voice.

"It's a special dictionary too," Tandy chirps. "Esoteric words. I got bored with the standard SAT stuff."

Sonya considers making another attempt at conversation, thinks of asking about the Puerto Rican boy. But she decides against it. She doesn't want Tandy to connect her to the shy white girl coming from Dr. Hillman's on the train. And she doesn't want to get shushed again.

"Now that *you're* here," Tandy says, "I don't have to cheat and look in my dictionary. You can read the words to me."

"You give yourself spelling tests?"

"I know." Tandy shrugs her shoulders. "I'm a nerd. But I'm a nerd at home. At school, nobody knows about my spelling bees or my SAT score." Tandy answers the question before Sonya can part her mouth to ask. "Twenty-two ninety," she says, motioning absentmindedly with her glass. "But I keep all of that to myself. At school, I'm just Tandy."

"If I made a twenty-two ninety I would get tee-shirts printed."

"And you'd probably wear it to school with your acid-wash jeans and your Kurt Cobain button."

"I don't know. Maybe."

Sonya recalls the anxiety she had this morning getting dressed. Somehow she knew the Kurt Cobain shirt was wrong for PLD, just as she knew that Lydia's biracialness made her features somehow less beautiful, less exotic. There was a code, unspoken but true. There was something to abide by.

"I learned from my old school," Tandy said. "People don't like different, doesn't matter where you are. Nerds aren't popular." She smiles and washes down her cake with milk. "I'm too smart to be stupid, so I keep my grades to myself. That way, I get to have my cake—" she lifts a piece of cake to her mouth "—and eat it too."

"What about, well," Sonya says, "awards and tests and stuff?"

"Who needs a plaque or a frilly piece of paper? I don't care about that stuff."

"No, I mean you must have gotten awards. Don't they give awards at PLD?"

"Oh that." Tandy tsks. "Principal Carlton and I have an arrangement." She doesn't go on to say what that arrangement is. Instead, she leans over and pinches Sonya hard on the forearm.

"Ouch."

"Just a reminder," Tandy says, "to keep my Cobain and my spelling bees top secret." Tandy's eyes sharpen and her face drops all of its whimsy. "You have to promise," she says. "Promise you won't put me on blast with Celesta and them."

"Why would I—"

Another pinch. But this one is hard and painful. "Say it," Tandy says. "Say it."

"Okay, okay," Sonya jerks her arm away. "I won't tell anyone." She looks into Tandy's eyes, which soften with relief. Sonya's vow seems to satisfy her. Still, something lies just beneath Tandy's smiling face. Some hard, dark thing, glowering sternly.

Tandy whizzes through the words, dashing down the spelling, part of speech, and definition at a breakneck speed.

"Slowdown," Sonya says. "You're finishing faster than I can turn the page."

"Any word," Tandy says fiendishly. "Don't be so methodic. Flip the page and pick a word."

Just then the door opens behind them and in barges the darkest man Sonya has ever seen. His lean, shirtless torso ripples with muscle. He stoops through the room searching behind stacks of books and under furniture. He has the same long neck and high cheekbones as Tandy's, but his skin is much darker. It is truly black. It shines as if it has been oiled.

Tandy snaps a finger in Sonya's face. "Hello," she says. "Earth to Sonya. Next word please."

"Kim-me," Sonya read. "Who is that?" she leaned in, whispering.

"C-H-E-M-I," Tandy said. "That's my brother. Noun," she says about the word. "The land of Egypt."

"Your brother?" Sonya's eyes follow the lean figure as he over-turns piles of books, grunting angrily all the while. "Poo-jah."

"P-U-J-A. Noun. The worship given to people or things less divine. He's a butt hole. Next word."

"Um." Sonya tries to focus on the page, but Tandy's brother draws her attention. "Lee-ah,"

"L-H-A," Tandy says, "and it's pronounced L'ha. *And,*" she announces loud enough for her brother to hear, "some people should learn to knock before they enter."

Her brother storms toward Tandy and wrestles a pillow away from her. He shoves his hands inside the pillowcase, his eyes glazed and intent.

"Next word," Tandy says with her lips pursed. But Sonya is too distracted to read. After a moment, Tandy's brother withdraws his hand. In it he holds a thin, black book.

"Hah!" He flashes the book quickly in Tandy's face. "Knew I would find it here."

"Happy?" Tandy says. "Now get the hell out of my room."

"Can't keep the black man down, baby," he says, backing away from Tandy slowly. A sarcastic, triumphant smile flares out under his nose. Sonya thinks it is the most beautiful smile she has ever seen. "Can't keep the black man down," he says again, walking backward all the way out of the door. Sonya's eyes lock on the space where he last stood.

"Goodbye, Livingston," Tandy says. Her voice is high and sardonic.

"Kush," her brother yells.

"Livingston! Livingston! Livingston!"

Sonya hears footsteps. Tandy's brother reappears in the doorway. "Kush," he says to both Tandy and Sonya. "My name is Kush." This time, he stomps down the hallway.

"What was that about?" Sonya asks. She can feel the blush washing across her face.

"Mother named him Livingston after her favorite book," Tandy says. "*Jonathan Livingston Seagull.* He's since then changed his name to Kush."

"Kush?" The name slides across Sonya's tongue, slick and sweet as butterscotch.

"He's been searching for that book all week. Some black revolutionary mess he's reading. Something about black folks from outer space and women walking seven paces behind their man." Tandy smacks her lips, displaying that black girl sass that captured Sonya months ago on the train. The gesture is out of place, Sonya thinks, with the grand house, the rock posters, the spelling bee and the way Tandy says *mother* in the voice of a spoiled debutante. "I got tired of hearing about his faux revolution, so I hid his book."

"Awe, Tandy," Sonya touches her hands to her lips. "That wasn't nice."

"He's gorgeous," Tandy sighs. "I know. Everybody falls for him."

"I didn't say that. I was just thinking, well, if somebody hid my favorite book, I would—"

"You don't have to say it. It's written all over your face, Yellow Mary," Tandy says.

Sonya touches her cheeks, which she knows are red and glowing.

"Had you met my bother two years ago, man, he was all khaki-wearing, George-W-Bush-loving. You would have thought he was a Crestman student." Tandy re-stuffs her pillowcase. "He's a senior." She surrenders this fact just as casually as she surrendered her brother's book.

"He goes to…" Sonya hears the elation in her voice and tries to calm it. "He's a student at PLD? I mean, I've never seen him around."

"You've only been there one day. You'll see him sooner or later. Believe me." Tandy idly flips through her book of esoteric words and glances down at her quiz list.

"Want me to check those?" Sonya asks.

"No," Tandy says. "They're all correct."

08

....

Shattered dreams

Sun cuts through the blinds of her bedroom, thick slants of light filled with twinkling dust. Sonya rises from a syrupy sleep. Something inside her smiles. In the bathroom, as she brushes her teeth, Sonya meets her face in the mirror and giggles. Last night's dream has drugged her, has made her dizzy and giddy, hazy with delight. Kush, she remembers from the dream. He was close to her. A vague but deep relationship, she and Kush had in her dream. An understanding. A love. They walked hand in hand through a park bedazzled with orange and yellow leaves. This is her third dream about him.

The happiness of the dream carries Sonya through her shower, through the choosing of what to wear (which is only mildly less torturous on this fourth day of school) and through her fuss with her frizzy crown of hair.

"Morning, little girl," Madison greets Sonya as she descends the stairs. "You sure are Smiling fucking Sally today." He leans back in his chair and massages his penis through his jeans. "Did you take a sniff of my stash while I wasn't looking?"

Silently, Sonya walks to the kitchen on iron legs. Her Kush dream fades to black. In its place is Madison's snide smile. She hadn't expected him this morning. He is usually gone by the time she wakes.

Sonya moves through the kitchen, nervous as a kicked dog, and pours juice that she will not drink.

Years ago, she and her mother sat up late one night eating ice cream and pickles and chocolate bars and salty chips. They did this once a month, pigged out on junk food. A "sweet and sour fest," they used to call it. An infomercial came on for Ginsu Knives. After watching the demonstration, her mother called the number on the screen and ordered two sets.

Sonya spies these knives on the counter now. She recalls the infomercial demonstrations, the way the knife zipped through a whole chicken, bone and all. The same knife cut a watermelon, a block of wood, a head of lettuce, and a slab of ham. Surely, one of these knives could slice Madison's throat.

Sonya stands at the counter with her back to Madison. The stainless steal handles of the knives gleam before her. She can hear Madison behind her spooning oatmeal into his mouth.

"Only seven o'clock." He speaks through a mouthful of oatmeal. "What time does school start?"

"Eight." Sonya's voice comes flat and automatic. Her eyes are locked on the knives. She will slip the smallest one, the paring knife, into her back pocket. If he asks her for a favor, she will walk over to him calmly. She will whip the knife from her pocket and plunge it into his belly. She will shove it deep, twist it. Her hand, like a spigot, will release the hot soup of his blood.

"Eight?" Madison sighs reflectively. "That gives you, oh…an hour. A favor shouldn't take but five, ten minutes tops."

Sonya slides her hand across the counter and fingers the base of the knife holder. Its cool metal hums on her fingers.

"Sonya." Doris yells from the other room. Her mother's call blinks Sonya out of her trance. "Sonya?" Sonya walks across the kitchen toward her mother's room. She can tell her mother is crying. Her voice is trembling and frail.

"Saved by the bell," Madison says.

When Sonya enters she finds her mother sitting on the floor of her closet. She wears a crumpled black business suit. Her stockings are twisted around her ankles and her hair sits atop her head in a tangled ponytail.

"Thought I'd get myself...together today," she says thickly. "Go to the office. Check the numbers. Get some prospect sheets."

Seeing her mother like this deflates Sonya's usual spite. It is like watching a disabled person toppled in a wheelchair, it is like watching the hobble of a one-legged dog.

"Then I realized," her mother says. "There is no office." Her mother falls forward in a slump. The laughter that escapes her rings clear as a flute. Sonya takes a step toward her and then stops.

"I would hate me too, if I were you," Doris says. "I'm such a fuck up." Her mother turns around and lifts up her skirt, revealing her bruised thighs. "Look at this." She rubs her legs, laughing and crying at the same time. "Look at me. Look at me. Look at me." Her voice shrinks to nothing.

"Mom," Sonya says. Seeing her mother this way frightens her. Her mother has reached a state beyond high, beyond pathetic, a state bordering on lunacy. Hot tears roll down Sonya's face.

Her mother looks up quickly. "No," she says. "I don't deserve that. Call me Doris."

Sonya opens her mouth to speak, but Doris waves her hand. "Don't," she says. "Don't. I'll be fine. I'm not high. This is the first sober moment I've had in months. I'll be fine." She pulls her skirt over her knees and draws them to her chest. "Just go to school."

Sonya misses the seven-twenty train. The favor took longer than Madison expected.

Sonya kneeled before Madison for what seemed like hours, though it was not longer than ten minutes. She kneeled before him with his vinegary penis in her hand, working his grimy shaft to orgasm.

By the time she gets to school, homeroom has already started. The halls are as empty as the belly of a ship. Sonya walks through them lethargically. A stew of emotions roils in her chest: disgust, anxiety, distress, indifference. By the time she reaches home-room, her hodgepodge of emotions has worked itself into a clump of misery.

"Thanks for joining us, Ms. Sonya Crane." Mrs. Larsen stands at the front of the class with her hands on her hips. She is a thin, dark, wiry woman of sixty. Her platinum hair tops her head like a windblown nest or a magnificent, metallic hat. Her thick-rimmed glasses sit uncomfortably close to her eyes.

Mrs. Larsen has made her dislike for Sonya no secret. "I know how you operate," she said to Sonya on the second day of homeroom. "You think you're the hottest dog on the grill." Sonya smiled tightly while the class looked on and giggled. Mrs. Larsen's words came out all slippery and wet, as if they were made of ice cream. She was obviously drunk. "But you don't fool me," she continued, waggling her finger at Sonya. "I know what you up to. When I was younger y'all yellow bitches got all the glory. But not in my class. Not this time, sister."

Sonya pauses in the doorway before entering. She does not know if she can face PLD today. She does not know if she can face Tandy and Maurice and the mixed illusion she has painted of herself. It is like the edge of a chasm on which she reels, the portal to Mrs. Larsen's homeroom. It is like the cliché nightmare of coming to school naked, only Sonya is fully dressed.

"You better get your yellow tail on in your seat," Mrs. Larsen says. "Y'all kill me with this CP time shit. Strolling in here smelling yourself." Some students cover the mouths and chuckle. Others look away, embarrassed for Sonya. Sonya ignores Mrs. Larsen and takes her seat. Her humiliation this morning with Madison over-shadows Mrs. Larsen's spite, numbs her to it. She flops down in her seat. She feels tired and heavy. She feels flaccid. Boneless.

Mrs. Larsen continues with the lesson, explaining to the class that they have to write a composition due on Thursday. She turns and writes in big squiggly letters, "Competition due on Thursday," then sits down in her chair and rests her chin in her hands.

"What's wrong girl?" Tandy whispers.

"Nothing," Sonya says. Then, spying the look of disbelief on

Tandy's face, she says, "My mother was just, you know, bugging out this morning."

"Your mother?" Tandy says. "You think your mother was tripping? My mother wouldn't get off my case about Kush's little book."

Tandy launches into a story about her morning woes. Celesta joins in from the desk behind her.

"She wanted to put me on punishment," Tandy says.

"Treating you like a pre-teen up in this bitch," Celesta says.

"I know," Tandy says. "But I was like whatever."

"My momma be trying to pull shit like that."

"Mine too," Tandy says. "But you know me." They both slap five.

These are the same complaints Sonya had wished to be a part of as she watched Tandy on the train, when Sonya lived in Buckhead in a sweeping loft, when the bills were paid and her mother's habit was at least under control, when notices of repossessions and liens had not clogged their mailbox.

"And Kush, man, he just straight sat there while she bugged out," Tandy says. Sonya tries to pull herself from her fog, tries to revel in the moment, but it loses its glamour.

The air around her warps and expands, until, she realizes, a capsule has been formed. Sonya sits in its center. Alone. She stares out beyond Tandy's irreverent, animated face, beyond the sickly green classroom walls and the field of starch white grass with its deformed track and bowed football goals. Beyond all this, Sonya sees her mother, still sitting in the closet. Her mother, holding herself with her thin, battered arms.

09

Pushed to the edge

Sonya waits and plots.

This morning Sonya took the longest of the Ginsu knives, a heavy square meat chopper, and hid it under her mattress. Now, in the cool dark of her room, Sonya slides her hand under her mattress and retrieves the knife. She sits on the edge of her bed with the knife cradled in her lap like a newborn. The curve of the blade glints in the moonlight.

The door to her mother's room squeaks open. Madison is done, Sonya can tell, because her mother has ceased her moaning. Doris's fight against her addiction has ended for the night, ended in another defeat.

Sonya waits.

And plots.

She knows Madison's routine. He comes in and smokes a cigarette on the couch, makes calls from the house phone and then goes to Doris's room. Sometimes Doris cries. Sometimes she yells. Madison speaks low and soft, so soft Sonya can never make out the words. In the end, he gives Doris her relief. Ties her off and pumps her veins with heroin. Then he goes to the living room and drugs himself into a nodding stupor.

Sonya waits to hear the click of the lighter and the rustle of the plastic bag that Madison ties to his arm. She listens for the clink of the needle casing and Madison's low sigh.

A car passes. Its headlights throw squares of yellow across the walls.

A dog barks three times and then is silent.

The knife glints in the moonlight.

Madison sighs.

The house is quiet.

Sonya waits.

And plots.

Slowly, she pulls her door open and peers down the hallway. Her mother's room faces hers at the opposite end of the corridor. The light is out. The door is closed. On sapling legs, Sonya tiptoes down the hallway. The knife pats softly against her thigh as she walks.

Just as she suspects, Sonya finds Madison in the corner of the living room. His eyes are low and glazed. His head slumps to the right.

Like a hunting cheetah, Sonya approaches with a quiet stealth. Suddenly, Madison's head jerks up. His hand slides down to the pocket that houses his razor blade. Sonya freezes mid-stride. Then, just a suddenly, Madison's lips part and his head drops. Nodding.

Sonya seizes the opportunity. Standing over him, she grabs a fistful of his hair. She jerks his head back and presses the knife against the skin of Madison's neck. A thin line of blood blossoms along the blade.

Madison's eyes open slowly. "Hi," he says.

Sonya's breath comes in ragged chucks. "You fucking asshole." Again, Madison's hand slides down toward his knife pocket. Sonya jerks his head back farther. "Don't even fucking think about it," she says.

Madison smiles his wry smile. "Doris's little girl's got chutzpah."

The clock ticks.

The dog barks.

Madison smiles. "That tickles."

"Fuck you!" Sonya says.

jd guilford

"We haven't worked up to that yet."

"Fuck you, Madison."

"You'll go to jail and I'll be dead," he says, still laughing. "You'll go to jail for life. Then who will take care of Doris?"

Nothing in the world exists. Nothing except the throbbing in Sonya's head, the cold steel of the knife, and Madison's pink neck. All she has to do is pull the knife across his neck, zip it from left to right and Madison is gone. She could load him up in his car and dump him somewhere. The police would find his stash and assume one of his druggy clients killed him. They'd never suspect her. Never.

A car passes. Its headlights blaze through the living room. In that flash of light Sonya spies the hump of Madison's Adam's apple and the goose bumps pimpling the underside of his neck. Terror dances like fire in his eyes. Sonya snaps out of her trance. The world resurfaces, all of its hard edges: the hinge of the door, the peach-colored walls, the wooden floors and the clump of Madison's hair gripped between her fingers.

The knife suddenly weighs a thousand pounds. It slides out of her fingers and thuds on the carpeted floor. A line of blood coats the knife's blade. Madison's mouth opens wide. There is a tick of time in which Sonya sees nothing but the hills of Madison's molars and the bright red cave of his mouth. Then, seconds behind his mouth's opening, laughter erupts and echoes through the room. Madison curls over, nods and jerks back up. Waves of laughter shake his body.

A fog of weariness curtains Sonya's eyes. Her joints wobble un-reliably. Sonya's spite failed her. She could not do it. She could not slit Madison's throat.

"Good-night, little girl," Madison says, nodding against the doorjamb. He chuckles sinisterly. Sonya slinks back to her room with its longish windows, its powdery walls and shellacked wood floors. She retires to her room like a gladiator who has not won but merely survived.

The next day, Sonya sits in a corner while Doris rocks back and forth on the edge of her bed, her body crackling with the first pains of withdrawal. Since coming home from school, Sonya has mopped up the clear green vomit her mother spewed over the bathroom floor. She has changed the sweat soaked sheets. She has bathed her mother slowly with a pail of lukewarm water. She has sat and cried and waited.

"I have to get clean," Doris chants. "I have to get clean."

Sonya tries rubbing her mother's back but Doris says it is too painful. There is nothing for Sonya to do but hold a pillow to her chest and watch as her mother fights against the hunger clawing at her insides.

Sonya remembered a time—a time before heroin stole her mother's light, before her mother became Atlanta's top broker—when she and Doris lived in a one-bedroom apartment in midtown. The floor slanted upwards from the front door and water from the upstairs tenant's pipes streaked the living room walls. After years of eating canned ravioli, after years of watching her mother on the phone with her head in her hands prospecting clients with a fake, exhausting perkiness, Doris came home and slapped a seven-thousand-dollar commission check on the table. She snatched her jacket off and twirled it over her head, skipping around the room and singing at the top of her lungs. "We're in the money. We're in the money." From that day on, houses flew out of Doris's hands like doves. Now, looking at the knobs of her mother's spine through the back of her gown, Sonya hopes for another such miracle. Sonya hopes her mother can walk through the door once again, smiling and happy and victorious. Sonya hopes her mother can overcome her addiction.

"You look like shit," Madison says. He stands in the hallway just outside Doris's room. He let himself in. He has Doris's key. Sonya looks at him with cold, hard eyes and reminds herself to chain the door later.

Before last night, Madison's appearance had always provoked in Sonya a wrenching fear. Before last night, she would have averted her eyes under Madison's harsh gaze. Now, she returns his stare. Now, she dares him.

Sonya eyes fall to Madison's neck. A jagged red line peeks out from the collar of his shirt.

"Sonya's taking good care of me," Doris says. Her voice is dry. Hollow.

"So I've heard." Madison does not take his eyes off Sonya. He trails his thumb along the fresh cut mark. Sonya glimpses a hint of something in his eyes, some sadistic mixture of reverence and malice.

Sonya touches her mother's shoulder lightly. Her eyes stay locked on Madison. "I enjoyed our conversation last night." Sonya slaps her spite on the table like a bet.

"Me too, kiddo," Madison says. Then, he sees Sonya's spite and raises her. "Thanks for the favor yesterday."

Madison's wide, leering smile makes a dough of Sonya's insult. It casts a bright light on her failed rebellion. Sonya does not have the guts for murder. If Madison ever had any doubts, last night erased them. Now, it will be even easier for Madison. He pushed Sonya to the edge and, as she stood teetering at the lip of the chasm, he knelt to draw chalk outlines of her feet. Sonya does not have to fear for her life. Madison will not kill her. He will do worse than that. He will use her up. After last night, Madison knows exactly how far he can go with Sonya. Now, he knows where she stands.

Last night, Sonya retired to her bed fully prepared to die. When she woke this morning to find both she and Doris unharmed, she thought Madison was simply biding his time. A slow torture she thought. No fear quaked within her. Just as the day when she took a razor to her wrist, Sonya faced the fact of her mortality with numb resolution. "I did not kill Madison," she thought on her way home from school. "So he will kill me."

Madison's smile tells Sonya she is wrong. Madison will not waste his time or risk prison on her. Since he has pushed Sonya to the edge, Madison knows exactly where it is for her.

Sonya looks into his steel eyes. Yes, Sonya thinks, he will use me up.

Madison sits beside Doris. "What are we going to do with you?" His voice is low and level, gentle almost.

Suddenly, the dynamics in the room shift. Before Madison entered, Sonya and Doris stood together against her invisible enemy. Like two priests exorcising a ghost, they faced Doris's darkest hour allied in their fear and determination. Now, Sonya stands outside the comradeship of Doris and Madison. They have their own secret society. They share knowledge of ache and famine darker than anything Sonya has ever experienced.

Madison gently pulls Doris to him. "You've done good," he whispers into her ear. "You done good. But now it's time for a little relief."

He turns to Sonya. "She's had enough pain for tonight," Madison says. "We're going to need some time alone."

Sonya realizes that, before today, Madison has been the one rubbing Doris's back and mopping up her vomit. He has been the one feeding and bathing her. He has been the one denying her heroin until she became hysterical with craving.

"I'll take it from here," Madison says.

Sonya opens her mouth to object but her mother looks up from Madison's shoulder. Her eyes throw up an apology and a plea.

There is no use, Sonya thinks as she walks back to her room. There is no use. Madison has my mother. Heroin has my mother. There is no use in fighting either of them. Now, it is only me. Now, I am completely alone.

10

Imposters and spies

Sonya has Tandy's house, at least, with its luscious green yard, with its slabs of windows and dark, cool innards. Zing welcomes her each day after school with a wide smile and open arms. Warm banana bread or ginger loaf steam on the counter, her and Tandy's mid-study-session treat. Jazz spins, crackling and antique, from Zing's record player ("CDs?" she scoffed. "It's not the same without the crackle.") The music berets its way through the rooms and up the stairs where Sonya and Tandy sit hunched over textbooks.

After Tandy deems their studies complete, they sit in the upstairs parlor with Zing and listen to her stories about the Black Panthers, about Ralph David Abernathy and the March on Washington. Zing whispers gossip about stars she's painted murals for. ("Boy laying up right there with him," she says. "Would have never guessed.") Tandy rolls her eyes every night when her mother calls from the parlor. "What does she want now," Tandy says with an annoyance so practiced and fake she smiles at herself. They both look forward to this time with Zing.

Each time, Sonya follows Tandy who shuffles to the parlor with slumped shoulders, who sighs as if put out. When they enter, Zing stands and smiles as if meeting a delegation from Zaire.

"My genius girls," she says, pulling them both toward her.

"Stop it Zing," Tandy says.

Once the candles are lit, once the bread is cut and the poured tea smokes from their cups, once Zing begins one of her fantastic tales, her eyes dark orbs, both Sonya and Tandy surrender and melt. They allow Zing her capture.

Sonya listens, rapt and buzzing. How comfortable, she thinks, how happy and whole Tandy's life is.

In the blank moments between Zing's call and Tandy's shuffle down the hall, or in the moment after an especially long story when everyone's tea needs refreshing, Sonya's attention dashes, like a child bringing news of war, to thoughts of Kush. Out of the corner of her eyes, she peeks for him. On luckier nights, she gets snatches of him: passing Tandy's bedroom door, coming in and out of the parlor for a book or a pair of boots, walking down the stairs or out the door.

On her second visit, Sonya had become confused getting from the downstairs bathroom to the upstairs parlor. She walked through the maze of hallways and came upon Kush and five other black men sitting in a semicircle on a plush rug. Candles blazed throughout the room. Kush spoke emphatically to the group, his face contorted, his hands a flare of gestures. The group paused and he looked up at her. "Peace, sista," he said. "The parlor is upstairs. A left, a right and another left." As she walked away from the semicircle, Sonya listened to Kush's voice, rising and falling, rising and falling. His words choreographed the swells of desire lurching within her.

Each time Kush passes Tandy's doorway or walks through the parlor, Sonya fights the urge to stand up and turn fully around, to take in the whole of his long shadowy figure. She imagines her mother staunchly refusing Madison's little brown packets, her mother sweating and moaning on the edge of the bed. In her own way, Sonya understands her mother's fight against longing. With Kush, Sonya is fighting a similar battle.

Tonight, there will be no Zing stories. She is on commission in Oxford, England. She is painting a mural of Nelson Mandela in the closet of some obscure, rich Arabian prince.

"Mandela?" Sonya said last night when Zing told them of the commission. "In a closet."

"Yep." Zing slurped her tea. "Whatever is clever."

Kush is downstairs in a meeting. Sonya heard the men filing in, all dressed in red, yellow and green sashes and berets. "Another gathering of the Imposter Rastas," Tandy mocked.

Sonya looks over at Tandy. Her eyes zip across the page of equations. She scribbles numbers and symbols on a pad of paper beside her.

"I need to go to the bathroom," Sonya says. She waits for Tandy to respond.

"Well go." Tandy does not look up from her numbers.

As Sonya steps out into the hallway, she knows she is not going to bathroom. She is going to spy on Kush's meeting.

Sonya walks along the hallway with her shoulders hunched and her eyes narrowed to slits. Her right hand trails the wall as if she is feeling for a secret doorway, as if she is reading brail. Realizing the obvious sneakiness of her posture, Sonya straightens and walks casually. "The house is too big," she will say if she runs into one of the men from the meeting. "I'm still learning my way around."

She will blink idiotically. She will ask to be pointed in the right direction.

She walks along the never-ending corridors, rounds a corner and finds another corridor. She had heard Kush directing the men to the third floor of the house. The meeting must be held there.

She passes one room that houses a wall of rugs. They are colorful, bold and intricate. Deep blues punctuated by fiery oranges and sharp greens. Another room reveals a large couch carved it seems, from a single tree. The arms and feet jut out in hard, knobby lumps. The L-shaped back, scooped out of the length of a tree's base, stretches from one end of the room to another. Velvety brown cushions are piled along the couch.

Sonya rounds another corner. Here she faces a huge set of double doors. They are closed. Desire throbs in her chest. She must get a glimpse of Kush. She must hear the sound of his voice again. "Peace, sista," he had said as if she was one of them, which, as far as anyone knows, she is.

But how can she get inside? What excuse would she have for opening the door?

Sonya walks boldly to the double doors. She will feign confusion. She will say she is lost. She will say she was looking for Zing, that she forgot Zing was out of town on commission.

She opens the doors prepared to meet the semicircle of men. But what lay beyond the door is no gathering. It is Kush's room.

The ceiling is vaulted and the floor is sunken, giving the room a huge, sandwiched, cavernous feeling. Sonya looks up at the high chandeliers and then down and the row of steps leading into the main part of Kush's room. It looks like a trap. If she walks in surely the ceiling and floor will rush toward each other and box her in. A ten-foot-high loft spans the left wall. On the loft Sonya can see the corner of a futon peeking out, as well as a television and several stacks of books. A desk sits below the loft. It is just as long as the loft and it is carved in the same tree fashion as the couch from the previous room. Posters, pictures and sketches stud the wall above the desk. A lone chair sits, like an ant among giants, in the far left corner.

Rounding the short inlet, Sonya steps into the room and down the stairs. And the sight of it sucks the air from her lungs: a wall of fantastic colors, fifteen feet long and twenty feet high. Shapes dash and curve—large ovals, cylinders, squares and arrows. They intertwine and separate. They fuse and explode. Shadows play along the sides of these figures, giving them dimension and depth. Sonya steps farther in. She has forgotten about finding Kush and the meeting. She has forgotten about Tandy and the equations. Kush's room is a trap. The wall has hypnotized her.

She approaches the wall tentatively, as if she is sneaking up on a sleeping dragon. She runs her hands along the cool curves and then steps back to take it all in. It is a word, she realizes. A message. But what? What does it say? Sonya squints. Steps back farther. Tries to decipher the shapes. *P. E.* She thinks she sees an *M.* Or is it an

N? She can't be sure. There is a star in the center, exploding. SUPERNOVA. Yes. No. Maybe. But where is the *V?*

"Selassie I." Kush's voice echoes through the room.

His room.

Sonya jumps, stutter steps and trips on a cluster of paint cans.

"I'm—I was just. I." She rises and smiles. "It's beautiful."

"Selassie I," Kush says again. His hands are tucked into his pockets. His eyes are blank with indifference. "Haile Selassie the First. Ras Tafari Makonnen. He started the whole dreadlocked Rasta thing. Well," Kush says, "not really. He was more like the inspiration for it, but…" He shrugs and says nothing more.

"I never knew his real—"

"Get out of my room," Kush says.

"Huh?" Sonya feels dizzy. Stung.

"Get out of my room, please." Kush's voice neither rises nor falls.

Sonya feels a prickle on her skin, humiliation setting her arm hairs on edge.

The space between the paint cans and the door to Kush's room becomes Saharan. Somehow, Sonya must walk its distance without collapsing under the heat of her shame. She manages. In quick, guilty steps, head down, eyes averted, Sonya manages her way to the door. Kush does not move. So she is forced to squeeze by him. Already, she can feel the world closing in on her. She does not cry, could not cry if she wanted to. Her eyes are dry as sand.

Seconds later, Sonya is in Tandy's room. She sits on the floor, picks up her math book and stares blankly at a column of numbers. Tandy does not look up from her page.

Sonya takes a deep breath and prepares to make her confession.

"I got—"

"Shh!" Tandy hisses.

"I was caught—"

"Girl, if you don't, grrr." Tandy bites down hard on her pencil. "I almost got this one."

Moments later, Sonya hears Kush's footfall. Each step, she can tell, is deliberate and angry. Closer. Closer until finally he is at the door.

He looks past Sonya. His eyes are on Tandy.

"Yes, Livingston?" Tandy says without looking up from her textbook. She scribbles furiously.

"If you want to sneak things from my room," Kush says, "at least be woman enough to do it yourself."

"Whatever, Livingston." Tandy taps her pencil against her chin. Her eyes shine with delight. "It's an inverse," she says to no one in particular. "It's an inverse. That's why." Then, back to her scribbling.

Kush scoffs and then walks away.

"I got lost." Sonya offers this explanation to Tandy, her voice small and whiny.

"He's so paranoid," Tandy says. "Since he started that group he thinks—negative. Okay, now we're cooking. Negative seventeen over four."

"What?" Sonya is confused.

"Negative seventeen over four. That's the answer to number forty-one. Negative four and one-fourth." Tandy hops off the bed and claps her hands briskly. "Tea time."

Sonya realizes Kush had not seen her in his room, not really. She is invisible to him. In all the time he has passed her in the hallway nodding a half greeting, in all the times he has stood near her during his conversations with Zing or his arguments with Tandy, Kush never noticed Sonya. To him, she is merely Tandy's friend, the mixed girl who comes by to study. So, when he came upon her in his room, he did not see Sonya. He only saw Tandy's friend—Tandy's accomplice.

The dryness that overtook Sonya subsides. Relief rushes tears to her eyes. Yes, she is infatuated with Kush. Yes, she will continue to dream about him. But this once, just this once, Sonya's invisibility brings her relief.

11

....

The whole truth

It has been over a week since Sonya crept into Kush's room. Madison continues to make nightly visits. Doris continues to fight, sweat, vomit and cry. And Sonya continues her escapes to Tandy's house.

Tandy seems especially distracted tonight. Several times, Sonya catches Tandy looking off into the distance or staring into Sonya's downturned face.

"What's up?" Sonya asks.

Tandy shrugs. "Nothing," she says. "Nothing."

Five minutes or so later, Sonya raises her head to find Tandy staring at her, her eyes wide and perplexed or thin and scanning. It is as if Tandy is trying to see through something, trying to figure something out.

Immediately Sonya retraces the past days, catalogs her lies. Has she betrayed herself? Has she told a lie that doesn't mesh? Or is this about Kush, about Sonya "getting lost" in the hallway, about her sneaking into Kush's room? When Tandy slams her book closed, Sonya readies herself for the worst.

"Have you ever lied?" Tandy asks.

Sonya's larynx drops to her stomach. She fiddles with her fingernails. Looks out across the room to avoid Tandy's eyes.

"We've all lied," she says. "I mean, haven't we?"

"I don't lie," Tandy says. "I try not to."

A beat of silence gives Sonya time to decide on her escape. She will confess. She will confess and walk away. She will transfer schools. She and Doris will move to a small apartment in an obscure neighborhood. She will revert to her other life, before PLD, before Crestman and the huge real estate sales. She will begin again.

"I haven't had many friends over to my house from PLD," Tandy says. "Actually, I haven't had any."

Sonya squeezes a question through her locked throat. "Why?"

"Because they'd hate me if they knew how I lived," Tandy says. "Because I'm rich. Because I haven't had a hard life like Celesta and Keeshawn. Because I'm a nerd. Celesta would see all these books and stuff." Tandy looks out into her vast room, the huge walls and columns, the teepees of books dotting the floor. "They wouldn't think I was, you know."

"I don't," Sonya says. But, somehow, she does. After seeing what lay behind Tandy's rough-around-the-edges facade, Sonya was surprised and a bit disappointed. Tandy proved to be something different from the Tandy Sonya had admired on the train. The house, the books, the money, all of it somehow discredits Tandy, makes her lesser-than.

"I'm not black enough," Tandy says. "At least not Celesta's and Meeka's definition of black."

Sonya steadies herself for what will come next. So, this is about being black enough. About race. Surely Tandy must know.

"There is one lie I've been telling for quite some time," Tandy says.

Good, Sonya thinks. This is about her. Not me. I'm in the clear. She does not suspect.

Sonya's insides settle down, click back into place.

"I lie about my grades," Tandy says. "Well, not to you. You obviously know. But I lie to Celesta and Meeka and the others."

"That's nothing," Sonya says. "I've lied about my grades. It was for the opposite reason," she says. "But I have."

"I love Zing," Tandy says. "But it's difficult being her daughter. She's so good at everything. Art. School. Everything. Did you know she got accepted to Harvard *and* Yale?" Tandy smiles, despite herself. "And everybody's drawn to her. Really, she does steal my friends. Kush's too." The mention of Kush's name warms Sonya's insides.

"When I began at PLD, I decided to be like Zing. At my other school, I was a nerd. I won lots of awards but nobody liked me. I was too, you know, uptight. Anal. So, I decided I'd keep my grades to myself at PLD. I needed friends more than I needed plaques and certificates."

Sonya listens as Tandy reveals the details of her deceit.

After attending private school from kindergarten through eighth grade, Tandy begged Zing to send her to public school. She had grown tired of the facade of prep school (these are her exact words to Sonya). "A real school," Tandy said to Zing. "Where I can meet real black people." Kush had already made his stand against private education.

In her first weeks at PLD, Tandy noticed the cold looks other students flashed when she raised her hand in class: to discuss a recent documentary on the Iroquois she had watched on the Discovery Channel; to read what she thought was an especially telling passage from the original, unabridged edition of Richard Wright's *Native Son;* or to suggest reading Margaret Walker's *Jubilee* as an extension to their coverage of the antebellum south. Intelligence, she gathered, would not win her friends. For a while, Tandy tried to actually make lower grades, but she couldn't force herself to write incorrect answers on test and quizzes. Parenthetic citations, sentence diagrams and quadratic formulas demanded her attention, drew her like metal to a magnet. Instead of denying her intelligence, Tandy hid it. Using her skills of composition and rhetoric, Tandy crafted a letter to Principal Carlton explaining her Quaker roots. "I request that my accomplishments not be publicized," she wrote. "I cannot accept accolades for my academic inclination. Celebrating the individual," she penned, "by default, shadows the accomplishments of many." Kush called it a lie. Tandy called it an exercise in persuasive writing.

"I'd never met a student so serious, so academically accomplished," Principal Carlton said to Tandy after reading her letter, "and yet so humble."

"Quakerism has shown me the true meaning of altruism."

And so it was done. Principal Carlton read Tandy's composition at the next faculty meeting. Teachers were perplexed. You mean *no* awards? they asked. No Honor Role? No Principal's List? No Certificates of Merit or even Most Improved? "Nothing," Principal Carlton said. For the last hour of the faculty meeting, Principal Carlton extolled the virtue of humility. He preached open-mindedness. He preached religious tolerance. Also, he reminded all teachers of the possibility of a lawsuit.

Kush had been sworn to secrecy (they'd both vowed to have each other's back) and Zing, with her flickering artist's mind—with her commissions and conferences, her rallies and round tables—paid little attention to Tandy's academics as long as she performed well. In this way, Tandy maintained her autonomy and anonymity. This allowed her to blend in with everyone else. When she met Celesta and later Meeka and Keeshawn, Tandy didn't wear the label of nerd. She was just another black girl at PLD. Over time, and with much practice and lying, Tandy became the sassiest, the prettiest, and the most popular. The leader of the group. This pushed any possibility of public scholarship out of the question. Nerds weren't popular and all smart people were nerds. Thus, Tandy lived her private, spelling bee persona alone. Alone, that is, until Sonya.

"I feel like we are going to be friends for a long time," Tandy says. "I know you knew some of it, about me keeping my grades secret and all that. But I wanted to tell you the whole thing," she says, "so we wouldn't begin our friendship with a lie."

"Thanks," Sonya says. "Thanks for, you know, trusting me." Sonya can barely find her voice.

12

Unbelievable catastrophe

Sonya is rolling with Tandy, Celesta and Meeka. At least, that's how Tandy puts it to Maurice Maitland who still leers and winks at Sonya.

"Leave her alone," Tandy says in homeroom while they await the arrival of the ever late, and, as Sonya learns later, ever drunk Mrs. Larsen. "Sonya's rolling with *us* now."

"Can I at least get your digits?" Maurice Maitland asks Sonya.

Tandy, Meeka, Celesta and Keeshawn look from one to another. Celesta nods a cue.

"Niggah huh?" Celesta rumbles.

"Niggah who?" Meeka squeaks.

"Niggah what?" Keeshawn smacks.

Tandy rolls her eyes, splays her fingers and pushes her hand into Maurice's face. "Niggah please!" She says, capping off their routine.

Up until now, Sonya's inclusion felt, to her, semi-permanent like something drawn with a preschooler marker, or like a cheap tattoo bought in a quarter vending machine—something that could be washed away or peeled off. But now, her status is official.

Tandy's words, *She's rolling with us now,* authenticates Sonya like a notary's stamp.

There are unspoken but understood rules to being a part of a crew, to rolling together. First of all, you meet frequently—between every class if possible and, at the very least, during locker breaks—to catch up on the day's happenings ("Mr. Zane is out today," Keeshawn said. "Something about his dog shitting everywhere." "Did you see what Kemah had on?" Celesta asked. Kemah was Celesta's, and therefore the entire crew's, sworn enemy. "She looked like a Lil' Kim wannabe."). Second, you take lunch together, sitting in the same seats in the same order. ("Meeka get up," Tandy said. "You know that's Celesta's seat."). Third, you are brutally honest with one another ("Sonya, girl, you too pale to be wearing that beige," Celesta said. "You look like you about to throw up.").

Sonya feels both relief and trepidation in being a part of Tandy's crew. Relief because she is no longer considered the new kid on the block. Before coming to PLD she had imagined an experience similar to that of her freshman year at Crestman. She'd imagined sitting in the back of the classroom, shoulders slightly hunched, being ignored by other students. She had imagined walking through the hallways among lumbering football players and heavily rouged cheerleaders. She'd imagined shoulders bumping into her, pushing her aside. In the lunchroom, she was sure she would face the horrifying decision of where to sit. She was certain the faces of other students would look up at her from the expanse of rectangular tables and flash hostility. But, more than any of these, Sonya was sure her whiteness, the very fact of her pale skin and light eyes, would isolate her.

Sonya had hoped against hope to meet Tandy and become her best friend. But alongside that hope ran the understanding that she would not be welcomed. That Tandy would not become her friend. Mirroring Sonya's fancy of rolling with Tandy and her crew was an image of her life as an outsider, the white girl, floating through the hallways lonely, disregarded, unnoticed for the most part, like a ghost of some abandoned mansion.

This has not happened. Tandy and the others have taken to her immediately, despite Sonya's lack of street smarts. "You live a real sheltered life," Celesta comments after having to explain to Sonya what she means when she says she got her bling on the low.

"My ring is stolen, fool," Celesta says. "Damn. We are going to have to enroll you in classes. Ghetto One-Oh-One or something. Get you a tutor."

"I grew up in the suburbs," Sonya says, which is a flat out lie. At this point, Sonya figures she is already in deep. One more lie doesn't matter. At this point, after the fact that she lets Tandy and the others continue to assume she is biracial, even plays it up a little with Maurice, the other fibs to follow are literally little white lies.

One little white lie becomes another and another until Sonya looks around herself to find she has built a life. She now walks through PLD as the confused and tragic mulatto. To Sonya's new friends, she is a white-black child with a family that disowned her mother (and, by default, Sonya) because of her mother's pregnancy out of wedlock and because of her mother's marriage to a white man. She is the daughter of an abusive and now absentee father ("I thought you said he left when you were three," Tandy asked. "He came back every now and again," Sonya said, "to kick me and my mother's ass."). Sonya's mother, to all concerned, is a reclusive alcoholic, scarred from years of neglect and abuse ("That's why I don't like studying at my house, you know." Here Sonya looks off, chokes up a little, borrowing grief from her mother's real story. "Because my mother's so fucked up all the time.").

Sonya constructs a colossal fabrication, a mammoth mansion of a lie. Sonya's faux past looms so huge, so blunt and obvious and tragic, so unbelievable in its catastrophe, that no one for one moment questions its legitimacy.

Today Sonya waits at her locker on the second floor near the science lab. She's meeting Tandy to check in. She is excited because today she has her first real bit of gossip. In days past, she'd thought of venturing out into the new territory, of offering something into the pot of tabloid Celesta and the other concocted for each other. But what Sonya comes up with never seems interesting enough to share aloud. Besides, she doesn't have Celesta's animated character, Celesta who can make you laugh at the fact of a nose in the center of your face. Also, Sonya still treads lightly. She feels the instability of her constructed life, a house of cards. She listens and laughs, drawing as little attention to herself and her biography as possible. Each time someone asks her a question, however ordinary, Sonya's heart shudders in her chest. Each time, she works hard in her head, shuffling through her catalogue of lies. Each time, she has to remember she is black.

Today is different. Today she will risk putting herself in the center of the group. Sonya is sure her news will be a hit. Surely they will want to know about the red stain on the back of Kemah's pants, how Mrs. Larsen had called Kemah to the board and how she had asked loudly in her gravelly, drunken voice, "Why you holding your book like that, baby?" Kemah froze. "If your period done messed your jeans," Mrs. Larsen announced, "go clean up yourself."

Mrs. Larsen continued to mumble to herself as Kemah skirted shyly out the door. "Girl is crazy, messing herself like that in Mrs. Larsen's class and not telling nobody. What she think she in, the second grade. Everybody know Mrs. Larsen let you go to the potty as long as you ask." If Sonya were Celesta, she could recreate the whole scene, with Kemah's humiliated face and Maurice's obnoxious laughter. If she were Celesta, she could do Mrs. Larsen's voice. She could mimic the way Mrs. Larsen says baby, drawing out the word into three syllables, *bay-ah-bee,* as Mrs. Larsen does.

Of course, Sonya will not do the voice of Mrs. Larsen. She will only tell the story. She attempted a retelling of the story, whispering it to herself on the way to her locker. She attempted Mrs. Larsen's voice, trying to get the correct tone of the "go clean up yourself." Recreating Mrs. Larsen in this way made Sonya feel the same way she felt when Madison fondled her breasts. It made her feel wrong. Embarrassed. It made her feel guilty, as if she were the molester. All at once, Sonya understood. Doing Mrs. Larsen's voice is different coming from Celesta, different because of the history Celesta brings to it (which is part of the reason, Sonya also realizes, why she is no good at it). It will be wrong and off-key, lewd, coming out of Sonya's mouth. The others, who think Sonya's black, will hear it as an elitist judgment from a yellow girl from the suburbs. Surely, one of them, most like Celesta, would say just that if Sonya attempted to do Mrs. Larsen. "Girl, yo yellow suburban ass don't sound even half right." To Sonya, who knows she is white regardless of what the others think, mimicking Mrs. Larsen or using the *N* word for that matter (which she has promised herself she will never do) will always be unacceptable because of her race. Sonya will always have to watch what she says, what she allows herself to do or not do, lest she becomes too comfortable. Lest she trips herself up on her own lies.

More teachers let their classes out. Now as the other students rush past, laughing and jeering their way to their lockers, Sonya spots Tandy. She feels her face lighting up. She feels her insides giggling with the fact of her gossip. "Your girl Kemah really embarrassed herself in Mrs. Larsen's class," Sonya will say. *Your girl* is one of Celesta's phrases. It is one of the few black expressions Sonya is comfortable with, one of the few that she adopted naturally. Sonya used it so naturally and effortlessly for the first time today at the lunch table that she almost stopped mid-sentence. She was even beginning to sound like them. She was even more satisfied that the others had not noticed.

So, yes, as Sonya spots Tandy with Celesta and Keeshawn trailing a few steps behind her, she readies her herself for her story.

"Your girl really—" she begins, but Tandy snatches her by the arm.

"What's the matter?" Sonya says. Tandy's grip is vice-tight. Sonya feels her arm throbbing under the crush of Tandy's fingers.

Tandy's eyes grow wide as wagons. She has a frantic, irritated expression on her face.

Sonya tries to pull her arm away, but this only causes Tandy to hold on tighter.

"Come on," Tandy says.

"What?" Sonya manages to free her arm. "What's your—"

Tandy locks Sonya's arms in another grip. She usher's Sonya down the hall and toward the fire exit. The more Sonya struggles the angrier Tandy becomes.

"I have to talk to you," Tandy hisses. "I have to talk to you right now."

....
76

13

Caught red-handed

Sonya allows herself to be led out of the fire exit by Tandy and down a far hill. This is where Keeshawn comes to smoke between classes. Sonya, Tandy, and Meeka accompany her and usually trade gossip while Keeshawn puffs. Once, during an excruciatingly cold morning when Keeshawn begged them to go with her for a cig, Celesta looked at Keeshawn and shook her head in mock reproach. "Girl, you're shaking like a crack baby," she said. "Look at you, puffing like P-Daddy. Puffing like the magic dragon." They all laughed at this. Even Keeshawn, who sucked on her cigarette vehemently with one hand pushed in her pocket, laughed almost to the point of choking. "We're going to change your name to Toby," Celesta had said. "Slave to the nicotine. 'Yessum Massah Marlboro. I'sa do whatevah you say, Massah Marlboro.'" Sonya remembers how she had laughed up to this point and how, afterwards, she looked around at Celesta and the other, at their earlobes and the backs of their hands. The joke—its reference to slavery and the way Tandy, Celesta and the others laughed at it casually— caused the same feelings of guilt to gurgle up in Sonya's gut. She remembers thinking, "I have to tell them. I have to tell them now." The day went on, of course. Tandy came to her crying about her grade on her physics exam (she is too embarrassed, she says, to tell the others the exact grade. Sonya found out later it was a B minus). Keeshawn announced she was moving to Texas in a week (I just didn't know how to tell y'all) and Celesta gave the fashion report at lunch ("Kemah looked like a goddamn Lollipop with all that pink on"). By the end of the day, Sonya had forgotten the moment outside. Sonya had forgotten her guilt and the fact of her lie.

She and Tandy have made it outside. Sonya knows this is her moment of conviction. Sonya feels the foundation of her mansion of lies trembling beneath her feet. The walls shake. Dust sifts down from the rafters. A blackbird abandons its nest in a high-up window, caws loudly and flies away with a clap of its wings. Sonya stands, as she knew she would eventually, in the center of her castle of lies, fully prepared for it to crumble around her. Even now, it seems surreal, the way Tandy does not look at her. The way Tandy paces, irritated and angry, at the bottom of the hill.

At first, Sonya thinks of apologizing. But she cannot think exactly how she will fashion this apology. In the midst of Tandy's obvious fury, her "I'm sorry" will ring false and insincere, partly because it will be too late to apologize. The damage is already done. More so, though, because Sonya will not mean it. Even as she prepares herself to take on the full blow of Tandy's scorn, even as she stands in the hollow of her castle looking up at the ponderous beams that are sure to crush her, Sonya cannot regret anything she has done. She wanted to belong; she wanted to be something more, something other than a rich white girl from Buckhead.

As she watches Tandy pace back and forth, as she watches the anger build in Tandy's face, Sonya tries to think of how to explain what she felt each time she saw Tandy and her friends on the train. *Envy* would not be the right word, though it seems close. What Sonya felt then and what she feels even now, when Celesta and Keeshawn exchange stories about going to the candy store, eating fish and grits for dinner, and growing up in black poverty, is longing. Their lives, their families and stories, are thick and rich and full of struggle and love. Her life feels skeletal in comparison. Her life feels and has always felt like something she has adopted. A small, unspeaking child that walks up to you on the street and takes your hand, a child who demands your guardianship but refuses to speak, a child with grey skin and a hacking cough. A child who eventually dies, that's what Sonya's life feels like to her.

There is no way to explain this to Tandy. So, Sonya doesn't. Instead, she prepares herself for the breadth of Tandy's anger. She will listen to Tandy. She will allow herself to be yelled at, slapped if it come to that, though, knowing Tandy, it won't come to that. Sonya will take it all without resistance or response. She will meet whatever chastisement Tandy issues. She will take it all and then walk away.

"So," Tandy says. She stops mid pace and looks directly at Sonya. Her statement is both a question and a dare. Sonya waits for the rest.

"Don't pretend you haven't heard." Sonya opens her mouth to speak, and then thinks better of it. "About The Rebels. About Kush." It takes Sonya a second to connect the name. Then she remembers: Kush. Tandy's brother.

"No," Sonya says. Suddenly, the castle ceases its rumble. The rafters still themselves. The sun burns away clouds of doom and the blackbird returns, settling into her nest with a caw. Sonya's face brightens with relief. This is not about her lie, about her not being black. This is about something else. The gods have smiled upon her again. She is saved.

"It's not funny," Tandy says. Her voice bubbles with anger. "My family's about to make an ass of themselves in front of the entire school and all you can do is laugh."

"Laugh," Sonya says. "I'm not laughing." Just as she says this, she realizes that she is. Her laughter is from relief, though Tandy can't know this.

"You are laughing," Tandy says. "You're laughing at my expense."

"I'm laughing because you're so angry and I don't know what about."

"You really haven't heard," Tandy says. "Celesta didn't tell you?"

"I haven't seen Celesta today," Sonya says.

All of Sonya's fear and repentance vanishes and she is back in the present. She has forgotten about the tragedy that almost befell her kingdom. She reassumes her role as Tandy's friend and, by default, her role as the mixed girl, with quickness and ease. Sonya listens with full attention. Whatever Tandy is about to reveal promises to be much less dangerous to Sonya than her lie and much more interesting than her story about Kemah's period.

"In five minutes, my mom, my brother and his idiot friends are about to hold a rally. You remember that book I took from by brother."

Sonya recalls that night. More than the book, she remembers Kush's dark, shining skin and his beautiful face.

"Yeah," she says. "But what's that got to—"

"That's like their bible or something. Their Black Rebels' Bible. They call it their little black book. What a cliché. It's got all this crap in it about overthrowing the government and taking up arms against the man, about black folks from outer space. It's some Angela-Davis-meets-Luke-Skywalker mess." Tandy speaks fast. Anger and annoyance tumble the words out of her mouth.

"Anyway, my mother is like the chairperson of the group. She and my brother and the other members are staging a rally at the school. They are going to have banners and a mic and all that madness. My mother! She's coming to PLD. I hope she doesn't wear those idiotic rubies and sapphires."

"Those are real?" Sonya asks, remembering the huge, twinkling rings on Zing's fingers.

"Yeah, but I don't want folks to know that. God, this is horrible."

"It will be okay."

"No it won't. Zing is crazy about mess like this. And I don't know what Kush is going to say, but if he says any of the crap he says to me at home, I'm going to have to transfer schools."

"Is it a school assembly?" Sonya asks.

"Please," Tandy says. "They wouldn't allow this kind of stuff at an assembly."

"That means it's not mandatory," Sonya says. "Just don't go."

"Don't go?" Tandy says. "Don't go! I live with these people. Now my brother, I could just ignore him. But my mother? I wouldn't hear the end of it. I have to go. If I don't, Zing would put me on a total restriction, no mall, no movies, no money and the longest guilt trip of my high school career."

"I'll stand beside you," Sonya said.

"Believe me," Tandy says. "You don't want to stand—"

"It's fine," Sonya shrugs. "I don't mind."

"You will mind once you—"

"I've been through worse. One time my mother came up to the school zonked out of her mind. Drunk, I mean, and accused the Lit teacher of molesting me. So I know embarrassment."

This really happened to Sonya. Her mother had stumbled through the halls yelling the teacher's name, "Zimmer! Zimmer you molesting son of a bitch!" Luckily it was a Saturday after band practice and only she and the coach were in the building. They had been waiting for an hour for Sonya's mother, who was late as usually. Sonya calmed her mother and escorted her to the car where Madison waited with a wry small on his face. "She needed a little fresh air," he said.

"You sure you don't mind standing by me?" Tandy asks.

"No, no. Of course I will." Sonya is so relieved to be in the clear she is ready to offer anything.

"Good." Tandy reaches into her book bag and pulls out red and black and gold scarves, two black berets and fire red gloves. "Put these on," she instructs. "And remember to stand at attention. Don't move. And, above all else, you have to look mad as sin."

Sonya holds the brightly colored accessories in her hand.

"Hurry up girl," Tandy says, fashioning the scarf around her neck. "We're going to be late."

Tandy slides her fingers into her gloves. They make her hands look as if they are on fire, as if they have been dipped in blood.

Sonya's scarf slides from her hand and falls limply to the ground. She has just volunteered herself to participate in a black revolution rally. This is almost as bad as using the *N* word, which Sonya will never ever do. Sonya knows she cannot go through with this. If there is any time to tell Tandy the truth, it is now.

14

Track marks

As they rush around the back of the building to help Kush and the others unload and set up, Tandy gives Sonya a brief history of the group. "My brother, my mother and three other artists founded the Black Rebels last year. My brother is a painter too," Tandy explains. "He did the mural in the foyer of our house."

"It began as a Rastafarian thing," she says, "but none of them had the patience to grow locks or eat the strict I-tal diet. So the Black Rebels developed into what it is now, a bunch of bourgeois black folks with too much money and time on their hands."

"Your mom," Sonya says. "She has dreadlocks."

"She's always had them, so that was kind of cheating." Tandy adjusts her tie. "Last year my brother went on a black culture binge. All of Maya Angelou's, Richard Wright's and Toni Morison's novels back-to-back, topped off with all of Malcolm's speeches, his autobiography and the teachings of Marcus Garvey. Plus a load of bullshit he got from the Internet and from those little Rasta markets in the West End."

Sonya listens and adjusts her own scarf and headgear. She is not really here, walking swiftly beside Tandy, listening to her talk about the Black Rebels. Sonya is not here, with a beret on her head, preparing to take part in a black power demonstration. She has retreated inside of herself. From there she looks out, watches the scene unfold. It is as if she is on autopilot, as if she is strapped down to a conveyor belt, which glides her slowly toward the mouth of a fiery pit. It is a dream in which she is horrified and wants to scream, but can't.

Tandy and Sonya arrive at the front of the school to find a band of red-, black- and green-clad people hustling about. The Rebels unload quickly: speakers, microphone, podium, rafters and plywood. Within five minutes they have set up shop.

"Who's the white chick," one of the members—a short, stubby boy with a bald head and full beard—asks. They call him Sergeant.

"The *white chick's* name is Sonya," Tandy answers in a sassy, perturbed voice loud enough for the others to hear. "And, unlike your grandparents on your father's side, Sergeant, Sonya isn't white."

The entire school crowds the lawn inside the school's circular drive. It is the end of the day, so the buses are parked. Their engines grumble and radiate heat like large, panting dogs. The bus drivers sit behind oversized steering wheels and fumble with the rigid beaks of their caps. Most are more irritated at being held up than interested in the scene at hand, though some look on the spectacle with distant curiosity.

Principal Carlton stands on the periphery of the crowd flanked by his nervy, white-haired secretary, Ms. Hurston, and the school security guards. He has decided he will not give the rabble-rousers what they were hoping for, resistance. He will not make a scene. He has decided to let them have their little rally.

Sonya and Tandy stand on the portable stage that the Black Rebels have set up. It is a long rickety structure of aluminum beams and thin wooden planks. Each time a member of the Rebels walks to the podium in the center, his footsteps shake the entire stage. Sonya has been told by several of the members to stand at attention, to never look any audience members in the eye. "Keep your eye on the struggle sister," Sergeant whispers in Sonya's ear from behind. She looks out and up, afraid to scan the audience, lest the fear in her eyes somehow betrays her whiteness.

Tandy stands beside her, shoulders erect, chest forward, eyes unwavering. No one, not even Sonya, would have known Tandy was the same girl who, just moments earlier, referred to the Rebels as imposter Rastas and imitation insurrectionists. As they were setting up, Sonya asked why Tandy participated when she disagreed with the group and its approach.

"Because he's my brother," Tandy answered coolly. "We may have our little fights, but that's my heart." She pointed to Kush who hoisted a speaker onto the stage. "I can't play him in public no matter what happens at home. And I definitely won't let anyone else play him."

Again, Sonya saw a hint of the glowering thing that peeked at her from behind Tandy's eyes.

So Tandy stands by her brother, literally, as he glances down at his notes. Zing sits at the far left of the stage, nodding and clapping when appropriate. To Tandy's relief, she did not wear her extravagant jewelry. For the most part, the audience is attentive as the leader of the Rebels reads the mission statement and lists the seven principals of conscious rebellion.

Next, Kush takes the podium. Before he speaks he looks back at Tandy and Sonya—at least, Sonya thinks she is included in the glance—for reassurance.

Kush begins steadily enough, restating the seven principles. He lists famous black leaders from Harriet Tubman to Oprah Winfrey and gives brief anecdotes from each leader's biography to illustrate the power of the principles. Next, Kush tells the history of the organization. From his telling, the idea of the Black Rebels came to him and his cohorts mystically. "As if from the voice of The One," he says. "The One, The Creator, The Divine."

Tandy, standing stock still next to Sonya, shakes her head ever so slightly. "Oh God," she says through her teeth. "As long as he doesn't pull out that book."

Kush pulls out the book.

"The Book of the One," he calls it. He reads passages written in a language Sonya recognizes as English, but barely. The phrases are jumbled and twisted, full of strange word combinations like *I-self* and *One-We*. "One-We will return to the original planet," Kush says, going on to explain that Earth to the Original Planet is just as the American colonies were to England—a debtors' camp of sorts, a exile planet for unwanted germs. "Since One-We have grown and matured, One-We are ready," Kush says. "Ready to return to Or-I and be accepted by The One."

The audience, which had been surprisingly attentive up to this point, begins to grumble and snicker. Some students, disappointed in the lack of spectacle, have already loaded the bus. Others listen, amused by the absurdity of Kush's pronouncements.

"The Creator is among us," Kush says. "The One. In the audience now, perhaps. The Creator, One-We, he watches. He watches. He watches." Here Kush decreases his voice to a whisper and walks away from the podium as if fading to black.

There is a moment during which the audience is completely silent, a moment of stillness like the pause after lightening and just before the explosion of thunder. And the audience does thunder, roaring and tumbling with laughter. Even Celesta and Meeka, who try to hold their faces rigid and serious, give in to the hilarity.

Sonya holds her at-attention stance. She can feel Tandy beside her, but is too afraid to look. Sonya fears if she looks, her face will betray her inner thoughts. And she thinks just what everyone else does, that the Black Rebels' philosophy is ridiculous. Sonya watches Kush and his straggly gang of rebels standing stock-still with their fists raised and their heads lowered. A sea of embarrassment rises in her gut. Her embarrassment is sad, removed and vicarious. It is as if she were sitting at a distant picnic table, watching children taunt a clown. Sonya thinks about stepping in, storming up to the microphone to chastise the audience. Even if she dared to break out of line, out of stance, even if she dared to walk across the stage in front of the already jeering, taunting eyes, even if she dared let her squeaky voice out into the huge amplifiers, what would she say? Stop it? What would she do, waggle her finger?

Eventually, Sergeant yells, "I-wards." They turn to the left military style. Sonya looks into the blades of Tandy's back and the shining strands of her hair, searching for a clue to her mood. She thinks she notices a slight dropping and heaving of Tandy's shoulders. She thinks Tandy is crying, but she is not sure. "I-ward," the bald one yells, and they march off the stage and down the drive. The crowd's laughter rumbles behind them.

It turns out Tandy's shoulders had been hunched with laughter. "I couldn't help it," she says to her mother who looks on Tandy with scalding eyes.

"Down right disrespectful," Zing says. "Remember what I said about restriction. I have to cut you off for a month."

This weekend was to be Sonya's first official outing with the crew. She eavesdropped as Zing scolded Tandy for laughing. Something in Sonya sighed with relief when Zing restricted Tandy. If Tandy didn't go, there was no reason why Sonya would go. Of course Sonya looked forward to hanging out with Tandy and the others, *posting up* as Celesta said ("We going to post up at Lenox Mall and check for niggahs"); but trepidation dwarfed her excitement. PLD and East Atlanta were safe. Sonya's life, if limited to these areas, held little threat of running into anyone from Crestman. At Lenox Mall on a Saturday night, at Lenox Mall, which was only five minutes away from her old house, ten minutes from Crestman, Sonya was sure to run into someone from her former life.

Samantha Klieg has called several times since Sonya moved. Each time she called, her voice bubbled and swooped valley-girl style, something Sonya hadn't noticed at Crestman. Sami peppered her last message with imperatives. "You *must* call me back," she said. "I simply *have* to tell you about Lydia's latest stunt. Oh my fucking God. You won't believe it," Sami overenunciated. Her voice boomed bright and annoying. "And I must—" here she scoffed "—I simply *must* see the new house. I heard it was humungous. Call me. Smooches."

Sonya eavesdropped as Tandy argued futilely with Zing. Even

from where she stood, Sonya could see that Zing had made up her mind. Tandy tried arguing. When that didn't' work, she fell into a pouty tantrum, flopping to the ground and refusing to help load the cars. "Suit yourself," Zing said.

"Can you believe it?" Tandy makes her way over to Sonya who busies herself rolling thick speaker cords.

"No mall, huh?" Sonya says. "That sucks." She digs deep for a let-down tone and tries to fashion her face to look concerned and disappointed. In reality, her heart swells with relief. She doesn't have to worry about what to wear, how to dress like a black girl who looks white instead of a white girl trying to look black. She doesn't have to worry about issuing the proper affect, that dim combination of embarrassment and insult she issues each time someone questions her race. Most of all, she doesn't have to worry about her former classmates from Crestman. She doesn't have to worry about Samantha Klieg.

Tandy drops the pile of cords she had begun to coil. "I'm out," she says. "Celesta has her mother's car. We're rolling to Checkers for burgers. You down?"

"I have to get home, check on my mother." As Sonya says this, she realizes, yes, she does have to check on Doris. For the last two nights Doris had been fighting with Madison and with her ad-diction. Sonya listened from her room as Doris pronounced her independence. "No more," she said, her voice trembling with effort. "I'm not like this, I'm not…"

"What," Madison said. His voice came even and cold. "A junkie. Then what do you call these?" He snatched up Doris's arm, exposing the scabby track marks on her inner arm and armpits.

"Mistakes," Doris said. "That's what they are. And I'm not making anymore." Sonya heard the strain in her mother's voice, a strain against the desire screaming out from every nerve in her skin.

"I know how this works," Madison said. "You need this right now."

Doris wanted the brown clump of heroin in Madison's hand. She wanted it bad. Still, she made her mouth say the words. "Go away, Madison."

Sonya listened, numb and unbelieving. She held a pillow to her chest and rocked back and forth on the edge of her bed. Her mother was in the living room fighting with her boyfriend who deals to her. Her mother was a heroin addict.

"I can't," Sonya says now to Tandy. "My mother's sick. Flu. I got to check up on her."

"You shouldn't take the train alone," Tandy says. "I guess Celesta can—"

"I'll take her." Kush says from across the lawn. Both Tandy and Sonya look up. Kush continues working as if he'd said nothing.

Celesta beeps her horn. "Come on y'all. I'm hungry. You know us big girls got to eat or else we get grouchy. I might end up slapping a motherfucker in a minute."

Keeshawn, who is visiting from Texas, waves from the car. "Hey, girl," she yells to Tandy. "Hey, Sonya."

"Hi," Sonya says.

Tandy is torn. Sonya can see it on her face. Tandy wants to go with Celesta, but she doesn't want to abandon Sonya. Sonya makes the decision for her.

"Girl, go on," Sonya says. Tandy looks from Sonya to Kush and the group of Rebels. "I'll be fine. I live less than ten minutes away."

Tandy and Sonya walk to the car together. Tandy hops in, cramming Meeka in the middle. "Girl you almost got my hair caught," Meeka says. She pulls her ponytail over her right shoulder and strokes it. It has grown rapidly, Sonya notices, over the past weeks. Now it falls down her shoulders, dark and whip-luscious, like the tail of a prized pony.

"Could you shut the hell up about that hair," Celesta says.

"I'm just saying," Meeka whimpers.

"There's more where that came from," Celesta says.

"What you talking about," Meeka says. "This ain't no weave."

"Whatever Meeka," Celesta says. "Let me yank that shit then." Celesta reaches back and Meeka shrieks.

"Stop girl. I'm tender headed."

"Me too, boo," Celesta says through pursed lips. "Me too."

Sergeant trots to the car.

"Good evening, sistas." His tips his beret.

"Oh lord," Celesta says, "let me turn my unholy music down. Don't want to offend Malcolm Luther Garvey."

"I could not help but notice—" Sergeant leans into the car and looks around at the four inside "—that none of you sistas remembered to wear your head wraps."

"Head wraps?" Celesta says. "What in the hell. Do I look like Erykah Badu?"

"I could use a rim shot though," Keeshawn says.

"You ain't never lied," Celesta says. She and Keeshawn slap five.

"Y'all so nasty," Meeka says.

Sergeant looks to Tandy for support.

"I'm down with the rebellion and all," Tandy says waving her scarf limply in her hand, "but I can't help you with this one, dog."

"A woman's hair is sacred," Sergeant says. He waggles his finger inside the car. "We have another gathering in a few weeks. I'm sure y'all will be there. The next time you attend a Rebel function, please come dressed appropriately. Do I make myself clear?"

"Do you make yourself *who?*" Celesta says.

"I said, do I make myself clear, ladies?"

Celesta meets the eyes of the others through her rearview mirror. Again, she nods the cue.

"Niggah huh?" Celesta says.

"Niggah what?" Meeka says.

"Niggah who?" Keeshawn says.

Tandy looks up at Sergeant. "I'm sorry, dog," she says. "But niggah, please!" Then, she says to Celesta. "Let's blow this joint." The car pulls away slowly.

"They'll be talking that mess all night," Tandy yells from the window. "Don't let them get inside your head."

"I'll be cool," Sonya says. Even she can hear the quiver of uncertainty in her voice.

The car skids forward then grumbles down the road.

Sonya looks at Sergeant who walks back toward the school. He is sure to grill her during the ride home. He is sure to try to convert her into a skirt-wearing, head-wrapping, black-book-reading Rebel woman. "Ten minutes," Sonya says to herself. "I can make it through ten minutes."

Celesta's car leaves track on the gravel, two gray-black question marks.

"I'll be cool," Sonya says to herself. "I'll be cool."

15
·······················

The revolution will not be televised

"If they start talking that black space revolution crap, just tell them to shut up." *Them,* Tandy had said, because she assumed Sonya would ride with Kush, Zing, the Sergeant and the other Rebels who helped load the van. Sonya assumed the same. As soon as Tandy left, plans changed.

Zing decides to stay after to talk to Principal Carlton and a few parents who were upset about the rally and the late buses. "Let me set these folks straight," Zing says, marching off to the principal's office. "Y'all don't have to wait around for me," she says. "Changing minds takes a little while. Kush, I'll call you to come get me when it's all over."

After loading up their SUV with the audio equipment, Sergeant and the other Rebels drive off to catch a speaker in the West End. They invite Kush and Sonya, but he declines for both of them. "Sista's got to get home to check after her mom," Kush says. "And I've had enough revolution for one day." Kush butts fists with Sergeant. Sergeant and his crew jet off in their oversized SUV leaving Kush and Sonya alone.

Later, when she is at home, sitting at the desk near her bedroom window or when she catches her own eyes in the mirror as she lifts to rinse her face, Sonya will look at herself hard and ask, "What the hell was I thinking?" This question won't be filled with regret or scolding. It will come from a pit of total and blank surprise. "What was I thinking?" Sonya will ask the hazy reflection of herself in her bedroom mirror. This will be later, of course, after she has actually had time to think.

Kush pulls the gearshift to drive. They slip smoothly out of the school parking lot. The February evening turns a deep, mellow blue, foreshadowing the early dark to come. Surprisingly, Sonya doesn't feel nervous. Awkward a little, being closed up in the hushed interior of the vehicle with Kush, a boy she barely knows, a boy she has a slight crush on. Awkward, but not nervous. She fiddles with the radio until she finds Hot 97, a radio station Celesta told her to check out. Sonya has been listening every night since her first day at PLD. She has been studying the commercials, songs and lyrics, familiarizing herself with the details of popular black culture. Now she sing-speaks the words to Salt and Peppa's "Push It." An eighties flashback, the DJ announces. Kush reaches over to turn up the volume and they sing the chorus together. Sonya smiles a huge, happy smile. Her studying has paid off.

"Nice car," she says when the song ends.

"It's Tandy's," Kush says. "She'll barely drive it. She's still trying to keep up that ghetto girl image for her friends."

"They see you driving it," Sonya says. "Wouldn't they connect the two?"

Kush shrugs his shoulders. "They probably think I sell drugs or something. Who knows what Tandy tells them? Besides, half of them have cars like this or nicer. Nigga rich syndrome."

"What?"

"Nigga rich. We'll spend three hundred on a cell phone before we spend three dollars on a calculator."

"They have to know who your mom is," Sonya says.

"They kind of know. They know she's sold some paintings. But they don't really know how much dough she's got. I think they

think she paints walls or something. I mean like a house painter."
He turns to look at Sonya. "I don't think *you* really know. Zing
has done shit for everybody from The President to Oprah. Everybody."

"Wow," Sonya says. Kush holds her gaze a little longer than necessary. She returns his stare. They both turn away, suddenly shy of
each other.

"What is the festival Sergeant kept going on about?"

"Fest-tee-vahl," Kush corrects her pronunciation. "It's the first
gathering of all major black underground movements in Atlanta.
It's going to be really dope."

"Oh, Fest-tee-vahl," Sonya repeats. "Like the Caribbean carnival."

"Only this won't be a carnival. It will be a mass political gathering, an exchange of ideas. There's going to be forums and
speakers." Kush and Sonya's eyes meet again in another prolonged
gaze. She looks away first. "It's going to be really cool."

Sonya stares down at her hands and then out of the window.
Other cars zoom past. Trees dash by, waving in the night breeze.

"What'd you think?" Kush's question comes out hesitant. Sonya
can tell he is unsure of himself.

At first, Sonya thinks Kush is asking about his looking at her;
then she realizes he is talking about today's rally.

"It was cool," she says. "It was cool." Her voice goes mellow
and hip, like a beatnik poet's.

"Cool?" Kush scoffs.

"It was a'ight," she says, another one of Celesta's words. Sonya
does not know where this new voice is coming from, but she
goes with it.

"Alright. That's all?"

"You know," Sonya says. "It was, well. I'm not trying to be
critical or anything, but you got to get your facts straight."

Sonya knows a lot about getting facts straight. Since coming
to PLD she has played catch-up, devouring every article and
book related to black people she can get her hands on. In
addition to her nightly study of R&B and rap via Hot 97,
Sonya rented DVDs of every black television show available,

from *The Jeffersons* and *The Cosby Show* to *In Living Color* and *Moesha*. Sonya viewed them all. By the third week, she had a kitty of blackness to pull from. When Celesta or Meeka mentioned an episode of *Good Times* ("You remember when Penny got burned with the iron") Sonya chimed in, laughing and adding details, with proper footnotes. If nothing else, Sonya had her facts straight.

"For real?" Kush's voice is timid and childlike, truly surprised, as if Sonya has just told him there is no Santa.

Sonya did not expect such shyness from Kush. Watching him bully Tandy in the way all big brothers bully their sisters, watching him at the microphone, his face twisted in misinformed rage, Sonya expected him to be more direct and challenging. This bashfulness of his leaves a huge void in the car's atmosphere. And just as a sponge that expands in water, Sonya feels herself swelling to fill it.

"All that alien shit," Sonya says. She jerks her arms forward in stiff gestures, fingers flared, to punctuate her words. "Man, you sounded straight twisted. I'm sorry, but it was kind of whack, yo."

"I wouldn't say wha—"

"It was definitely whack." Sonya says. Something cracks inside of Sonya, spills open. An alter ego. A higher self. She feels brazen and sassy talking this way. She feels as if she's doing an impression of someone, but doing it well. Her voice loses its Crestman chirp. It fills out, grows thick and syrupy like Tandy's. Like Celesta's and Keeshawn's.

"It was just, I don't know…" Sonya says. A word Celesta often uses gurgles in Sonya's throat. She opens her mouth and spits it out. "It was bootleg. You can't talk about revolution in one breath and talk about space invaders in another. Dog, come on!"

"Bootleg?" Kush has parked the car. They are in front of Sonya's house. Outside, the sky bleeds a heavy indigo. A lone dog barks in a nearby yard. "Bootleg?" He says again, slapping his hands on the steering wheel.

Sonya looks at his face, which seems both amused and offended. She can't decide if Kush is about to laugh at her. She doesn't give him a chance to.

"The Revolution will not be televised," she says. "Have you ever heard that?" Sonya stares flat and waveringly into Kush's eyes. It is a challenge. A dare. She has no idea where she is headed with this statement. Still, she barrels forward.

"The revolution ain't about making speeches or marching down the street or having sit-ins and rallies," she says. "Man, that stuff is outdated. It worked for our forefathers, King and Garvey and Davis." She says *our;* she is aware that she says *our,* that she is including herself in a struggle that does not belong to her. She has put her mouth to the trumpet and begun blowing a garbled, tragic song. She must finish. She must see it to its end. "It was cool then. But the time for that type of demonstration is over. Man, we have to take it to the streets. We have to mobilize the masses." And here are her hands again, flaring and flapping, the hands of a gansta rapper spitting lyrics. "Son, we have to get back to our roots, yo."

Kush returns Sonya's stare again. He is not flirting, nor is he challenging her. He sits, mesmerized.

"Man." Sonya leans back in her seat. "Race relations and all that stuff. It's more complicated than your little black book. Even Garvey had it mixed up. Even Malcolm had it mixed up earlier in his life, when he was still dealing with The Nation. It's not just about the white man trying to get everybody." The voice that comes now is more her own, reflecting on her short time at PLD. "There is a definite gap in achievement and resources and all of that, don't get me wrong. At my old school—it was mostly white— I mean, we had everything. New books, new computers, all the AP classes we wanted. And it wasn't just because we were, I mean, because the school was white. It was because the school had money."

Kush opens his mouth to interrupt, but Sonya continues. "But you kind of knew that the money came from being white. That it was one in the same. The few black folks that were there were like, well, exceptions. There were a few black families that the school adopted and allowed into its circle of whiteness. Still, you couldn't be black like PLD black. No matter how smart you were, you could just go into class talking like, you know, ethnic."

"You had to be an Oreo," Kush says. "A sellout."

"Yeah, I guess." Sonya thinks of Lydia Grant—the boisterous, popular, outspoken class leader—and how quiet she was standing next to her brown mother on Parent Visitation Day. "But I don't think it's about selling out. I don't think people consciously betray their race. I think people just want to fit in and they do what they have to do to fit." She sighs and stares out into the darkening night. "I've done my share of trying to fit in," she says.

Sonya feels them before she sees them, Kush's lips pressed softly against hers. When he pulls away, they both sigh.

He lays back in his seat and stares up at the ceiling. "When I first saw you in Tandy's room, I looked at you and thought, 'Another yellow girl trying to be down.' But then I would see you around PLD, you know, off to yourself. And I could tell there was something else happening in your head beyond all that ghetto shit Celesta and Meeka are concerned with. I knew you were different. I just didn't know how different."

Sonya hears Kush's voice as if it is coming from inside her head. She gives her body to the contours of the seat and the lull of the blue-black sky. This is her first moment of relief—the first time she has not had to pretend, or hide, or think hard to catalog the lies she has told.

"I don't know how it is to be you," Kush says. His sharp chin and high cheekbones jut up to the ceiling. "To look white on the outside but be black on the inside. That must be hell." His face is rapt with sincerity. Sonya looks at his dark, shining skin. She could say it in this moment. Under such a sky, with the dog's lonely yelp and the car's dense, quiet interior, she could tell Kush the truth. Perhaps he would become her ally. They could exchange knowing looks, have profound conversations. Perhaps he has a secret of his own to share, some deep tragedy from childhood. Tandy has never mentioned their father. Perhaps there is something there.

Sonya looks into Kush's face, his wide gleaming eyes. His hard, high cheeks. Yes, she thinks. I can tell him. I can tell him now.

16

....

"Just joking. I'm as white as salt."

The knock on the passenger-side window startles both Kush and Sonya. Sonya sees the white knuckles and thin, track-marked arms through the frosted glass. Mother, Sonya thinks, coming out to the car to see if she is okay. Sonya hadn't considered this. She was sure Doris would be in the house sweating the sheets through, fighting against her urge for more smack. She hadn't thought ahead enough to this. How could Sonya have known Kush would park the car, that he would kiss her?

An old hate for Doris smolders in Sonya's chest. Now, just when Sonya has what she wants—real friends, a sprouting social life—now, with the after image of Kush's kiss lingering on lips, Doris wants to fuck it all up by playing mother, by coming out to the car. For once, Sonya would rather her mother was in the house slumping and fluttery-eyed.

Sonya readies her lips for the words she will hiss. "No needles tonight?" she will say through bared teeth. "Thanks for wrecking my only chance at happiness," she will say. "Thanks for fucking it all up Doris." She won't say this in front of Kush, of course. She will say it later, after Kush sees her white mother, after Sonya stumbles over an explanation, after she storms into the house and slams the door.

After, which is only seconds away. After, when her short sweet time with Kush, Tandy and the others will be all over.

"Sonya. Little girl, it's past your bedtime," the knocker says. Immediately Sonya recognizes the flat sarcastic voice. It is not Doris. It is Madison.

Even worse.

"Who is that?" Kush asks.

"My uncle," Sonya says. Then, remembering Madison's obvious whiteness, she adds, "On my father's side. He's here to help with my mom." Kush's face twists in confusion. "Long story," Sonya says.

The air around Sonya turns to cotton. She cannot move through it. She cannot breath. Her heart swells and shrivels in her chest. Her bladder fills to capacity.

Now, Sonya faces the problem of making it out the car and into the house without Madison blowing her cover. She takes a deep breath and opens the door.

"Hi, Uncle Maddy." Sonya's voice is high and nervous. Pleading.

Madison immediately recognizes the desperation in Sonya's voice. The entreaty. The need. It is a tone he has heard many times before from Doris and others. Madison smiles wide. He doesn't know what advantage he has here, but he won't leave until he finds out.

"Well, hello, Sonny," Madison says to Sonya, making up a nickname equally as foolish as the one Sonya has given him. Madison licks his lips like a greedy cat. The shine in his eyes tells Sonya he's not going to make this easy.

She shoves her books down in her bag and steps out of the car. She flashes a look at Madison that says, "Please let me pass, I'll do anything." He returns one that says, "Not so quick, kiddo."

"Who's your friend?" Madison says. His voice is booming and falsely fatherly. Demonic. "Somebody from your new school?" He slides his arm around Sonya's waist and gathers her to his hip.

"Kush, Madison. Madison, Kush." Sonya rushes the introduction.

"What's up, Uncle Maddy," Kush says.

"Well, hello yourself." Madison shakes heartily. "Are you and Sonya in the same classes?"

"In the same struggle is more like it," Kush says. "Sonya just joined the Black Rebels. We had a rally today."

"Wow." Madison looks off into the distance. "The Black Rebels. Interesting." He runs his hand along Sonya's lower back and stops just shy of her buttocks.

"Yeah," Kush says. "But don't worry. There are a couple of other biracial members in the group. We're just lucky to have a strong sister like Sonya to help us get our facts straight." Kush winks at Sonya.

Sonya tries to smile. A train wreck settles into the pit of her stomach. Her face numbs, partly from the cold and partly from sheer dread. She is afraid to look at Kush or at Madison who she can feel beaming evilly down at her.

"That's just great," Madison says. "You know, I'm biracial myself."

"Really," Kush says. "Damn, I could have never—"

"Naw," Madison laughs. "Just joking. I'm as white as salt. But Sonya here—" he squeezes Sonya to his chest "—well, she's the genuine article."

Kush's cell phone blinks and rings on the dashboard. "That's Zing," he says to Sonya. "Sorry, I got to go. But it was nice to meet you, Uncle Maddy."

"See you around, I'm sure." Madison holds Sonya tight to his side.

"Bye, Kush," Sonya says. Her voice comes out dreary. Defeated.

Kush speeds off. The red eyes of the taillights blink twice before disappearing down the narrow boulevard. Madison stands for a moment with one hand in his pocket. Sonya wriggles her way out of his arm. He tucks the other hand in his pocket and breathes heartily as if he is admiring the freshness of a country pasture. He pulls out a cigarette, lights and takes quick starter puffs.

"Sami called," he says, "again." Then, with a lilt in his voice, "Maybe you could invite her to one of your Black Rebel meetings."

Sonya walks past him stiff with humiliation. "Go to hell," she says.

"Sonya," Madison calls without turning around. "I'll be needing a favor tonight."

Madison drags hard on his cigarette. He stubs it out and follows Sonya inside the house.

17

Passing

Sonya stands in the center of the living room. It is no use going to her room. He'd call her out. Or worse, come inside for his favor, and Sonya doesn't want it to happen there. Her back is to the door. She hears it open and then close. She hears the thud of Madison's boots as he crosses the room. He'll take his time, Sonya knows. He'll want to see her sweat. The spicy smoke of his cigarette fills Sonya's nostrils, makes her want to gag. Her stomach tightens, loops, twists and squirms in a thousand different directions.

Sonya is prepared for the knife, which Madison always uses, though by now, of course, he knows he no longer has to. He knows Sonya's limits. Madison whips it out, a long, shiny switchblade—Sonya hears the click of it—and sidles up behind Sonya.

Sonya is prepared for the knife. She is not prepared for the harsh tug of her hair, yanking her head back, exposing her neck.

"Go to hell?" Madison says. "I'd slice your throat," Madison says, "except I haven't gotten my favor yet. Plus, it'll break Doris's heart."

"Go to—" Sonya begins, but Madison interrupts her words with a quick slap.

"Don't fuck with me you black bitch." He laughs at own joke, a dry harsh cackle. "Black bitch. I want your big black lips. Get down on your knees."

Sonya collapses to her knees and faces Madison's groin. She knows what she is down there to do, but Sonya does not move, cannot move. Revulsion, like a slick fat frog, leaps in her throat, a combination of nausea and anger. She has held a knife to Madison's throat. She has seen a plea for mercy in his eyes, if only for an instant. Sonya cannot go back to her role as his pubescent whore after that. She thinks about the protractor in her back pocket, made of sharp pink plastic. Yes, she thinks. It's sharp enough to cut.

She takes too long to get to work. Usually, Madison would have yelled at her by now, or slapped her, or both. Tonight, he looks down at Sonya as if she is a new pair of loafers being tried on at Macy's. His eyes, empty of spite and indifference, are inquiring, indecisive.

"Aw, get the fuck up," he says. But he doesn't give her time to. He walks away, leaving Sonya on her knees in the hollow of the living room. Sonya's heart ceases its sloshing in her chest. Moonlight streams through the living room windows. Sonya looks out into the crisp purple night and listens as Madison runs a tub of water for Doris. She hears Madison's voice as he coaxes Doris awake and walks her to the bathroom.

Mr. Davenvort paces through the rows of desks. His tall chestnut figure casts a long shadow over the class. He voice is as dark as coffee. It swells theatrically, reverberating against the classroom walls. "It was the best of times," he says, slapping down Maurice's Maitland's exam, which is nearly clean of correction marks. "It was the worst of times." He slides Meeka's exam slowly across her desk. "It was the age of wisdom." Celesta receives her exam. "It was the age of foolishness." Mr. Davenvort winks at Tandy as he hands over her test.

Sonya watches Tandy survey her quiz. Tandy's face brightens and her eyes twinkle. She flips through the stapled papers searching for her lost points. Number seven: negative eight. She had forgotten the negative sign. Quickly Tandy looks around the room for the reaction of the other students. Satisfied with the grunts and frowns, she stuffs her quiz into her book bag.

"Congratulations are in order for the student who scored highest in the class," Mr. Davenvort says. "Maurice Maitland with a whopping eighty-nine point four."

Maurice stands amidst the mixture of boos and applause and bows exaggeratedly. Tandy is among those few students who applaud.

"He cheated," Meeka whispers.

"No," Celesta says. "He's just a motherfucking nerd." Celesta's pronouncement is not spiteful, but mater-of-fact. "That's why he clowns all the time. He's trying to make up for being so smart."

"You ain't nothing but a nerd," Meeka says to Maurice.

"Shut up, Blacky." Maurice flips his middle finger at Meeka.

"How quickly we fall from grace," Mr. Davenvort says. "Maitland, step out into the hallway."

The class hisses and boos as Maurice exits the class. Mr. Davenvort follows behind him and shuts the door.

"What's your damage?" Celesta asks Sonya.

"Seventy-two," Sonya says.

"You're five steps ahead of me." Celesta rolls her paper into a horn and bellows her score. "Sixty-nine."

"That's three," Tandy says off-handedly.

"What?" Celesta asks.

"You said five steps, but the difference between sixty-nine and seventy-two is three."

"Well whatever," Celesta says. "At least I made it to retirement. How go ye, dog?"

"Girl please," Tandy rolls her eyes shyly. "I'm just glad I passed."

Sonya does not immediately notice when she comes upon Meeka exiting the far left stall of the bathroom. Meeka sidles past with a hand over one side of her face. No one else is in the bathroom. The locker room stalls are ususally empty when there are no gym classes in session, which there aren't at this hour. Sonya often walks across the school to this bathroom for privacy. She can pull herself together in here. She can take a moment and step off the stage on which she performs her new, made up life. She can check in with herself her. She can get her bearings.

Not today. Meeka is here, with her hand over her face. Oh great, Sonya thinks. Meeka is having another crying fit. Maurice Maitland has been taunting her about her dark skin again. Now Sonya must comfort Meeka when all Sonya really wants to do is pull off her mask and let her real skin breath.

Meeka tries to slide by Sonya. She is shy and embarrassed. Sonya can't just let her walk by. Comforting a friend is part of the pact of rolling with a crew.

"What's wrong, Meeka?"

"Nothing," Meeka says from behind her hand. She walks quickly toward the door.

"Come on." Sonya stands in her path. "You can tell me. Did Maurice say something to you?"

"No."

"Have you been crying?"

"No. No. Leave me alone." She sounds like a child, impetuous, obstinate and babyish.

"Meeka?"

"Leave me alone," Meeka says. The sniffling starts now, quick, moist gasps. "Please, just go."

"Meeka come on."

Meeka tries to walk past, but Sonya grabs her arm, the one covering her face. Meeka lowers her head and, after a moment, looks up at Sonya, defiantly almost, like a woman who has just been slapped but refuses to cry. It takes Sonya a second to realize the oddity on Meeka's face: her eyes, psychotically mismatched, one dark brown and one a cloudy hazel color.

Sonya can see Meeka steeling herself inside, waiting for some quip, some snide remark. Sonya smiles. "I'm cool," she says. "It's cool. I'll just go to another bathroom."

Sonya returns to class. She flops down in her seat, slouching.

"Have you seen Meeka?" Tandy asks.

Sonya considers offering the information about Meeka's eyes, about how they are really contacts. But she doesn't. She has made a pledge, however silent. Plus, Tandy doesn't deserve this, sitting under everyone's noses with her almost-perfect test tucked into her book bag, with her arrangement with Principal Carlton, with her holier-than-thou smile curling up her lips. If Sonya were to tell about Meeka's eyes, Tandy would seize on this. She would use Meeka as a stepping-stone for her virtue. Tandy would do this without realizing her own hypocrisy.

"There she is," Sonya says as Meeka walks into the door. Then to Meeka, "Girl, are you done with your crying spell?" She says this a little meanly. It is a cover-up for Meeka's eyes, which are cracked with red. She hopes Meeka gets it.

"What?"

"Your crying fit? In the bathroom?" She winks and immediately feels silly for doing it. But Meeka needs a little assistance. "Are you over it?"

"Oh that?" Meeka says. Both hazel contacts are intact. "I'm cool. I'm cool."

Looking at Meeka, Sonya realizes the thinness of veils, how, with time or lack of attention or mere circumstance, they can grow dry and brittle, they can be eaten away by moths. Meeka's veil has fallen. Sonya has glimpsed the true face beneath. Sonya has seen Meeka for what she is: A beautifully dark girl with an inferiority complex, a girl fallen prey to prejudice, a girl who wants to be something other than black. Sonya vows to keep Meeka's secret to herself. Sonya knows it could just as easily have been her caught in the bathroom, exposed and unbeknownst.

18

....

Madison pays

Music blares out of the speakers. Windows rattle and figurines shake on shelves. Tandy dances around the room, flailing her arms and singing at the top of her lungs.

> "Zom-bies
> Zom-bies
> Zom-be-ee-ee-ee-eez
> Do do do do do do do do do
> Ah-ah-ah-ah"

Zing and Kush are away at a Black Nationalist Movement Conference at the Auburn Avenue Library. Tandy holds her calculus test to the sky, every now and again screaming out ninety-eight which is her score. Her face glows with exuberance. Sonya sits on the bed watching Tandy's pathetic attempts at dance.

Usually, Sonya indulges Tandy's scholastic revelry. But today she cannot muster up the necessary enthusiasm.

"What's your problem?" Tandy turns the music down and

flounces on the bed. Her breath comes out in huge huffs. "You look like somebody's died or something."

"I'm tired," Sonya says. Last night, she managed two hours of sleep. Between her mother's moaning and sweating, between changing sheets, fetching water, making ice packs and then heat pads, Sonya managed two measly hours. Even still she came to Tandy's study session, more in hopes of seeing Kush than watching Tandy's celebration dance. Kush, who had kissed her last night then walked past her coolly in school today.

"Better take a power nap," Tandy says. "We have two tests next week." Tandy's face lights up. "Physics and Lit."

"I'm really tired," Sonya says. "I was up all night."

"Hmph." Tandy scoffs disbelievingly. She opens her book of esoteric words and sets it in front of Sonya. "A C-minus on an exam does enervate." She fans herself with her *A* exam. "At least, that's what I've heard."

"My mother's still sick." Sonya feels the pang of headache squeezing the back of her eyeballs.

"Excuses are like butt holes." Tandy slaps the book of esoteric words in front of Sonya. "We all have them and they all stink."

Two days later, Madison shows up in the middle of the night. Sonya is in the kitchen getting water for her mother when she notices the red smolder of Madison's cigarette in the dark living room. Madison has taken Doris's keys. He comes and goes as he pleases.

"How is she holding up?" Madison says.

"Go see for yourself."

He brushes past Sonya who stands in the center of the kitchen. Minutes later, Doris's moans subside.

"I guess she called you," Sonya says as Madison emerges from the bedroom. Sonya can't take it anymore. She will not restrain her spite now. She allows it to seep into her voice. If Madison asks for a favor tonight, Sonya will go for the Ginsu knives, only this time she will use them on herself.

"Your mother hasn't worked in a long time," Madison says. "Even when she was working she wasn't making any money."

"So that's what this is about." Anger makes a razor of Sonya's voice. "Money? Well, there's none left. So if she owes you, get in line. The realtor, the car dealership, everyone's taking a goddamn number."

"She hasn't paid on the house." Madison sucks hard on his cigarette. "It'll be up for auction in a couple of weeks."

Sonya slams the glass down on the counter. "I know that Madison. I know. I know. I know. Who do you think gets the mail? Who do you think buys the groceries and feeds Doris when you're not around pumping her veins full of smack and fucking her brains out? Who do you think does the real work?"

Tears slide down Sonya's face, but she is ignorant to them. Her rage is that strong.

"No one comes back from heroin," he says. "At least, they don't come back the same. You always want it. It's like air." His voice is calm, carrying none of its usual leering wickedness. "Your body produces false hormones. Dopamine, I think it's called. Or some endorphins. Either way, your body thinks it needs it. It rebels when you take the heroin away. That's what's happening to your mother now. Best Doris can hope for is to carry on with a little decency."

"Like you?" Sonya says

"I'm not decent," Madison says staring into the smoldering tip of his cigarette. "Not by a long shot. You and I both know that," he says. "And no. She didn't call me. I came myself."

"To make sure Doris is all loopy," Sonya says. "To keep her on her leash." Anger washes over her in waves. Sonya makes no effort to control herself. She knows how far to go with Madison. She knows he won't kill her over words.

Madison sighs. "This isn't her first bout with withdrawal. We've been trying to clean her up for a while. Remember that trip to Puerto Rico?" He waits for Sonya's response. She nods. "It was actually two weeks of intensive rehab." He smiles. "As you can see, it wasn't intense enough."

"So now you're making it a little easier for Doris." Sonya fights to hold on to her anger. Imagining Madison mopping her mother's vomit, icing her back and washing her sheets softens Sonya. "If Doris is trying to clean up, why are you here?"

"I'm the only one who can really help her." Madison rubs the *Tommy* tattoo on the back of his neck. "I've been through it. Several times before."

An image of Madison floats before Sonya's eyes. Madison naked and sweating, his body pulsing with pain. Madison, heaving foamy green puke. Madison shivering cold and then suddenly boiling hot. *Several times before,* he'd said.

"Actually," Madison leans back on the couch. "I came to see you."

Immediately, Sonya's stomach tightens. He wants another favor. Motherfucker, she thinks. You dirty motherfucker. She doesn't say this. At this point, what's the use?

"No, not that," Madison says, responding to the cross expression on Sonya's face. "I need a real favor this time. I need your help."

Law arrives late in the night. Pulling up to the house in a squeaky, grumbling truck. He is broad and tall and muscled as a tree trunk. His skin is as dark as Kush's. His eyes sit deep in his head. They take in Sonya, the yard and the house in quick darting glances. Sonya walks out of the front door and down the drive with her arms folded over her chest. Her pajamas billow in the breeze. As Sonya approaches Law, she wills herself to not be intimidated by his size.

Sonya has agreed to allow Law, Madison's "business partner," to move in. She has agreed because she has no other choice

"Hello," Law says. Sonya is taken aback. She cannot attach the small voice she hears to the massive body from which it escapes. This voice is the voice of a prepubescent boy or of a cartoon mouse. It is high and soft, slightly feminine. Law's voice makes it easier for Sonya to snub him.

"*You're* Law?" She folds her arms across her chest and looks him up and down as if he is a sorry substitute with which she must somehow manage.

"Yes." He smiles. "And you're Sonya. Right?"

Law stands opposite Sonya just in front of the driveway.

February has died with a last breath of bitter cold. March arrives, bringing with it the delicious body heat of spring. Even in the 3 a.m. hour, the air is merely cool. It holds an undertone of warmth. The sky above is clear and dark.

Sonya notices the truck Law drives. She thought the truck would be fancier. She expected something similar to Zing's Mercedes SUV. Or she expected the Porsche, though, when she sees what the truck holds, she understands why Law drives it. All of the rusty metal parts and piping and tubes peeking from under the tarp would have ruined the interior of any car.

He stands beside the pickup with its large double tank and extended cab. The purple house paint with which the truck is painted crumbles and flakes. Law explains that he borrowed it from a man who owes him a favor. Sonya has a visceral reaction to that word, *favor*. Madison has ruined it for her forever.

"Much better than that piece of crud Madison drives." Law makes his attempt at a joke, at small talk.

"I'll get the keys to the basement," Sonya says. She marches toward the house somberly. Her back is pole straight.

Law pulls the truck up to the back of the house. They unload the equipment in the basement. He takes the heavier metal parts, leaving Sonya to carry the plastic tube, dram viles and beakers.

"Anything else?" Sonya asks and she slides the box of beakers through the door with her foot. She did this with the other boxes, slamming them down haphazardly, breaking some of the viles. This is her little revenge. Law allows her this tantrum, grimacing every now and again when she slams down an especially fragile package.

"That's it," Law says.

Sonya crosses her arms and stands with her legs slightly apart. Hate steams off her skin.

The rafters above them creak.

Nothing in the basement moves.

"I'm sorry about Doris," Law says. "If it makes any difference, I'm clean. I never touch the stuff."

"It doesn't make a difference," Sonya says.

"I know you don't approve of what we do, Mad Man and I," Law says. "But it's what he knows. It's all I know now. Believe it or not

Madison wasn't always…" A melancholy smile floats across Law's face then vanishes. "He was a regular guy once. Decent. Clean."

Sonya makes a show of wiping her hands on her pants. She sighs a heavy, put-out sigh. As Sonya walks up the stairs she hears Law's voice, small and slight in the dark. "Thank you," he says.

Madison makes several promises. One: he will leave Sonya be. He will ask her for no more favors and he will not threaten her. "I won't be around enough to fuck with you," is how he put it. Two: he will provide for everything. He will give Law enough to pay the mortgage and utilities, to buy food and toiletries and to cover any other expenses. And three: he will get Doris cleaned up.

"I have a private guy," Madison says. "Went to him myself when things got out of hand."

"A lot of good it did you," Sonya says.

Law watches this exchange from behind the kitchen counter. His eyes are on Sonya. A flash of warning lights up his face.

Madison makes a fist and juts out his track-marked arm for Sonya to see. "I chose to come back to this. I chose to be fucked up. Doris doesn't have to. She's stronger than me." He looks up at Sonya. "She's got something to live for."

In his voice Sonya hears a controlled fury, something leashed and dangerous, different from his usually chilled malice. Madison pulls his arm back slowly and runs his hands absentmindedly across his wrecked veins. "There's nothing else for me in the world," he says. "I had my chance. I played my cards and lost."

A mixture of sympathy and fear washes over Sonya. She, Madison, and Law sit silently in the space Madison's anger carves out.

A clock hangs on the far wall. They listen to it tick.

"When I started on smack, there were no real PSAs, no war against drugs. You had 'Say Nope to Dope' and all the anti-drug campaigns, but there was none of that in the late seventies. Not really. So I tried everything: PCP, LSD, barbs, 'shrooms. Then came the needle. I was fucked up for years."

"The stuff got a hold of me bad. Dropped out of college." He smiles at the surprise that registers on Sonya face. "Yep. Berkeley.

You're looking at a real live Rhodes Scholar. Didn't do me any good when I was snatching purses, burglarizing houses or sucking cock in an alley for smack."

Sonya looks from Madison to Law who listens to the story with a patient sadness. He has heard it before, Sonya can tell. Still, she can see the mourning in Law's face. He truly feels for Madison.

"Eventually I got tired of it. Like Doris." He flicks ashes off his cigarette. "Most do. I'd gotten cleaned up, I guess, if you can call methadone clean. I got a real job. Got married." He looks up at Sonya. "Even had a kid." Madison smiles to himself. "Who'd've thunk it?"

Law smiles. "Good old Mad Man had a son."

"Tommy?" Sonya says.

Madison rubs the back of his neck again and sighs.

"Yep." Tears tremble at the rim of his eyes. "Tommy. When things got rough, I fell off. Went back to smack. My wife was smart enough to keep me away from our son. One day I came home to an empty house. Haven't seen Tommy since."

Madison pats his thighs, rises and walks briskly out of the room.

Law pays for everything. In exchange, Sonya agrees to let Madison and Law use the basement of the house to store their stash and equipment. "I had to move fast," Madison says. "Things were getting a little too hot in my other place." This is the only explanation he offers. Sonya doesn't ask any questions.

Sonya also agrees to allow Law to stay in Doris's empty room. "He'll keep an eye on the fan," Madison says, "in case shit hits it. He won't fuck with you either. He's a real pussycat."

Law grins at Madison's side. "I'm just not an a–hole like Mad Man," he says.

"See what I mean." Madison chucks Law on the arm. "I've known this fucker for twelve fucking years and not once have I ever heard a fucking swear grace his motherfucking lips."

Sonya places her mother's suitcase beside the door and sits down next to her on her bed. Her mother leans forward with her hands under her chin, prayer-style.

"Mom," Sonya speaks softly, as if her mother is a sleeping child.

"I look like shit," Doris says. "I've looked like shit for almost a year now."

"Two years," Sonya says. "But who's counting?"

Her mother laughs. It is the first time Sonya has heard her mother laugh in months. Sonya laughs too, until she realizes her mother's laughter has become tears. Doris brushes them away and then looks down at her mascara-smeared hands.

"Can't even put on makeup anymore."

Sonya takes a brush from a nearby dresser and begins brushing her mother's hair.

"Remember when I was strong?" Doris says. "Remember how I gave your father the boot then started the firm the very next day? I was naive then. I didn't know jack shit about property or taxes or a business license. Maybe it wasn't strength at all. Maybe it was just stupidity and luck."

"You're still strong," Sonya says.

Her mother stares out at nothing, envisioning her past self. Sonya can't bring herself to believe that this woman whose life is embrangled in drug addiction is the same woman who once closed million-dollar contracts. This is the same woman who chased away Danny Panatelas, the kid who used to wait outside of their apartment to pull Sonya's hair. This is the same woman who, every year at Christmas time, dressed as Mrs. Claus and baked cookies because Santa had the flu. All the anger, all the hostility and disappointment Sonya has felt toward her mother melts.

"How long will you be away," Sonya asks.

"Who knows? Six months. Maybe a year," Doris says. "Some private doctor. 'The Specialist,' Madison calls him. Says it's my only hope."

"What am I going to do?" Sonya says.

"The same thing you've been doing for the past two years," Doris says. "Make your own way. Handle my fuck ups." Though Doris's face streams with black tears, her shoulders stand erect. She looks staunchly at the difficult months of rehab ahead. Already, Sonya can see some of her mother's old strength returning.

"Law's great," Doris says. "Really. I mean, he's a dealer and all, but other than that, he's the nicest man…" Her mother wipes her hands on her pant legs. "I've talked to Madison," she says. "He won't bother you anymore." Doris sighs a quivering sigh. "I'm sorry Sonya. I've been away so long."

They lock in their first true embrace. "I've been away so long," her mother says again. Sonya pulls her mother into her and is surprised how small she has become. Beneath her mother's skin, Sonya can feel thin brittle bone. Doris's skin smells salty and warm, unwashed.

"That's okay," Sonya says into the crux of her mother's neck. "You'll be okay."

"I have to." Doris pulls back, straightens her blouse and pants. "I have to."

"Madison says it's going to be hard," Sonya says, "and painful."

"Can't be anymore painful…" Doris says, "can't be anymore painful than what I've put you through."

19

....

Law and order

For the first few days after Doris leaves for The Specialist, Sonya avoids the house. She spends all of her time at Tandy's. Each night, Kush drives her home. They stare up at the sky through the moon roof. They philosophize about race and revolution. They talk about school. They kiss.

Sonya takes the vow of the Nazarite and joins the Black Rebels. They hold Nyahbinghi gatherings, sitting in a circle with the sweet smolder of patchouli incenses clouding the room. They smoke marijuana from a communal chalice. It is a flute pipe, intricately carved with Yoruba Orisa idols. They read Garvey, Fanon, Malcolm X and the Rastafarian Holy Piby. Some nights, they plan for Festival, making phone calls, folding flyers, debating the benefits of one auditorium venue over another. Tandy sits in on the meetings, more out of obligation to Zing, Kush and Sonya than out of genuine interest. At every meeting, she keeps her head lifted stubbornly as Kush reads I-doctrine and pours libation to the ancestors. Tandy is like a mother, sitting obstinately at her son's wedding, disapproving of his choice of bride.

Last night, as Zing read from a book called *The Nazarite Lives* which was translated from Amharic by a Jamaican prophet. Tandy leaned over to Sonya. "Why is it…" she whispered and then paused. "Never mind."

"What?" Sonya said, pulling a string of alertness up from the marijuana fog under which her mind drifted. "Why is what?"

Sonya heard the words of *The Nazarite Lives*. She understood their meaning. These meetings gave Sonya time and space to clear her head. They gave her purpose, which was the purpose of all true Rastafari (though she would never claim to be that). Sonya's purpose during Nyahbinghi, under the release of ganja, was I-and-I, Overstanding. Her purpose was to connect to God, Jah. At Nyahbinghi, Madison's ultimatum, Doris's sickness and even the lie of blackness under which Sonya now lives all float away—and she, Sonya, is left. She is lifted. Absolved. During Nyahbinghi Sonya tries to make this gathering of New-Age Rastas, the circle of Orthodox black revolutionaries, her family. Sonya searches for something real, something true.

Sonya was in this state of transcendence when Tandy asked her question. "Why is it what?" Sonya asked again. She listened, expecting Tandy to speak on Jah, on I-and-I, on Overstanding.

Instead, Tandy sucked her teeth. "Why is this book so grammatically incorrect?" Tandy said. "Didn't they have editors in Jamaica?"

Sonya bowed her head. She had to avoid Tandy's eyes lest Tandy see the rage bubbling beneath her skin. *Didn't they have editors in Jamaica?* Tandy had asked. Her voice twanged inside Sonya's head like a gnat's buzz, like a bang of cymbals. *Didn't they have editors in Jamaica?* Sonya's hands curled to fists. She breathed deeply and dug her fist into the carpet. She fought a civil war with her hands to keep them from slapping Tandy.

On the rare occasions that she and Law are in the house together, Sonya confines herself to her room. She sleeps with a Ginsu knife tucked under her pillow and waits for Law to show the opposite of his gentlemanly self. She waits for Madison to renege on his promise. Law proves a real gentleman and Madison keeps true to his word. By the second week, Madison no longer appears at the house. He only calls to check in with Law and to make sure shipments are arriving and leaving on time.

In the common areas of the house, Sonya and Law walk past each other in silence, nodding to each other like executives sharing a bathroom. One day at breakfast, Law breaks the silence.

"My ex-wife's name was Judy," he says. He opens a brown pill bottle and pops two white pills into his mouth. Sonya does not ask what they are. If it's Mad Man's brew, Law will be zonked within the hour.

"And?" Sonya says. She finds it easy to be mean to him, like kicking a puppy.

Law's eyes fall into his bowl of oatmeal. Sonya stands at the sink, rinsing a large platter. She sees Law's bulbous shoulders and the top of his gleaming black head. Despite the pills, she feels sorry for what she has said.

"Judy's a pretty name." She offers this compliment, handing it to him delicately, like a bone-shaped doggy treat.

Law looks up and smiles. "Yep," he says. "She was named after a Jetson."

This is the first laugh they share.

Over time, Law fills in his and Madison's story. He talks about their days at Berkeley together, about a mutual friend named Jimmy who introduced them to marijuana. "The gateway drug," he says. "Such a freaking cliché, or so I thought. Mad Man and I entered those gates together with a couple of other friends. But we're the only ones who lived to talk about it."

"You and Madison were in school together?" Looking into Law's smooth brown face—the face of a twenty-two-year-old—Sonya cannot believe he is the same age as Madison.

As if he has read her mind, Law says, "Thirty-nine. I'll be forty this year. Started Berkeley at fifteen. That's what made me so naïve to drugs."

"You said you were clean," Sonya says. "When we first met, you said you never touch—"

"I don't," Law says. "Not anymore. I've been drug-free for what eleven, twelve years now? Can't stand the stuff. But I know its power. I know the grip it has on your soul once you tried it. That's what makes me a good salesman."

Law talks to her about his time in prison, about his release, his bout with heroin and his cleanup via The Specialist. "Your mom is going through H–E–L–L," he says. Then, to soften the blow to Sonya, he says, "But Mad Man says she's strong. She'll make it."

A week later, Sonya and Law embark on spring cleaning together, scouring and scrubbing all surfaces of the house. Law does the windows. Sonya does the floors. He never explains the pills that he takes twice a day. Sonya finds out for herself, reads the label this morning while Law was in the bathroom. Lithium. An anti-depressant. That explains his sullenness at night and in the mornings before he's taken his dose.

Sonya works up a froth of blue suds on the counter. She considers asking Law about his depression, but decides against it. Every once in a while, she looks up from her work to find him staring at her.

"What?" she finally asks.

"Well, I just…nothing. Never mind." Something resembling a blush curls Law's too-young face.

"Now that's not fair," Sonya says. "You can't start and then say 'nothing.'"

"I was just thinking," Law says. "You're one of those girls who doesn't know how beautiful you are."

Sonya's heart falls. So is this it? Is this the source of Law's politeness, a boyish crush? Probably, he'd been working up to this moment all this time, Sonya thinks.

What is Sonya to say? "Thank you" would be encouragement. She does not want to do that. First, because she has Kush and, second, Law is old enough to be her father, though no one would believe it. She could tell him to fuck off. But that would be declining a perceived invitation, an invitation Law may or may not be making. Sonya catches sight of Law's shy smile. Definitely, he's making a pass. Despite Law's good looks, she does not feel this way for him. Still, she can't say nothing. Already, her silence is becoming awkward.

"You…you think I'm pretty?" No one has every said this before to Sonya, not Tandy, not Celesta, not even Kush. Sonya assumes from the kisses that Kush is attracted to her. But Tandy assured Sonya it's because Sonya is mixed. "Kush is on that yellow thing too. Color-struck," Tandy said. "Worse even than Maurice Maitland. Most black men are color-struck one way or another. Either they want a mixed girl or a white girl or some Asian-type chick. To them, anything is more beautiful than a plain old black girl."

Doris has called Sonya beautiful, of course, but isn't that what mothers are suppose to say?

Sonya falls briefly in love with Law whose smile is both gentle and lusty, the smile of a eunuch priest. Then she thinks: Kush!

"Yeah," Law says. "You are pretty. Pretty ugly."

He chucks a wet sponge at Sonya. She shrieks and chases him with a bucket of water, splashes it down the back of his shirt. They are both saved by Law's comedy, lifted out of the awkward silence, the uncomfortable awareness of their situation: man and woman, strangers, with sexual organs glowing like beacons between their thighs, alone in a room, looking into each others' eyes.

"Dog, it sounds like everything was set up for you," Sonya says later that same night as Law polishes the silver. She has begun doing this naturally, peppering her speech with black slang.

Law lies on his stomach—all six foot five of him—and squeeks the service clean with a tiny rag. They have both silently agreed to forget Law's comment this morning.

"You were rich. Sounds like it at least."

"My parents were so darn-gone-it pushy. In addition to school, I sat with private tutors all the way through junior high and high school. They wanted to be sure I grew up in their spitting image, two anal retentive overachievers."

"Lot of pressure," Sonya says.

"Two corporate lawyers in one house," he says. "No wonder I'm so messed up."

"Is that how you got the name? 'Cause your parents are lawyers?"

"That—" Law works the small rag into the crevice of a fork "—and because, well, Mad Man calls me Mr. Morals."

"Because you don't fuck with people like he does," Sonya says.

"And because I don't smoke, drink, do drugs…"

"Well, me either. Except a little green."

"…Eat meat or any non-organic foods…"

"You're just health conscious."

"…Swear, raise my voice, use my hands in any non-helpful way…"

"Non-violence. That's good."

"…Wear any colors of aggression, especially red, orange and shades of green resembling money…"

"Oh."

"I never wear the same socks twice."

"Seems like you've got a little of your parents in you after all."

A couple of days later, Law hands Sonya a checkbook and a debit card. *Doris Crane,* the card reads.

"I dropped cash in your mother's account," he says, "so you shouldn't have trouble writing checks. I'll leave you in charge of the bills."

"How will I know if there is enough?" she says.

It appears on his face again, the lingering, lustful look, the look of a starved dog. Law pulls wads of bills from each pocket of his backpack—thousands of dollars—and begins counting his day's earnings. He masks his desire with a wry smile. "There's enough," he says, "and then some."

Law leaves Sonya her privacy.

Law doesn't ask for favors.

Law stays sober.

Every check Sonya writes clears.

Law does not mention anything more about Sonya being beautiful.

With each of his anecdotes, Sonya softens. She even shares stories of her own, stories about Doris's antics as a realtor. She tells Law how, once, Doris went from house to house dressed as a human-sized tarantula.

"Why a tarantula?"

"I don't know," Sonya says. "Something to do with cobwebs and making folks feel like they needed to move."

They both laugh. Though Law makes no further comment about her looks, Sonya notices the smile on his face. It is shy and quick. He is smitten by her. He is a little in love.

part two

20

. . . .

The all-seeing, all-knowing Zing

Sonya walks up the tree-lined boulevard and waves to her neighbors. She wears a long white skirt and colorful dashiki. Her earlobes hang under the weight of large copper earrings in the shape of the continent of Africa. Her face is tanned a smooth beige. April has arrived and, with it, the sugary air of spring. People are outside mowing laws or washing cars. Some lounge on porches or wave from high-up windows.

A child of five or six runs up to Sonya pointing and smiling.

"Your hair. Your hair," the child shrieks. "You have snakes in your hair."

Sonya kneels to meet the child's round, brown face. "They're called Senegalese Twists," Sonya says to the little boy. She lifts a rope of her hair. "Want to feel." The boy reaches out shyly and takes Sonya's hair in his hand.

"It's crunchy," he says, giggling.

"My twists aren't locked yet. It's only been a couple of months." She examines the tip of another lock. "But when they do lock, they will be long and pretty, like a lion's mane. The Conquering Lion of Zion. You know about The Lion?"

"You have hair like Mr. Snuffleupagus."

"Well," Sonya says, and nothing more.

Sonya darts around the living room dusting and polishing. The clock above the mantel reads three-forty-seven. He said he would come by at four-thirty.

She can't measure up. Compared to Kush's palatial home with its columns and gargoyles and domed ceilings, her house is meek and humble. She feels embarrassed about the framed prints on the wall and the throw rug of bright squares and triangles. There is no use, Sonya thinks as she reshuffles the pillows on the couch. The house is what it is.

Law walks up from the basement with a piece of mail in his hand. "This is for you, *Sonya Crane*."

"Give me those," Sonya snatches the mail playfully. It is her cell phone bill. "I thought I told them to change my name to Sonya on this," she says. "I'll have to call them."

And there are Law's eyes again with their wet wanting, eyes as heavy as sponges. Sonya feels hypersensitive under Law's gaze. All of her feminine parts become blatant to her, heated, ultra-violet. It is as if her vagina and her breasts are electrified. The heat happens against her will. It happens despite her lack of at-traction to Law.

"Dog, this place is a mess," she says, moving around Law to wipe the counter a third time. "Don't want Kush coming by—" she catches herself, pauses, then continues "—don't want him coming by for the meeting and see all this shit everywhere. I thought you were supposed to be so germ-phobic. You're slipping, dog."

"Kush is coming by again?" Law's voice is icy. He still has his back to her.

"It's New-Age Rasta stuff. We're planning for Festivale," she says. "It's getting out of control. I mean, man, we have about four hundred tickets already sold. Pretty soon all of Atlanta will be on this black righteous shit. It's cool though. It's cool as shit. This thing is going to be big. We are about to blow up."

Her mouth continues ahead of her, babbling out of control. She feels guilty speaking of Kush in front of Law this way. It is as if she is flaunting her relationship with Kush, taunting Law. Also, she feels apologetic. She feels as if she owes something to the desperation that haunts Law's eyes.

"I'll leave you your privacy," Law says.

"We're only planning our big gathering," she says. "Festivale. It's not a date, L. A. Law." This has been her nickname for him since she found out he was from Los Angeles. It is a private joke between them. Using this nickname now is like chucking Law on the shoulder. It is a reminder of their platonic relationship.

"Festivale? That's the black thing right?" He has turned slightly around, hands in his pockets. She has noticed that lately he can't bear to look at her. On the rare occasions that he does, his face gives it all away.

"The black thing?" Sonya says. "If you mean the largest gathering of the black political underground in forever, then yeah, dog, it is the black thing. The NARC is about to blow the fuck up."

"I thought you called yourself the Black Rebellion."

"Changed our name," Sonya says. "Now we're NARC. The New Age Rasta Circle."

"Oh," Law smiles. "I get it. I think."

Law has never broached the subject of Sonya's race. In the beginning, Sonya assumed he was being respectful, that he didn't want to pry. Later, she realized he believed she was biracial. Only Law believed her father was black.

"I have to go anyway for a day or two," Law said. "I have some packages to deliver." He clicks off quotation marks around *packages*. Sonya winks and shoots an okay sign. Their exchange is heavy with a forced friendliness, strained. They are doing impressions of their former selves and doing them badly. Since the night Law told her she was beautiful this strain has swelled between them like a balloon that threatens with each exhalation of breath to burst.

Sonya hears the engine of Law's pickup and then the skid of the tires as he pulls out of the driveway and down the street. She flops down on the couch and stares up at the clock on the wall.

Her hair no longer falls in her face. It lies in thick brownish ropes, framing her head like a lion's mane.

Sonya changed her name and began dreadlocking her hair the week after her mother left. "I need change," she told Kush. They stood in the foyer of his house just after Sonya's study session with Tandy.

"Lock your hair," Kush said. "Give yourself over to the revolution."

"Lock her hair?" Tandy came from the study, where she went to get a book of quotes for Sonya. "Who's locking their hair?"

"Me and Sonya," Kush said.

"Sonya, you have a good grade of hair. Why would you want to go around looking like Bob Marley?"

Sonya had heard this phrase before, *good hair*. Celesta used it. Meeka used it. Even Mrs. Larsen who seemed to have a personal vendetta against everyone lighter than a chocolate bar used it ("Sonya Crane, you better stop passing notes in my class before I snatch all that good hair out your green-eyed head"). Everyone at PLD used the term *good hair,* which, as Sonya understood it, simply meant straight hair, which meant hair that was difficult to style, hair that went frizzy in rain, hair that was less dense and dark and luxurious than black people's hair, hair that made Sonya look whiter, which wasn't good at all.

"Lock my hair," Sonya repeated Kush's proposal to herself. It seemed so obvious it was ingenious. Locking her hair. That was the answer.

"You can join us?" Kush pulled Tandy close to him.

She wiggled away. "No thanks, Jonathan Livingston Seagull."

"Dreadlocks." Zing came from the other direction. Now the entire cast was on stage. Sonya felt as if she were caught in some hilarious, over-the-top stage play. "Who?"

"We're locking our hair," Kush said. "Me, Sonya and Tandy."

"Not me. I'm not walking around with that nappy mess in my head."

"Well me and Sonya then."

Before Sonya could object, Zing threw her arms around her. "Welcome, baby," Zing said. "Welcome to the family."

Sonya's heart swelled in her chest. She felt like a tragic hero in a novel. She felt huge and changed and victorious. Yes, she thought, I'm going to lock my hair. I'm going to give myself over to the revolution.

Tandy walked off. "Y'all will just have to excommunicate me because I'm not putting that mess in my hair."

Zing chose Sonya's name. It happened later, at the end of a Nyahbinghi gathering. The NARC sat on the floor in a semicircle. Candlelight flickered around the room. Zing pulled out a bag of stones, shook them out over the mud cloth on the floor, and read each member's life. Sonya was first.

Fear danced in Sonya's chest as Zing shuffled through the pile of stones, her eyes squinting in concentration. She thought Zing might see right through her.

"Something's not right," Zing says. "Not true."

Sonya's heart leapt.

The other members of New Age Rasta Circle leaned in, peering at the stones as if they too had the power of sight.

"There is internal dissonance," Zing said.

Sergeant's face crinkled. "Huh?"

Tandy chucked him on the shoulder. "Inner conflict, idiot."

"You are fighting with yourself," Zing said. Sonya found herself leaning in, trying to see what Zing saw in the stones. Everything Zing said was true. Hopefully, Zing's powers of sight had limits.

Suddenly, Zing looked up. Her eyes were glazed and bright. "Sonya," she said. "That's it. You are trying to unite two opposing forces within yourself. You should carry the name of unity. *Sonya.*"

"Sonya," the group chanted in unison. "Sonya."

Now Sonya, formerly Sonya, fumbles around the apartment, dusting vases and straightening cushions. The clock reads four-oh-four. When the doorbell rings Sonya knows it is not Kush. Never early and never late, Kush is prompt to the minute. This is his personal vendetta against the myth of CP time—colored people's time—another term Sonya had to research. Sonya assumed it was Law. Perhaps he left his house keys or forgot one of his "packages."

The smile Sonya prepares for Law and the little joke (Forgetful Fred, she thinks to call him) she plans when she opens the door withers when sees the face greeting her on the other side.

21

....

Time bomb

Samantha Klieg is fat. Her cheeks puff out from either side of her face and her hips ride high and wide in her jeans. Her neck is thick, sitting under her head like a squashed tree trunk. Still she has the same bright blue eyes and over-zealous smile. She has dyed her hair a shade of blonde so bright and unconvincing it is obnoxious.

"Sonya." Sami opens her arms, fingers splayed, preparing for a hug. Sonya does not step into Sami's meaty arms. Instead she stands in the doorway, shocked, as much by Sami's plumpness as by her unannounced appearance.

Sami closes her hands in a clap. "So," she says, looking around with an antsy smile on her face, "aren't you going to invite me in?"

"Oh, yeah," Sonya says. "Sure. Come in."

Sami takes in the living room in one big sweep. "This is...this is nice," she says. "Not as fab as your former residence, but nice."

"Thanks," Sonya says blankly. She looks at the clock. Four-ten, it says. Kush will arrive in exactly twenty minutes.

"Wow," Sami says. "It's been eons."

"Months," Sonya says.

"So." Sami takes a seat and slaps her hands on her now fleshy thighs. "I want to know everything about your new life," she says. "You *must* fill me in."

Sonya tries desperately to think of an excuse. She could say she's on her way out, but to where? There is no car in the drive and where would she be walking? Tandy's house? Yes. No, not Tandy's. Samantha would offer to drive her. Then Samantha would want to come in and see the house. If she told Sami she is expecting company, Sami would wait around, eager to meet whomever is coming.

"I go to PLD now," Sonya says, keeping her eye on the window for Kush's car. "I'm in a couple of groups. I'm dreading my hair." She pulls absently at one of her knotted locks.

"So I see," Sami says. "Well, I just came back from France. And can we just say overrated. Michael Benton. Do you remember him? Anyway, he's been accepted to Andover. So of course Julie Shays is all in a stink thinking he will go to boarding school and forget all about her, which of course, he probably will but, hey, like I told her, why get yourself all in a huff now. My God—" Sami nearly screeches the word *God* "—the guy hasn't even packed his bags yet. I mean, like come on, they practically have another whole semester together."

Listening to Sami talk is like listening to Celesta when she does her white girl voice. "Like, Ohmygod," Celesta says, feigning surprise at some announcement one of the crew has just made. Sonya never took offense to Celesta's mimicking because she thought it didn't include her. Even at Crestman, Sonya thought, she never talked like that. Now, listening to Samantha Klieg—a living, breathing flashback of her Crestman days—Sonya realizes she did once talk that way. She must have.

"And Mr. Flange didn't even change my grade, despite the fact that it was *so,* so obvious I deserved at least a B minus." Sami looks at Sonya as if noticing her for the first time. "You look different. What have you done to yourself?"

Sonya glances between the clock and the window. Four-eighteen. Twelve minutes until Kush arrives. "I told you I'm locking my hair."

Sami stands and smiles wryly. "It's not just that," she says. "You have a certain glow. A certain—" she clicks her tongue "—womanly *je ne sais quoi*."

Sami's playful chiding and squeaky voice come to Sonya like a poke to the ribs. Four-twenty-one and Sami circles Sonya, smiling her wry, knowing smile. Annoyance chugs away in Sonya's gut.

"Did you commit a lascivious act?"

"What?" Sonya says.

"Sex," Sami says. "Did you lose your virginity?"

In fact, Sonya had had her first sexual encounter with Kush not more than a week ago. Law left early that morning. "A road trip," he said, using his patented quotations. He was due back at the end of the week. Sonya and Kush had decided to consummate their relationship in the natural way, the African way, Kush had said, with no animal skin between them. Without protection. The pull-out method, he said. They had both learned about it in health class. It seemed safe enough to Sonya. That night, Sonya lit candles and put on a CD compilation she had burned just the day before. *Love,* she had called the CD. Sonya lay under Kush with her eyes closed, willing images of Madison out of her head. She cringed when Kush entered her and cried the entire time. He panted and apologized. It was over in less than five minutes. It was Kush's first time also.

In the days that followed, no one, not even Zing the all-knowing prophet, had noticed a change in Sonya. Now it annoyed her that Samantha Klieg, a girl who'd built her social career degrading Sonya, saw the glow of virginity lost on Sonya's face.

It also annoyed Sonya that the clock read four-twenty-four, Kush would arrive at four-thirty and Samantha is still here.

"Cut the crap, Sami," Sonya says.

"What do you mean?"

"You came by here for something."

"It's just," Sami flutters and stammers, "well, I hadn't heard from you in so long. I mean, you hadn't returned any of my phone calls."

Four-twenty-five.

"Hmm." Sonya places a finger on her chin in faux contemplation. The gesture is deliciously sarcastic. "And why do you think that is, *Samantha?*"

"I—I," Sami says. "I have no—"

"It's because you were such a cunt to me at Crestwood," Sonya says. "That's why I took a razor to my wrist, Sami. You drove me to suicide Sami. You and your bitchy friends. *Sami!*"

"Sonya—" Sami tries to break in, but Sonya continues.

"You called me a pug. You know what a pug is, Sami? It's a fucking dog. A dog!"

"Please, Sonya," Sami says. "Just listen."

"You said I was fat." Now Sonya is the one circling. Sami stands stiffly, wringing her plump hands. "Remember your notes, Sami? Your fat notes? 'This little piggy went to market'? 'Attila the Ton'? Remember *Sami?*" Four-twenty-seven. "Now who's the fat bitch?" Sonya spits her words. "Who's the pig? The cow? The sloppy cunt?"

"Sonya," Sami says. "I'm sorry. That's why I came, partly. I've been very sick," she says. "They put me on steroids and I've gained so much weight. Now I know. Now I know how cruel I was to you." Samantha wrings her hands and stammers. "I came to say, well…I came to say I'm sorry."

"Sorry? I tried to slit my wrists and you're sorry." Sonya looks at Sami's fat, red, tear-streaked face. "Fuck you, Sami. Fuck you like you were fucking Mr. Stemma, like you were fucking half of Crestman. Fuck you and the fat-ass horse you rode in on."

Sami gallops to the door with her head in her hands. She chokes on her own tears. Sonya is close behind her.

"Fuck you, Sami," Sonya yells from the door.

Sami slides into her car and speeds off.

"Fuck you!"

Four-twenty-nine.

Back in the house, Sonya changes the sheets on the bed. She lights candles even though it is daylight out.

Four-thirty.

She cues up her Love CD and dims the lights.

22

....

Nothing to say

The first time Sonya saw the uniform was when Tandy held it; the gloves, scarf and beret. "Put these on," Tandy said then. "Remember to stand at attention. Don't move. And, above all else, you got to look mad as sin." All of this still applies when wearing the Rebel colors, only now, Sonya understands what it means.

The first time Sonya saw the uniform, it was out of context, an elephant in an ice cream shop. She could not make sense of it— a hurried exchange behind the school building where Keeshawn took her furtive cigarette break. "Put these on," Tandy had said without explanation. And so she did.

Now, as she fashions the Rebel scarf around her neck in the pre-scribed double-knotted flare, as she cocks her black beret at the proper angle atop her head (Sergeant is sure to correct this later), Sonya understands the significance of the colors. Red for the blood spilled during slavery and apartheid, green for the lushness and fer-tility of the motherland, and black for the rich dark heritage of their culture, black for unity, black for sincerity, black for mourning our forefathers and foremothers, black for respect and pride. Black for strength.

Sonya emerges from her room and floats across the living room in her black beret, black turtleneck, and black ankle-length skirt. The accent of the fiery gloves and the scarf makes her look like an eccentric artist or like the last bit of a flame caught in a smolder of black smoke.

"Ready," Law says. He will drive Sonya to the Rebel gathering. Not directly to the gathering of course. She will have him drop her off within a block or two, though he won't know this. She cannot show up to the gathering, where Meeka, Celesta, Tandy, Kush and others from PLD will be, with this tall, muscled black man. As far as they are concerned, Sonya and her mother live alone. As far as they know, she has been disowned by her family because of her bi-racialness. How will she explain Law? Instead of suffering the risk of another lie, Sonya will keep Law secret from her PLD friends.

"Yep," she says to Law. "I'm ready."

"Aren't you hot?"

Sonya pulls at her scarf.

"No," Law says. "The turtleneck. And that skirt. Why are your skirts so gosh darn long?"

"Humility of the female body," she says, curtsying. "It keeps the boys guessing."

A sly look shadows Law's face. "You're right," he says. "I've been wondering what's under that skirt for a while."

Like a cloud crossing the sun's path, creating a second or two of shade, this moment of raw, innocent flirtation between Sonya and Law passes quickly. The phone rings and Law answers it, speaks in quick, hushed whispers. Sonya stands in the aftermath of his words. Sonya feels Law has done something physical to her. It is as if he has slipped his hands under the tresses of her long skirt and danced his fingers lightly along her thighs. Sonya cringes.

"How have you been?" Law says into the receiver of the phone.

Sonya taps her hand on her wrist and widens her eyes.

"Oh," Law says to the person on the other end. "Oh, I remember that. That's tough. That stuff will make you vomit for days." He places a hand over the receiver and mouths, "Doris."

Shit! Sonya thinks. Doris. Her mother. Of all the times to call. Sonya shakes her head, No! and waves her hands in front of her face.

"Wow. You finished all of that in such short a time. Well, I can believe it," Law says to Doris. "I can believe that coming from you." There is a pause in which Sonya hears wisps of her mother's voice escaping the receiver. The old anger stirs in Sonya, the same anger she felt when her mother begged her to make her appointments with Dr. Hillman so that she, Doris, could have Sonya's meds. It is the same anger Sonya felt when her mother missed Parent's Day and teacher conferences and every important event of her Crestman career.

On the verge of Sonya's big debut with the New Age Rasta Circle, when she only has twenty minutes to make it to the West End Auditorium (which is only ten minutes away, but still!), as she stands fully garbed in her new NARC gear, Doris calls and interrupts another important moment, perhaps the most important moment, of Sonya's high school career. How dare she? Sonya thinks. How fucking dare she!

"Sonya?" Law says, then looks over to Sonya who has her arms folded stubbornly across her chest. "She's out somewhere, ripping and running." Another beat of silence as he listens, as Doris sighs or clucks expressing her exasperation. Sonya has missed most of Doris's phone calls. She is either at school, at Tandy's or out with Kush. The Specialist has a phone which blocks all out-going calls to cellular phones just in case his patients are trying to contact a dealer. Thus Doris is not able to contact Sonya that way.

"Oh she's doing great," Law continues. "She's got a hog pile of friends at school. She's even joined a study group." He looks at Sonya, his face desperate and pleading, and holds the phone out to her.

No! Sonya mouths emphatically. Then, more staunchly. No.

"All right," Law says to Doris. "You hang in there. You've seen the worst of it, believe me. Just coast on down the road to cleanliness and follow the Specialist's orders." He chuckles. "You're right about that. You don't have a choice."

Sonya taps her wrist again and then turns away.

"All right now, Doris," Law says. "I will. I'll tell her."

Law hangs up the phone with a click as definite as death.

"That was Doris," he says to Sonya's back. "Remember her? Your mother?"

Sonya has her hand on the doorknob. She wants to escape the living room where Law lied for her, where she avoided her mother's call from rehab for the tenth time. All of these facts linger in the air, which press down on her with guilt.

"That was Doris," Law says again.

"Oh." Sonya cannot turn around to face his disapproving eyes.

"Yeah, she's going through it, but she's doing fine."

"That—" Sonya's voice falters in her throat. After some time, she catches it. "That's good."

"It is, isn't it?" Law says. "She told me to tell you that she misses you and she loves you."

She will mount the stage to speak in five minutes and she has no idea what she is going to say.

In the backstage area, Sonya paces from one end of the green room to the other. Back and forth from the walnut veneer coffee table, past the vending machine filled with Lance cheese crackers, across the coarse avocado colored carpet to the opposite wall where a poster of a clown holding a rose and tooting his red nose urges her to smile.

"Five minutes," the woman with the headset said, holding up her hand of four flaring fingers and a thumb. It had not hit Sonya until then, concerned as she was with the guilt of avoiding her mother's call. Concerned that her mother is going through hell and she, Sonya, has not been there to support her. In five minutes Sonya will be onstage at a conference organized by the Model of Black Brotherhood (MOBB), the Congregation of Immigrant Africans (CIA) and the New Age Rasta Circle (NARC). Earlier, Kush rushed backstage, his eyes gleaming and his breath panting with excitement to tell her the auditorium was full. Two-hundred-plus people. Standing room only. Sonya managed a meager smile. Inside she cringed. How is Sonya to speak at Festivale, where there will be at least twice as many people, when she cannot manage this?

Five minutes and Sonya will be at the podium standing before a tide of brown, expectant faces. She closes her eyes and tries to calm the storm in her head. With her eyes shut, she searches the blackness of her thoughts in an attempt to snag something, a word, a phrase, some seed of inspiration that might blossom into the three to five minute oration she is scheduled to give. Sonya opens her eyes. She can think of nothing.

A rumbling applause escapes the crowd. The previous speaker has finished, Sonya knows. It is her turn to take the podium. Zing enters the backstage area bringing with her a breath of light.

"Ready?"

"No." This truth escapes Sonya's mouth without her permission.

"No?" Zing says.

"I'm not prepared. I haven't written anything. No outline. No nothing."

"And?"

"And? And! I'm going to make an ass of myself," Sonya says. "I can't go out there. Tell them I'm sick. Tell them something."

Zing places her hands on Sonya's shoulders. Her eyes sharpen to knives. "You can," Zing says, "and you will."

"Zing, you don't understand. I can't think of—"

"You think I write outlines before I paint. Hell naw, girl, I just walk up to those walls, or stones or closets, take a deep breath and start slapping on color. This is not one of your study sessions with Tandy. There is no magic formula to this."

"Zing." Sonya's eyes are wide and watery. Her voice comes out small and pleading.

"Sonya, baby, listen. Sometimes you don't know until you know. Speeches aren't always written on paper. Life is your preparation. Truth is your outline. Now," Zing sighs, "go out there and say whatever it is you have to say."

The silence feels lonely and taunting and accusatory. Sonya stares out at the cloud of brown faces, all upturned and alert. They are like a crowd of spectators watching the aerial stunts of a plane. They are like baby birds, beaks wide and anxious, waiting to be fed. Among the crowd, Sonya sees Tandy, Celesta and Meeka.

Meeka winks a fake hazel eye. Sonya opens her mouth and the words flow out.

"I have a friend," she says, "that does not know her beauty. I have a friend who does not know she is loved."

Moments after she speaks these words, Sonya hears them. She looks out at the audience. She is not sure if something more will come. Just as expectantly as the audience does, Sonya waits.

"Though I identify as biracial, as black you may as well say, I am trapped in a white body. I have never belonged anywhere. Since I can remember what physical features were, I can remember that mine were not acceptable. Every morning in grade school my mother fought with the mass of curly hair on my head. We woke early in the morning, showered and ate, preparing for the task at hand. Then we sat at the kitchen table in our one-bedroom apartment where my mother tussled with my hair. If my mother knew how to braid my hair she probably would have. If she knew anything about dreadlocks and how they formed, that may have been an option too. But she didn't. So she brushed and brushed and brushed until my tresses were calmed enough to accept a comb. Then, for twenty or so minutes, she combed, tugging my head this way and that. After some time, she would manage to get my hair into two pigtails. These were sure to unravel by the end of the day.

"High school—my other high school, not PLD—taught me to hate myself even more. I was called fat because I have naturally wide hips. I was called a pug because I have a nose that is less than narrow. I was called brillo head because of my curly hair. I did not know my beauty.

"This is the first time I've felt accepted. My mother and I moved to East Atlanta partly to escape the tragedy of our former life. I didn't know how people would take me at PLD, trapped as I am in this white body. I did not know if I would belong.

"I have friends here. Tandy, Celesta, Meeka." She gives each of them a nod. "Kush. Even Maurice Maitland, with your crazy self. You have all welcomed me. Now, I feel beautiful."

There is a smattering of applause. Sonya holds her hand up to signal that she is not done.

"I hated myself for a long time. For years I would watch other black girls with their dark hair and brown skin. That is what I wanted to be. At my old school, I didn't have many black friends, partly because there were very few black people there. Now, *all* of my friends are black.

"To these friends I want to say that you are beautiful. You are beautiful black women. You, with your deep eyes and full lips, with your chocolate-coated skin and your crown of dark hair, you are the source of my envy."

It comes to her, from a long ago literary class where students chose from a basket the title of a poem to memorize. It comes to her, her poem from that class.

"Pretty women wonder where our secrets lie. They say we're not cute or built to suit a fashion model's size. But when we start to tell them they think we're telling lies. We are women! Phenomenally. Phenomenal *black* women. You and me."

Sonya knows it is over, partly because no more words come. The flow ends here. Also, she can tell by the crowd's reaction she is done. They rise to their feet and applaud, stomping and whistling. She has said something moving and true. Almost true. Sonya's first NARC speech is a success.

The nickname comes from the speeches she makes at almost every Nyahbinghi. Sonya takes the reins of the New Age Rasta Circle as the lead orator. She opens every gathering with Libations and words of inspiration. Today, as she makes her way to the center of the weekly gathering, she hears calls from the crowd.

All right, Sonya!

You better come with it!

Take it to the bridge, Soul Sista!

This is her new title, Soul Sister, reserved for use by members of the black conscious crowd. Now Sonya, the Soul Sista, stands front and center with her hands tucked behind her back. Just as with her first speech, she has prepared no notes. Instead she lifts her head and waits for the words to come.

"Praise be to Jah Rastafari." Sonya places her hand over her heart and bows her head in respect. When she lifts it, the words are there, right behind her eyelids, twinkling like stars. They wait to be released. "There is an answer, brothers and sisters. Believe it or not, there is an answer. There is a key to life." Sonya's voice takes on a thick, peppery timber. "The answer, my brothers and sisters, is Kugichaculia. Self-determination. So much of what we do relies on the assistance of The Man. To buy a car, we go to The Man. To buy a house, we go to The Man. To get an education, we go to The Man. My mother owes seventeen thousand dollars in private school loans to The Man."

Sonya looks to Zing. "Excuse my French, Sista Zing, but fuck The Man. Fuck The White Man and his master plan of institution-alized racism. Say it with me, brothers and sisters. Say it. Fuck The Man."

"Fuck The Man," the gathering chants.

"Fuck The Man." Sonya makes a fist and holds it before her.

"Fuck The Man." They are louder, more fervent.

"Fuck The Man and his master plan."

"Fuck The Man," they repeat, "and his master plan."

"Come on," Sonya says. "Give it to me three times brothers and sisters."

Sonya and the crowd chant together. "Fuck The Man and his master plan! Fuck The Man and his master plan! Fuck The Man and his master plan!"

"Thank you brothers and sisters. Thank you for speaking truth to power. This is our first step toward Kugichaculia. Thanks brothers and sisters. Let's begin Nyahbinghi with meditations by Sista Zing."

It is Zing's suggestions, the shirts. "If you don't stand for some-thing," she says as they pick up the box from the printers. They dis-tribute two hundred of them, mostly to friends, family, and members of the New Age Rasta Circle. The shirts are red and green of course, with bold black letters across the front. The back features a montage of prominent black leaders—Maya, Malcolm, Martin and Garvey, of course. The front of the shirt boasts Sonya's fiery words, "Fuck The Man and his master plan." Two asterisks replace the *U* and *C* in Fuck.

When Sonya and Kush walk past Principal Carlton wearing matching Fuck The Man shirts, he shakes his head and smiles. He won't give them what they want, a spectacle. He will allow them their little rebellion.

23

....

Pimp-slapped

Sonya wants more.

Her hair sits atop her head in a gauzy, khaki-colored wrap. Her shirt boasts a profile of Angela Davis. The right side of Sonya's nose winks and sparkles, freshly pierced with a sapphire stud. Her skirt, thick and billowy and gathered in a hundred places, swings from her hips to her ankles like a curtain. Every now and again someone calls to her in the hallway. "Hey, Sonya," they say, or "Greetings, Soul Sista." Sonya responds with a modest wave, bowing her head, mouthing, "Greetings," ever so humbly. Copper bangles jangle from her wrists and silver rings clink on her fingers as she waves. Sonya walks down the hall with Celesta and Meeka trailing behind her. In Tandy's absence, Sonya is the leader.

But Sonya wants more.

Kush rushes past juggling an armload of books and flyers.

"King Man," Sonya calls.

"Queen Woman," Kush responds as he trots back. He encircles Sonya's waist and she looks up to him, blinking demurely. Kush leans down and gobbles under Sonya's neck. She giggles and tweaks his ears.

"Could somebody shoot me," Celesta says.

Meeka smiles. "I think it's cute."

"How are you going to just rush past me?" Sonya says to Kush. "Come to lunch with us."

Kush looks over at Celesta and Meeka. "I heard men aren't allowed at your table."

"I'm sure we can make an exception." Sonya snuggles her head to Kush's chest and slides her torso over his waist, sidling up against him like a cat. "Can't we, ladies?" Her voice goes high and singsongy, playful and chiding as a nanny's.

"Whatever," Celesta says. "He's your man."

"My King Man," Sonya singsongs.

"I don't have time anyway," Kush says. "I'm meeting Sergeant to discuss our next meeting. I'm sure I'll see you sistas there."

Kush takes two steps down the hall and Sonya yanks him back. Pushing up on her tiptoes, she kisses him long and hard. It is a performance, her kissing Kush this way. It is a marking of territory. Sonya is a child waving her ice cream cone in the face of her friends. Sonya is boasting.

"See you tonight," he says.

"Bye, King Man." She gathers her skirt and turns in the direction of the cafeteria.

Celesta watches the bunch and ruffle of Sonya's skirt from behind.

"Girl," Celesta says, "I don't know how you're going to manage in the summertime with them Massa-I'sa-comin' skirts you be wearing."

"They breath," Sonya says a bit annoyed. Celesta has made such comments before. "They're made of cotton."

"Cotton my ass," Celesta says. "You look hot as Satan on Sunday."

"You do be looking hot," Meeka says.

"And dry and thirsty too, like The Wind Done Gone up in this bitch," Celesta says in a scratchy, parched voice. "Looking at you is like licking a block of salt," she continues. "You make a niggah thirsty."

Celesta laughs riotously. Meeka covers the giggle escaping her mouth.

Sonya stops and turns swiftly to face Meeka and Celesta. She gathers clumps of her skirt in her fist to keep it from dragging on the floor. "The Books says, 'Women keep thee modest. Keep thee whole and covered and pure. Keep thy feminine powers of body.'" Here, she looks down at Meeka's short skirt and exposed legs. "'And thy lashing, passionate tongues,'" she shoots this line at Celesta, "'clean, pleasant and bridled.'"

The book from which Sonya quotes is the newly adopted bible of The Rebels, *The Book of Ancient African Thought*. Sonya has been reading it every night during her study sessions with Tandy.

"What about American History?" Tandy said a few nights ago during one of their study sessions. "We have a test coming up."

"You mean His-story. The *Man's* version of the way things went."

"*Ancient African Thought,*" Tandy read the last words of the book's title. "What's African thought anyway?"

Sonya looked up with searing eyes.

"Just asking." Tandy threw up her hands in surrender. Then, under her voice, she said, "'Cause there are more than eight hundred cultures and religions in *ancient* Africa. They don't all think the same. Y'all must be practicing some fusion religion or something."

"Whatever," Sonya responded. "Just go on learning His-story." Her face parted in a condescending smile.

"You better learn *His*-story too if you want to pass *His* class and go to *His* college."

"The Man got your head straight twisted."

"You can't very well be the one talking about twisted heads, Ms. Dreadlock Queen. Ms. Righteous Indignation."

Lately, she and Tandy clash this way, little arguments about school or The Rebels. At first Sonya backed down, deferred to Tandy's opinion. As she grew into her Rebelliousness, as she became known around PLD and East Atlanta, Sonya began objecting. Now she argues back. By hinting that Tandy is brainwashed, that she is a sellout in some ways, Sonya quashes Tandy's sharp pronouncements—paper to scissors. Sometimes, Tandy acquiesces. "I can kind of see that," Tandy will say. Or, "To each her own," allowing Sonya a slender victory.

Still, Sonya wants more.

Tandy walks up just as Sonya finishes her last line from The Book. Noticing the expression on Sonya's face, her upturned head, her fiery eyes and pursed lips, Tandy smiles.

"Is she quoting that dumb book again?"

Like the jerk of a knee when dinged with a mallet, or like the pull of flowers toward sunlight, Meeka's and Celesta's attention sways toward Tandy. Sonya feels a cold lonely overcast, a deep, gray cloud—Tandy's shadow. The true queen returns. Reluctantly, Sonya surrenders the throne.

For now.

Sonya wants more.

From first hour to lunch, Sonya enjoys her reign over Celesta and Meeka, her reign over PLD. She walks through the halls greeting her court.

When's that Festivale thing?

Hey, sista.

Like the new head wrap.

Your hair's really coming along.

In the past months, Sonya has successfully erased Sonya, the furtive, curly-haired white girl, the girl with the pug nose and the ugly hands, the girl who sat in the corner of Mrs. Larsen's homeroom with her mouth sewn shut by reticence. She is Sonya, Kush's Queen Woman. Kush, the jet-black revolutionary, thin bodied, long fingered; Kush, who toured her through the West End, Morehouse, Spellman, Clark, the African Braid Salon where she began her locks, the Patty Hut where she had her first taste of coco bread (he'd fed it to her, sliding his fingers along her lips and the ridges of her teeth). Kush, Sonya's King Man, who introduced Sonya to Mos, Common, L-Boogie, and KRS-1.

"It's more than just words put to a beat." Kush stood behind Sonya and pressed the oversized headphones to her ears. He was so close she could smell the thick, coarse wool of his sweater and feel his heartbeat against her shoulder blade.

Lauryn Hill's voice came through the wires, all syrup and salt.

> How can dominant wisdom
> Be recognized in a system
> Of anti-christs and majority rules
> Intelligent fools
> PhDs in illusions
> Masters of mass confusion
> Bachelors of past illusions

Now, she is Sonya, the girl who's "on that black righteous shit, on it hard," as Celesta says. Sonya, one of the keynote speakers for Festivale. Sonya, the girlfriend of the most popular, most beautiful boy in school. She has much more than she had every dreamed when Doris announced their financial distress and subsequent move to East Atlanta. Back then, Sonya would have settled for mere inclusion into the group of black girls. She would have settled for a relationship similar to the one she had with Samantha Klieg— to be allowed to stand near Tandy and the others, to be tolerated like a bad smell. Sonya would have settled for this. What she inherits, creates, forges from a slab of lies is much more than the sidekick status for which she had originally dreamed. Sonya is popular and beautiful. All the things that made her "ugly" at Crestman—her wide hips, her curly hair, and her dirty brown eyes—serve the opposite purpose at PLD. Here, her hips make her thick. Her hair is "good hair." Most of all her eyes, which where muddy compared to Samantha's baby blues, shine a dazzling gray-brown, a gray-brown that, as far as everyone else is concerned, boasts her tragic mulatto heritage.

Still, Sonya wants more.

In the morning, Tandy attends advanced tutoring, the classes at PLD proving too remedial for her sharp brain. Of course, this is not what she has told Celesta and Meeka. "Some mess Principal Carlton's got me doing," is what she said. "I barely pay attention to that lady." Every day, from first hour to lunch, while Tandy devours logarithms and Tolstoy, Sonya floats through the halls with Celesta and Meeka trailing behind her like bridesmaids. For those few hours of the day, Sonya reigns as the most popular girl in PLD. Sonya is the leader of the group. Sonya is queen. Until Tandy arrives.

"Excuse me, Mrs. Malcolm Garvey King," Tandy says now to Sonya. "Are you finished with your freedom song, because we're hungry."

Tandy walks down the hall with Meeka and Celesta in her wake. Sonya stands for a moment staring at the backs of the three black girls, the three black girls from the train, the ones with whom she desperately wanted to be friends. Sonya watches as they walk away from her, their figures thinning, thinning, thinning before disappearing into the crowd. Slowly, Sonya gathers up her skirt, which seems heavier now, and follows the black girls into the cafeteria.

She does not plan to say it. She could not have. Her lips would have betrayed her. They would have trembled, stammered. Halted. Sonya does not plan to say it. Actually, she made a promise to herself early on that she would never say it, ever, no matter how far things went. But today, at the lunch table, with Tandy, Meeka and Celesta sitting beside her and Maurice Maitland standing at the table's head, Sonya says what she promised herself she never would.

The boys at the other table snicker as Maurice approaches. Celesta flashes Sonya and the others a knowing glance.

"Here he comes with some bullshit," Celesta says. "Ladies, don't shoot until you see the whites of his eyes."

Maurice bows theatrically. "Good evening, madams. How are you enjoying today's feast."

"Hmm," Sonya says, rolling her eyes and pursing her lips. After much practice, she has black-girl sass down to a science.

"Hey, Maurice," Tandy says. Her lips, too, are pushed together in a pout.

"What a fine meal we are having here." Maurice looks back at his crew from the other table, the table for popular boys, and winks. They snicker like sly cats. "How are you—"

"What in the hell do you want?" Celesta asks.

Meeka giggles and then covers her mouth.

"Would you be so kind as to help a hungry young man such as myself by providing a meal."

"You ain't getting my pizza," Celesta says.

Sonya uses this opportunity to work in her new phrase. "You straight bent shorty," she says. She and Celesta slap five.

Meeka looks up with big eyes. "You can have mine."

"Girl," Celesta slaps the square of pizza down which Meeka had held up for Maurice.

"I'm just saying," Meeka squeaks.

Celesta casts Meeka an angry eye. "You always just saying"

"Cut to the chase, Maurice," Tandy says.

"I'm quite hungry," Maurice says, glancing over his shoulder at the other table. "And, well, Sonya—" Maurice turns and bows to her "—I was wondering. Can I eat you out?"

The group at the next table turns around. "Did you hear what he said?" the girl nearest Tandy asks her neighbor. Pokes and nudges travel around the table, alerting nearby students to the action.

Though Celesta begins it, it is Meeka's voice that gains the attention of the entire cafeteria.

"Niggah huh?" Sonya can tell by the steel in Celesta's eyes that indignation is real, not the mock, comedic scorn she usually musters for such occasions.

Meeka, who rarely speaks above a squeak, bawls her outrage. "Niggah who?" Her voice—shrill and loud—pierces through the atrium of students. It announces commotion and possible spectacle. Students turn in their seat. Some rise to get a better view. A wave of whispers passes over the cafeteria.

Maurice said something.

Meeka's pissed off.

To Sonya?

Something about eating her out.

Sonya looks up at Maurice. Her eyes lock on him, hard and gray-brown. The lewdness of his question hangs over her, sticky and damp. An image of Madison servicing her mother, an image of him in his leather jacket, with his head of thorned hair, his head of horns, crashes before Sonya's eyes.

There is a pause in which nothing is said.

"Niggah what?" Tandy says.

Usually, Tandy issues the last pronouncement. Before Keeshawn left for Texas, the order remained the same: Celesta, Meeka, Keeshawn and, last, Tandy. Always Tandy to issue the final edict. Always Tandy, to put a cap on it. Always, the most coveted and most gratifying part, the leading role, went to Tandy.

But that was before, when Sonya sat as a spectator, when Keeshawn was here to complete the quartet. In Keeshawn's absence, Sonya becomes the fourth, and, by default of Tandy's "Niggah what?" the last.

In the pat of silence between Tandy's words and the next, Sonya's heart thumps. She stands up to face Maurice. Her head wrap and skirt giving her height and heft over him. Maurice's hands are tucked behind his back butler fashion. His lips part in a wry smile.

"I said, Can I eat you out?" Maurice enunciates each word, speaking loud enough for the entire cafeteria to hear.

It is reflexive, the rise of Sonya's hand, just as reflexive and just as natural as the words that topple out of her mouth. Sonya draws her hand back and slaps Maurice sharply, quickly, with the backs of her fingers. Her head rolls as if it is connected to her neck by ball and socket.

"Niggah please!" Sonya says.

The cafeteria explodes in cacophony of whistles, ooohs, giggles and high-fives. Sonya feels the electricity of attention in the crowd. Only after Maurice Maitland fails to strike her back, only after he lowers his head and slinks back to his seat, only after she looks around the cafeteria and see that the jeering is not at her but *for* her, only after she looks at Celesta and Meeka whose faces are split with wide grins, then at Tandy, whose nostrils flare with anger and jealousy, only after all these things does Sonya understand the scale of her victory. Her name will float through classes and in the hallway.

Did you hear what happened?

No. She didn't!
He said something to set her off.
Sonya is gangsta.
Shorty don't play.
Meeka and Celesta slap five at the table.

Sonya sits calmly, modestly. She agrees with Meeka that, yes, Maurice is nasty, that he had it coming. The jeering dies down to rustle. Still, Sonya can feel the eyes of reverence hot on her back. Outside, her face is calm, languid even. Inside, Sonya revels in the commotion, stretches her arms out to it, scoops it up like a bouquet of roses tossed at her feet.

Silently, Tandy swivels her pizza across her tray with a fork. She recognizes the pert grin on Sonya's face, the smirk, the held-in merriment of it. For two years Tandy held such silent celebrations. Sonya sees Tandy eyeing her. She shoots Tandy a quick, tight smile.

"You showed him," Meeka says.

"Goddamn, girl," Celesta rears her head to look at Sonya.

"What?" Sonya looks for Celesta to Meeka. "What?"

"I didn't know you had it in you," Celesta says. "You straight pimped that niggah."

From across the table, Sonya sees wholly the thing living behind Tandy's face. It stares straight at her. It is envy—fanged and growling and green.

24

....

This is a hoot!

Sonya saunters into Principal Carlton's office and drapes herself over the chair, sitting with her back slouched and her hips pushed slightly forward. She leans into the seat like someone fed up and exhausted. Her insides tingle and wheeze with a dreadful excitement. In slapping Maurice and saying "Niggah please," Sonya has stepped sideways and crossed into another dimension. In this dimension, rules no longer apply. In this dimension, Sonya is rude and brash and fierce. She is the type of black girl she once imagined Tandy to be, the type of black girl who slaps one of the most popular PLD boys in the face—straight pimps him—and says, "Niggah please."

Sonya understands more now. As an outsider, she once listened to comedians like Chris Rock, Dave Chappelle and MoNique on the television. She once listened to rappers like Jay Z and Nas. The word *niggah* peppered their jokes and music. The work of these performers seemed to be hinged on this one word. From the outside, back when Sonya was Sonya, she listened with a baffled, slightly condescending criticism. Listening to black performers as they employed this word, which had been used historically to oppress them, Sonya (then Sonya) felt as if she were watching a dog, ignorant of its own anatomy, chase his own tail. To Sonya when she was Sonya, to call yourself *nigger,* a term of hatred and oppression, seemed so obviously self-destructive.

Now Sonya realizes that it was she, not the black community, who was the ignorant one. A mysterious and magical alchemy has been performed on *niggah*. It has been exonerated of its harsh meaning and given a purple cloak of royalty, a shiny veneer.

But the luster of *niggah* is more than a coating, more than plating or a chunk of fool's gold. *Niggah* shines through and through with layers upon layers of meaning. Only after employing the word herself does Sonya understand this. Before, when Sonya was Sonya, she saw the word as either a term of hatred used by racist whites (I hate niggers!) or as a term of endearment used by urban blacks (What's up, niggah?) Before, when Sonya was Sonya and newly landed at PLD, she avoided the term because of her limited understanding of its various implements. Using it, she thought, would indict her as a racist and would offend others.

In fact, *niggah* was the bridge over which Sonya needed to cross, a suspension bridge swaggering above a lake of rushing, icy waters and dark, jagged rocks. Crossing this bridge acted as Sonya's initiation, her rite of passage. Now she understands the difference between *nigger,* N-I-G-G-E-R, and *niggah,* N-I-G-G-*A*-H.

The other *nigger,* the new *nigger* (N-I-G-G-*A*-H) serves a myriad of functions. *Niggah* can be friendly (S'up, niggah?), or hostile (Fuck you, niggah!). *Niggah* can be comedic (That niggah just farted) or serious (That niggah got shot). *Niggah* can be an adjective (I acted the niggah fool), an adverb (I niggah rigged the TV), or a root word (I got niggahitus). A *niggah* can be black (Dave Chappelle! Now that niggah is crazy) or white (George Bush! Now that niggah is crazy) or other (Tiger Woods! Now that niggah is crazy).

Niggah has been lifted from the sludge of water hoses and the Mississippi River. *Niggah* has been snatched from the fanged mouths of Bull Conner and police dogs. *Niggah* has been torn down from the trees of Georgia and the flaming crosses of the KKK. *Niggah,* absolved of its former infamy, has been scoured by Nikki Giovanni, scrubbed by Oprah Winfrey, washed by Malcolm and rinsed by Martin Luther King. Lauryn Hill, KRS1, H. Rap Brown and Richard Pryor have polished *niggah. Niggah* shines glorious and round and bright like a sun in the center of all that is blackness.

Sonya stares up at Mr. Carlton and thinks, "What is this niggah going to do to me?"

Mr. Carlton's face is stern and serious, an outline of reproach. He circles behind Sonya like an interrogating officer.

"So?" He says. It is understood to be a question, Sonya's segue into an explanation. She feigns ignorance.

"So…what?" She pops gum on her back teeth and pulls at a loose lock of her hair. Inside her heart beats in quick rabbit breaths. But the pulse of cool power she feels humming inside her devours her nervousness.

"You slapped a fellow student," Principal Carlton says. "That's what. Now explain how this came about."

Sonya recounts the lunchroom scene for Principal Carlton, altering it a bit to make herself more offended, more victimized. In Sonya's version, Maurice flicks his tongue at her. He gropes her. He calls her a bitch.

"So I pimped him," Sonya says. She flares her hands and shrugs her shoulders. Inside, her heart takes short doggy breaths. This is the first time Sonya has had to visit the principal's office in her life. At Crestman, Sonya practically lived in the counselor's office. But that was for the opposite reason—for hardly ever saying or doing anything. Sonya has never had to go to the principal's office. She has never done something so blatantly wrong.

"You 'pimped' him?" Principal Carlton scrunches his brow. "Expound, please."

"Well, you know. Maurice pushed up on me and my girls like we were straight tricks so I had to represent," she says. "I slapped him." Sonya stares over Carlton's shoulder at the placards hanging on the wall, golden-colored certificates, a Morehouse diploma, and a framed picture of Martin Luther King, Jr. "I've been to the mountain top," the King poster reads. This is exactly how Sonya feels now, as if she is standing on the precipice of a high mountain—prophetic, unwavering, immaculate—with cold clouds smoking above her and crisp mountain wind whipping at her skirt.

As Sonya looks at Principal Carlton who looks at her, she composes the retelling of this incident for Celesta and Meeka. "And when I told him I pimped Maurice, Carlton was looking at me all crazy," she will say. "That niggah didn't even know what 'pimped' meant," she will say. Meeka will cover her mouth and giggle. Celesta will guffaw. Tandy will be away in her special studies.

Sitting on the edge of his desk, Principal Carlton sighs. "I'll have to call your parents." His tone carries a practiced gravity. It is as if he is reading from cue cards flashing up from behind Sonya's shoulder.

"Handle yours, dog," Sonya says, one of Celesta's phrases. If she had hesitated a second longer in her retort to Maurice, Celesta would have said just that. "Girl, you better handle yours."

Principal Carlton has pulled Sonya's file and dialed the home number listed there. At this moment, Sonya is happy for everything that has happened in her life. She is happy that they moved to East Atlanta. She is happy that her mother is in some clandestine rehab, and that she only hears from Doris during Doris's one allotted phone call. Most of all, Sonya is happy for the alliance she and Law have formed. They are partners now, both involved in illicit activities. She is even happy for Law's little crush, which gives her an upper hand, a certain level of control over him. Sonya relaxes her seating position even more, bunching herself up in the chair and throwing her legs over the chair's right arm. She is sure Law will cover for her.

Sonya listens at Principal Carlton's *Mmm-hmm*'s and *I see*'s. She can only imagine what Law is saying. "Exactly," Principal Carlton agrees. "We need more involved adults like you." Principal Carlton issues a few more *Mmm-hmm*'s and then listens at length. His face beams down at Sonya victoriously.

Principal Carlton hands the phone to Sonya. "Your uncle would like to speak with you." Her face contorts in the mock reproof of a B-movie actor.

"Don't miss any more of her phone calls," Law says. His voice is thick, reprimanding. It catches Sonya off guard. "The Specialist only allows one a week. Two for good behavior. You missed the last one."

"I didn't mean to," Sonya says. "I've just...been under a lot of stress."

"Well," Law says, "I talked to her. She's not doing so well. She'll make it, hopefully. But it would be nice for her to hear from her daughter every now and again.

"I moved some packages in the basement," he continues. "It's a lot of stuff. It will have to stay there for a month or so, until I can move it."

"Yes, sir," she says for Principal Carlton's benefit. Sonya adds a tremble in her voice. Principal Carlton turns around respectful as if Sonya is changing clothes.

"Well," Laws sighs. This is when Sonya hears it in his voice, the dampness of depression. She remembers this sound in her voice back at Crestman when she was under Samantha's rule. He hasn't taken his medication.

"I'll bring the slip for you to sign."

"Apologize to Carlton," Law says. "I promised him you would."

"Yes, sir." Sonya returns the phone to the receiver. She makes a note to herself to reprimand Law about skipping his meds.

"Do you have anything to say for yourself?"

Sonya looks up to Principal Carlton with wide wet eyes. A handful of laughter tickles the inside of her stomach. She can barely contain herself.

Principal Carlton paints his face a mask of disapproval and regret.

"Principal Carlton," Sonya says.

"Yes." Principal Carlton nods, already accepting the apology he is sure Sonya will give.

"Fuck you and fuck this white man's establishment you call a school."

★ ★ ★

It is a parade of triumph, Sonya's walk back to her locker to get her books. She has been suspended for two days. More importantly, she told Carlton to fuck off to his face. She told Carlton to fuck off and got away with it, more or less. Sonya heard some of what Law said on the phone. She heard her mother's name and assumed Law was giving Carlton the alcoholism story. They had agreed to speak of it as alcoholism, for everyone's safety. Otherwise the Department of Family and Children Services was sure to come in. And if counselors happened to arrive on one of the days when Law and Madison had a large delivery, they would all be busted.

Law delivered the alcoholism story, Sonya was sure. Carlton explained to Sonya that most students would be expelled for her action. "But," he sighed, "considering your family circumstances…"

Sonya makes a beeline for the second-floor theater. Most of the juniors will be gathered there for junior seminar. Mrs. Larsen is the teacher, which means there will be no teacher for another fifteen minutes. Already she can imagine the whispers and wide eyes as she enters the theater. Already, they would have heard. News travels that quickly at PLD. And, if they haven't, Sonya will retell the story. "Girl, what's the verdict?" Celesta will ask. A crowd will gather around Sonya. They will lean in close. They will wait.

"Man," Sonya will say. She'll be sure to suck her teeth and roll her eyes. She'll be sure to shrug her shoulders. "I told Carlton to fuck off."

This will be her crowning moment. Her coronation. Her coup. Sonya, the tortured mulatto, Sonya the conscious revolutionary has now become Sonya the Brazen, Sonya the Badass.

Now Sonya will be the definite leader. How can she not be? She slapped Maurice Maitland. She told Carlton to fuck off. If this does not knock Tandy off her throne, nothing will.

Sonya rounds the corner to the gym. Kemah walks past her, swooshing down the hall in her fire red tights. Her hair sits atop her head in a complicated basket of braids.

"We heard about you," Kemah said.

"Whatever," Sonya says. The surly indifference comes easily to Sonya now. She feels the power of popularity buzzing through her like lightening. She feels as if she is about to bungee jump, or as if she is walking up to a stage to accept a Grammy.

A crowd has already gathered in the theater. In the center, she can hear a familiar voice. She hears her name. "But I've known Sonya forever," the voice says. Sonya smiles. Yes, she thinks. They are shocked. Appalled. They are waiting for me. They all want to know.

"Hey, Sonya," Tandy says. She stands on the edge of the crowd. Her voice sings with sarcasm. "You're just in time." A demented smile sits under Tandy's nose.

Self-righteous bitch, Sonya thinks. She marches past Tandy into the center of the crowd. Sitting in a seat with a small photo album in her hand is Lydia Grant.

"Ohmygod." Lydia pops up and hugs Sonya. "Sonya. Sonya. Sonya. I heard you were here. I just transferred. Isn't this a hoot?" Lydia's words zoom out of her mouth like a speeding train. But Sonya cannot hear them. Her eardrums swell in her head. Her brain contracts and expands like a large beating heart. Sonya cannot see anything, save Lydia's beaming brown face.

"I mean, who would have thought you and I would end up in the same school," Lydia shrieks. "I mean, from Crestman to here." She turns to the crowd. "Not that here is bad," she says. "I'm happy to be out of that snooty school. I love our new house. It is so huge. I mean, gigantic. It would have cost a zillion dollars in Buckhead. Sonya. Oh, Sonya. Wow. I told them we'd gone to school together and I just happened to have my photo album. I have pictures from freshman year. When you were all Goth."

The room blackens and then is suddenly bright. Sonya must find something to hold on to or else she will faint.

"Well," Lydia says. "Say something. Isn't this a hoot?" She turns and addresses the crowd. "This is a hoot!"

25

....

Yellow Mary convention

Blue. Red. White.

  Blue. Red. White.

  The lights flanking the stage become Sonya's anchor. It takes all of her energy to stare forward and feign attention to Lydia Grant's speeding words. Blue. Red. White. The stage lights are the color of police cars, the color of emergency. If Sonya could concentrate, she might think to herself, "How ironic." But she can't. An alarm clangs inside her head. Her castle has been flooded. It is submerged in water. Everything around her wavers, gurgling and slow. Doom, like a scattering of sharpshooters on high-up buildings, has her locked in its targets.

  Sonya feels her face flush. She feels the hot tears rushing to the rims of her eyes.

  Most other students engage in their own antics, gossiping or shooting spitballs or reading ahead for the next class. Sonya's frantic paranoia makes her think all eyes are on her. Tandy is the most attentive of the spectators. She looks from Lydia to Sonya and sees the dread in Sonya's eyes. Tandy recognizes the crease of opportunity.

Mrs. Larsen arrives just as Lydia begins talking about her ride over to PLD.

"And then we couldn't find any parking and there was this like homeless man knocking at our window and I was like, 'Go away from me please.' But he kept knocking so I was like 'Ohmygod, here is a dollar now skiddaddle.'"

Mrs. Larsen totters to the stage and pulls the microphone screechingly down to her mouth. "Oh, BeJesus me," Mrs. Larsen says looking down at Lydia Grant. "Another hybrid. What's your name, baby?"

Lydia smiles a wide silly smile. She answers Mrs. Larsen singingly. "I'm Lydia Denise Grant from Crestman which is way far away from here but my family just moved so here I am at PLD. I'm so excited. This is my first day. Have I missed anything?"

"Baby that's the longest name I done ever heard," Mrs. Larsen says. "How about I just call you Lydia."

"Great," Lydia's voice booms across the theater.

Mrs. Larsen addresses the students surrounding Lydia and Sonya. "I know we are still a color-struck people but can we save the Yellow Mary Convention for lunchtime. I do have to earn this here eight cents they call a paycheck."

Other students shuffle to their seats. No one wants to fall prey to Mrs. Larsen's stinging sarcasm. As the students move to their various seats, Sonya looses sight of Lydia. Then she spots Lydia two rows up. Just as Sonya moves to intercept her, to pull Lydia outside and make up some lie to cover her tracks, Tandy hitches Lydia Grant's arm and ushers her to a seat up-front.

Then Sonya remembers: she has been suspended. Principal Carlton instructed her to leave the campus immediately. But how can she leave now, with Lydia Grant fresh on the scene. Lydia Grant, the beautiful brown-haired girl, the girl with the boisterous personality (which will be a real disaster at PLD), Lydia Grant, who'd lived in Sonya's neighborhood, close enough to have seen Sonya and Doris sitting side by side in their car, driving around on one of their many mother-and-daughter excursions. Lydia Grant, who had attended Crestman with Sonya for two whole years. Lydia Grant who said she has brought pictures!

Sonya watches as Tandy flips through the pictures Lydia brought. Tandy and Lydia sit front and center with the other smart students. On one side of them is Cindy Hargrove, class president and on the other is a skinny girl whose name Sonya does not know. Neither of them is interested in the pictures.

Sonya's skin grows hot and her pulse throbs inside her head. She can only imagine the things Lydia Grant it telling Tandy. Luckily, Doris never attended school events, so it is unlikely Lydia will have a picture of her. Does Lydia know Sonya's mother? Sonya can't remember if they ever met. Doris didn't show up for Crestman's Parent's Day. She was either working or stoned. Samantha Klieg knew Doris. Samantha and Lydia weren't friends, but still. Lydia could know, somehow.

The lights flanking the stage blare at Sonya—blue, red, white— taunting as a poked out tongue. Sonya can see Mrs. Larsen on the stage giving weekly announcements and deadlines. She can hear Celesta next to Meeka making a wisecrack about Mrs. Larsen's plaid dress. She can even see Tandy and Lydia several rows up, the backs of their heads leaning into each other as they talk. Tandy glances over her shoulder at Sonya with a bright, mean smirk on her face. Sonya notices all of these things, but in the far-off hollow way, the way a dreaming person recognizes the first buzz of an alarm clock.

Sonya has been suspended. She must leave.

She must leave while Lydia Grant sits beside Tandy, the black girl from the train, Sonya's new enemy and former friend, the girl from which Sonya has been siphoning popularity. The girl Sonya recently dethroned. Festivale is less than a week away. It is supposed to be Sonya's big debut. Tandy could ruin it all if Lydia runs her mouth. That's exactly what Lydia is doing as Sonya watches her from several rows away. She is flipping through photos with Tandy. She is pointing and laughing. She is running her fucking mouth.

Sonya has been suspended. So she must leave while Tandy plots her demise.

Sonya stands and heads for the door. Her head wrap wobbles on her head like a bowl of marbles. Her skirt pulls at her legs like an anchor. Celesta was right: It is too hot for the summer.

"Excuse me, Miss Clairol," Mrs. Larsen says into the micro-phone. "Where, do tell, do you think you're going?"

"I've been suspended," Sonya says. "I'm going home."

"Baby, we don't just walk out of Mrs. Larsen's class like we're president of the world. We ask to be excused."

Sonya sees the familiar faces: Tandy, Celesta, Meeka, the skinny girl whose name she does not know. This time everyone really watches and waits. Everyone listens for the crackle of Mrs. Larsen's words.

"Who do you think you are?" Mrs. Larsen says. "Walking in here cavalierly to announce you—"

"Save it Larsen," Sonya says. "I don't have time for your shit today."

Sonya hears the wave of *ooh*'s in the crowd. She feels the hot bright eyes on her back. She walks out of the theater doors. She does not wait for Mrs. Larsen's response.

Sonya walks down the halls toward the back of the school where the gymnasium is located. A plan blossoms in her head, a vivid red flower.

A way out.

"I need you to pick me up from school," Sonya says. Her cell phone feels cold and hard against her face, like the barrel of a gun.

"Sonya?" Law says. His voice is slow, plaintive. Depressed.

"Have you skipped your pills?" Sonya is more annoyed than concerned. Law's bout of depression might spoil her plan.

"I'm not doing that anymore. They fuck up my head."

Sonya's ears snag on the profanity. It sounds foreign coming out of Law's mouth, more crass coming from him, like a grandmother burping. Sonya decides to ignore the profanity. She has other things to worry about.

"Take your pills," she says "At least one. Dog, you can't just go cold. It might shock your system or something."

"What happened with Carlton?"

"Man that niggah was trying to fuck with my head," Sonya says. "But never mind that. I only got suspended for two days. I need you to come get me, yo."

"Now?"

"Ten minutes." Sonya says.

"I got to get myself together first," Law says.

"Law," Sonya says. "Ten minutes. Okay?"

She is certain Law will come. He has become captivated with Sonya to the point of worship. Several times, Law has missed appointments with Madison or has made late deliveries in order to drive Sonya to the mall or take her to the movies. Though he is twenty years her senior, Law has become like the kid brother of a best friend with his wide, watery eyes and his juvenile yearning.

Sonya snaps her phone shut and heads down to the east wing of the school. What Law said reminds her of something. Only, it isn't what he said, it's how he said it. She had heard that tone before—flat, resigned. Defeated. She heard it in her own voice back at Crestman just before she went for her wrists.

Sonya turns the corner and glances at her watch. She hopes the lack of medication will not affect Law's promptness.

It is easier than Sonya thinks. The glass has already been broken, probably by someone who'd been dared to pull it but chickened out at the last minute, or by someone who got caught in the act. Sonya has nothing to loose now. She yanks down the red lever to the fire alarm. Waits for the bells. Nothing.

Nearby, she spies a trashcan. Eureka.

Sonya retrieves fingernail polish remover from her book bag and pours it over the pile of papers in the metal can. Her heart thumps inside her chest. She feels sneaky and daring, righteous as a Black Panther. The ignited match sizzles in her hand. She drops it on the pile of papers. For a moment, nothing happens. Then a breath of fire rises from the trashcan. The black liner of the can burns off in black smoke. Sonya walks away.

As she rounds the corner to the main hallway, the lights along the top of the wall flash and a symphony of bells clang throughout the school.

26

....

No holds barred

The designated gathering place for classes in the theater is the front of the building where the buses park and where parents come to pick up their students. Sonya waits on the steps. She leans back with her legs crossed in front of her. She feels as indestructible as a supervillain. Students trickle out along the side exits and occupy the lawn on either side of the building. After a minute or so, Sonya hears the juniors descend the stairs behind her.

"Ohmygod," Lydia Grant says. "A fire on my first day. How utterly horrible."

"Calm down, girl," Celesta says. "It's a bootleg fire. Somebody got bored and pulled the shit."

"Either way," Lydia says. "It must be an omen. Do you believe in omens? I don't. But an alarm on your first day of school. I mean, come on. If that's not an omen then what is?"

Tandy pushes past the crowd like a minor celebrity. "Hey, it's Sonya," she says. "Lydia. Everybody. Sonya's still here." Tandy's voice is high and false and diabolical.

Sonya raises her voice to the same level of cheerful wickedness. "Hi, Tandy. Hi, Lydia."

"Girl," Celesta says. "I thought you would've gotten the boot by now."

"That niggah Carlton suspended me," Sonya says.

Meeka joins the group. "Mrs. Larsen was pissed."

"I'm already on the chopping block." Sonya shrugs her shoulders. "Not much more she can do."

"Expel you," Tandy says.

Sonya meets her eyes. "She would have to go through Carlton and he would never do that. Carlton and I have an arrangement." She pulls out this phrase, Tandy's own words about hiding her grades. It is like the tip of her sword trembling at Tandy's larynx.

"Lydia has pictures," Tandy says, as if to slap Sonya's sword away. Her voice booms over the crowd of students. "Hey, Celesta, Meeka, y'all want to see pictures of Sonya before she was all righteous."

Celesta, Meeka, and others gather around. "You got pictures of Sonya when she was a straight white girl?" Celesta asks Lydia.

"I have every freshman year event."

Tandy sidles up beside Sonya. "She even has pictures of your mother."

In Tandy's eyes is the deep, sly shine. Her mouth parts sinisterly showing a flash of teeth. She has caught Sonya red-handed. Or so she thinks.

Sonya knows Tandy would never play her, ruin her social career, and her Festivale. Sonya and Tandy made a promise early on not to play each other no matter what. Tandy's loyalty has anchored her in every New Age Rasta Circle gathering, every NARC bake sale and rally, though she disagrees with their politics. Tandy's loyalty has kept her from calling Kush by his former name, Livingston, or even arguing with him in public. Sonya knows Tandy will not disclose what Lydia has told her, if Lydia has told her anything. Tandy only wants to see Sonya squirm.

"I'd love to see the pictures." Sonya stands beside Lydia and narrates. She remembers a deodorant commercial from when she was younger. *Never let them see you sweat,* the caption read. She won't.

She won't.

"Wow, Mr. Stemma? I haven't seen him in forever." Sonya flips through the drama club pictures. "He left quick," she says.

"Heard it had something to do with Samantha Klieg," Lydia says.

"Oh really." Sonya continues through the pictures. "You have the picnic, too. What did I have on?" Sonya faces a picture of Sonya, her former self, a frail child with limp hair and dark, glowering eyes.

Celesta takes the picture. "You do look like a straight bumpkin here."

The pictures float around various hands. Each student in turn laughs at the Sonya when she was Sonya.

"If I didn't know you," Tandy says, "I'd think you were white."

Lydia looks from Sonya to Tandy and blinks ignorantly. "What does she mean—"

"Lydia. Lydia. Where's the one of Sonya's mother?" Tandy asks. "Show us *that* one."

So, Sonya thinks, Tandy means to go for the gut.

"That's the funniest one of them all," Tandy says.

"Oh," Sonya says. "I doubt she has pictures of my mother. My mom never came to any events."

"Wait," Lydia says. "I think…oh, here. From Spring Concert."

Tandy snatches the picture. "You mean the white woman here? This can't be Sonya's mother. Sonya?" Tandy turns to meet Sonya's eyes. She speaks cheerleader loud, as if into a megaphone. "Sonya, this can't be your mother. Your mother's black. Right?"

Sonya laughs wryly. Silly bitch, she thinks as she looks into Tandy's face.

"Let me see that." Sonya stares at the picture and pretends to ruminate. "Her? In the blue? That's my aunt."

"You introduced her as your mother," Lydia says.

"Well she's not," Sonya says. "I know who my mother is."

"Do you?" Tandy asks.

"She does look like you," Celesta says. "Look at her nose and her eyes."

"Y'all, I think she would know better than us who her mother is," Meeka says. Her voice is unusually assertive. This must be Sonya's repayment for keeping Meeka's hazel contacts a secret.

"Girl," Celesta says, "this aunt of yours could be your twin."

"My aunt and I do look alike, I guess," Sonya says. She is surprised at the evenness of her voice. And she can tell without looking that Tandy is too.

"But Lydia says that's your mother," Tandy says. "Right, Lydia?"

Lydia Grant nods her head in agreement. "I remember when you introduced us because she had on this fabulous fur coat and this huge diamond. I mean it was huge. Like Ohmygod huge. And I was like, wow, is this your mother because she is really really fabulous and you were, well, really really not."

"I thought you said your momma was black," Celesta asks.

"She *is*," Sonya sings. "That's my aunt. My mother was, well…" She lowers her head, averts her eyes—the same victimized mope. She has become a method actress of the highest caliber, making her voice guttural with sorrow, producing tears on command. "She was in rehab and I didn't want anyone to know. I was too embarrassed. And people at Crestman aren't nearly as open and accepting as people at PLD. If they had known my family was half black. Well, Lydia you know how it is."

"Oh do I ever," Lydia chirps. "That's one of the reasons why we moved to this part of town. Crestman was great, but it was also, well, so, blah. Did she tell you I was one of the most popular freshmen at Crestman until everyone found out *my* mother was black? I mean, come on. It wasn't like I was hiding it. I was just well, I was just—"

"Passing," Celesta says.

"You're black?" Meeka says. "I thought you were a straight up white girl."

"Biracial," Lydia nods. "My mom's black and my father's white." Then, to Sonya. "I guess we're twins. Get it? Twins?"

"I knew she was black," Celesta boasts. "Look at her hair. And her eyes. Same way I knew Sonya was nigra."

Tandy pushes through and grabs the picture. "This doesn't make any sense. Sonya you have too many stories. First you're father left you when you were three. You're estranged from your family. Your aunt who looks like your mother is not your mother. Then your mother's all messed up. Next, you'll tell us you're Michael Jackson's secret love child." Tandy turns to Celesta, Meeka and the others. "Don't you think it sounds suspicious?"

"You do have a lot going on," Celesta says.

"It is like a soap opera," Lydia beams.

Celesta peers hard into the photograph. "I need a Venn diagram to keep up with your shit."

Tandy crosses her arms obstinately. "I don't believe it. I think you're lying."

So, here it is, finally, the challenge.

Sonya cackles at Tandy's statement as if she has just said the moon is made of cheese.

"What's there to lie about, dog? Why would I want to be a minority within a minority, double oppression at the hands of The Man? Come on, yo. What fool would choose that?"

"I don't know," Tandy says. "Why would you?"

"Well, what can I say?" Sonya sighs. "Everybody's life is not as easy as yours, Tandy. Everybody can't live in a mansion. Everybody can't be the child of a famous painter."

Sonya watches as the sparkle of malice in Tandy's eyes dims. Tandy's wry smile deflates.

Tandy meant to go in for the kill, but she failed, just as Sonya failed to slice Madison's throat with the Ginsu knife. Tandy's earlier challenge in the theater sent a bolt of fear through Sonya. Tandy drew first blood. Now, the battle is on. There are no holds barred.

"Tandy's momma ain't nobody," Celesta says. "She's just a painter."

Sonya sees the look Tandy had hoped to inspire in her; an electrified panic, a panic as raw as a side of beef. Sonya makes her voice high and naïve. "Y'all don't know?"

"Your momma's famous?" Meeka asks.

"She paints pictures on people's walls." Tandy rolls her eyes to the sky as if to dismiss it all. She tries for indifference, but her voice is thin and fretful. "It's nothing really."

Sonya turns to Lydia. "You know Tandy's mother. Nzinga Herman. You know, the mural painter. We studied her in—"

jd guilford

"Ohmygod," Lydia shrieks. "Nzinga Herman is your mother. She's like the most famous muralist in the nation. I mean, her heyday was in the seventies, but still, anyone who's anyone in the art world knows her. She did the mural for a family at Crestman and they paid her like some ludicrous amount like seventy thousand dollars or something. For a wall! Can you believe it? Your mom's amazing. I'd love to meet her."

"Girl, why didn't you tell nobody you was rich?" Celesta says. "All this time, you been crying broke and you been sitting on loot like that? Man."

"That's crazy," Meeka says. "If I was rich…"

"I'm *not* rich," Tandy says. "Mother paints somebody's wall every now and again, that's all."

"But you made it seem like she was a house painter," Meeka says. "You even told us she paints houses."

"So you been faking broke all this time?" Celesta asks.

"I haven't been 'faking' anything." Tandy tries to muster up her old huff, her command of the group. "How did we get to talking about some stupid paintings anyway? Weren't we looking at pictures of Sonya's mother?"

"Her aunt," Meeka says flatly.

"You bootleg as hell, Tandy." Celesta says. "Ain't nothing worse than a faker."

A clunky purple truck pulls up to the school. It's Law. He waves from the driver's seat. Sonya can see by the look on his face that this show of cheerfulness, however small, takes extreme effort.

"That's my brother," Sonya says, tapping the last piece into place. "He came down to help me out with—" she pauses her for dramatic effect "—with my mother and her, well, you know." Sonya looks directly at Tandy as if to say, "Now what?"

"Your brother?" Tandy's voice whines with disbelief. "Now you have a brother. Out of nowhere. Really? You never said you had a brother."

"Well, I do," she says.

"You never said you was a millionaire," Celesta says, "so shut the hell up, Tandy. God, to be so righteous, you sure are so…so…so ugh."

"I can't believe you're rich," Meeka says. "You don't even look rich."

"Well, I don't look black," Lydia says. "At least, that's what most of the folks at Crestman said when I first arrived and I guess that was due to my wearing all—"

"Damn, dog," Celesta barks, "do you ever take a breath?"

"I was a swimmer," Lydia chirps.

Law sits behind the steering wheel, large and handsome and gloriously black. Ha! Sonya thinks. Ha! Ha! Ha!

"Got to go."

As Sonya walks toward the car, something lurches in her stomach. An egg yoke of nausea slides down her throat. Like the village elder who ties a beautiful maiden to the base of a mountain for offering, Sonya has made the necessary sacrifice. She has escaped turmoil for a time.

She spies Tandy who has moved slightly apart from the others. Sonya's heart sinks. She thought she would enjoy this moment. She thought she would feel exuberant and triumphant. Instead, she feels carved out, hollow as a pumpkin. She feels both utterly exhausted and utter relieved, like a person who has barely escaped, which she is.

"He's a cutie," Lydia says as she waves to Law. "Tell your brother I said hello."

Sonya calls from the passenger seat. "Girl, he's too old for you." An urge to cry rinses over her. She shakes it off. Smiles. "Way too old."

"What's the deal with the Sanford and Son truck?" Tandy asks. She tries to sound normal, like the leader of the group, which she no longer is. Yesterday, Tandy would have sounded like a friend poking fun, joshing another friend. Now, she sounds desperate and bratty. Snobbish. A rich bitch.

"Sorry he didn't drive up in a Benz," Celesta says. "But everybody ain't ballin' like you."

Sonya waves at Celesta and Meeka. "Tell that niggah Carlton I said kiss my ass." The truck rumbles away. She watches Tandy walk into the building while the others stand outside waving at the truck. Another douse of grief comes. It is like an ice cube along her spine. Sonya shivers.

"You okay?" Law asks. He pats her thigh and then slides his hand up her leg. It rests there for a while. She can feel it pulsing and sucking like a parasite. She can feel the hard, hot waves of lust glowing within him.

"I'm fine." Sonya lifts Law's hand and places it between them on the seat next to her. His eyes go glassy with tears. His head drops.

27

Witch's brew

Back home, Sonya holds the phone to her ear as if it were a seashell into which she is listening to the roar of the ocean. It has become both fragile and sacred, the phone—a pendant that has just granted her a wish. On the other end of the phone is amnesty. Sonya can't believe she has been forgiven. And so quickly.

"I'm sorry," Sonya says. "It just slipped."

Her stomach rolls and riots, but Sonya ignores it. She won't put the phone down now. It is too fragile. She fears breaking this delicate connection.

Even now it seems too obvious, too simple, like a box held up by a stick—a perfect little trap. And Tandy walked right into it. Sonya's stomach tilts again. Inside, Sonya whispers *I repent. I repent.* She whispers this with the conviction of a chaste nun. But also, she feels triumphant. Defiant. It was such a simple trap. Sonya showed Tandy she is not so smart after all. *Silly bitch,* Sonya thinks. She does not say this out loud, of course. She has said enough.

"Celesta and the others would have found out eventually. PBS is running a special on Zing next week, so…"

"Oh," Sonya says. Again the lurching, the slosh and sway of Sonya's stomach, which she fights hard to ignore. Guilt, she thinks. It is guilt manifesting itself physically, like a ghost reincarnate.

Sonya betrayed Tandy. She reneged on her pinch promise to never play Tandy in public. The realization of this sits, rock heavy, in the center of her chest. It is like spending stolen money, the combination of exhilaration and guilt Sonya feels when she replays the scene on the steps: Lydia's pictures; the beat up truck; Tandy's desperate attempt to regain ground; Law's cameo appearance as her brother. *Everybody ain't rich like you,* Celesta had said when Tandy made the comment about the truck. In swift brushstrokes, Sonya had painted a picture of Tandy as a fake, rich brat. She'd turned Tandy's closest friends against her. Most importantly, Sonya secured her place as leader of the group.

Sonya betrayed Tandy. It was her only choice, she felt. Sonya has come so far, crawling from the obscurities of Crestman where she lived under the shadow of Samantha Klieg and friends. She has come so far from the girl who had slit her wrists, who had been a sex toy for her mother's drug dealing boyfriend, who had watched the black girls on the train with a yearning reverence. At PLD, Sonya built a new life—a precarious castle of cards, which Tandy threatened to topple with Lydia Grant's pictures. Tandy meant to banish Sonya back into the shadows, to excise her. It was self-defense, Sonya tries to tell herself. What happened during that fire drill was a face-off, a cage match, a battle in the Thunderdome. Two women enter, one woman leaves. It was either Sonya or Tandy.

Sonya has exited as the victor.

Most importantly, she has been forgiven.

"So." A sigh issues from the other end of the phone. It is like a thumb held up to test the wind. "What are you doing tomorrow?"

"Not much," Sonya answers, "I won't be in school, as you already know."

"Yeah, well." Then, another sigh.

Yes, Sonya betrayed Tandy. In doing so, she wrote off her relationship with Kush. Surely, he would have nothing to do with her after finding out what Sonya did to his sister.

During the ride home with Law, Sonya recounted the day's events. She quashed Tandy's insurgence. She won over Meeka and Celesta and got her story in order with Lydia Grant. Lydia is now on the same page with the others. Lydia understands Sonya's tragic plight as a student with black and white parents. Sonya knows this because Lydia passed a note to Sonya just before Sonya climbed into Law's truck. *We'll talk later,* it said. The note was written in Lydia's curvy script with a smiley face on the corner just above her phone number. As she rode home with Law, Sonya chalked Kush up as one of her losses. Surely, he will never talk to me again, she thought. But she was wrong.

"I won't be in school either then," Kush says. "I'll take off, in solidarity with my Queen Woman."

Kush called minutes after Sonya walked into the house. "How's my Queen Woman holding up?" he asked. Sonya was so baffled, so relieved and overjoyed that she could think of nothing to say but, "Fine."

Sonya has not lost her Kush, her King Man after all.

"How long are you out for?" Kush asks now.

"Two days," Sonya says.

"Then I'm out two. I'm due for another vacation."

"You don't have to do—"

"I want to," he says. "We could use the time to plan Festivale. It's right around the corner. Besides, I can't deal with Tandy right now. She's been moping around the house all day. We left right after you left. I don't think she'll be in school for a while, either. She's too embarrassed."

This time, Sonya's stomach twists in on itself.

"I'm sorry," Sonya says and some part of her really means it. Of course, there is another part of her that twirls, does a little victory dance while tossing up a shower of stolen bills.

"Whatever," Kush says. "So folks at PLD found out we're rich. So. Who cares? My friends don't care. Like I told Tandy, it's not that her friends don't like her for who she is. Is that she never gave them a chance to know the real her. It's the lie I think Celesta and Meeka are mad about. Not the money."

Lurch. Roll. Tilt. Twist. Sonya's stomach becomes an acrobat, whirling and flipping and twirling around inside of her. Salty saliva rises in the back of her throat. Her mouth becomes hollow and wet, full of nothing. She can no longer ignore the feats of her innards. Sonya drops the phone and runs to the bathroom where she spews green all over the toilet and the floor.

While Law drives, Sonya leans forward with her head between her knees. It is like drinking sour milk and pickle juice while zipping around the loop of a sonic rollercoaster. It is like watching someone slather himself with his own shit. But Sonya manages the ride to the drugstore, which is less than a mile away from the house.

She grabs the square box, makes her purchase and reels across the parking lot back to the truck. In the bathroom at home, she provides the necessary sample and waits. If it were a witch's brew, then the window on the tip of the plastic applicator would bubble and hiss like a cauldron. Only, Sonya's nausea is not some mystical happening and the plastic wand in Sonya's hand holds no magical powers. Sonya has purchased a home-pregnancy test, which holds a whole different power altogether.

When Sonya was Sonya—cynical, boyfriendless and unpopular—she never had need for such a thing. She never had sex, unprotected or otherwise. Now, Sonya sits on the bathroom toilet fully clothed with her wrists pressed between her knees. She sits and awaits the wand's prediction.

28

....

Party pooper

She finds Law standing outside the bathroom door. His face holds a contrite, guilty expression, as if he has been eavesdropping. For a moment, Sonya thinks he has been. Anger boils inside of her. She realizes she's being paranoid. Law would not eavesdrop. And if he had, so what? There was nothing for him to hear in the bathroom except the tearing open of the box and the unraveling of the plastic package. He would have heard the long silence as Sonya held her breath and waited for a verdict. Also, Law would have heard the sigh, which was a mixture of doubt, relief and agitation.

"What's wrong?" Law asks.

Sonya stands at the bathroom door paralyzed. It takes a second for the question to register.

"Sonya. Sonya." The sound of Law's voice comes just behind his actually speaking. It is like a bad dub, like a B-movie karate flick, like Doppler effect. She hears his question and the sound of her name as something muffled and distant, some commotion two rooms away in an adjacent apartment. An argument perhaps. Or sex. It is as if Law is yelling Sonya's name from the surface of a cold deep lake into which she is sinking. The undertow of the day's events locks around her ankles and yanks Sonya, pulls her down and down and down.

"Sonya." Law approaches her slowly.

She cannot speak. *Maybe he thinks I'm crazy*, Sonya thinks to herself. She is not crazy, only numb. It is a numbness she has not felt for a long time. Not since Crestman. Not since before her visits to Dr. Hillman. Sonya felt this way right around the time she opened her wrists.

"Sonya. What's wrong?"

Law's hand on her shoulder awakens her. A cacophony of emotions—distress, guilt, loneliness, joy—blossoms inside of Sonya, spills open like something sliced. She falls into Law's arms. Sonya knows it is the wrong thing to do, but she is too drained to fight her need for comfort. For weeks she has been keeping a careful distance with Law, measuring out niceties like sugar rations in wartime. She remained friendly in a sisterly way. She ignored his furtive glances. She overlooked his leering smile.

Now, in his warm, large arms, Sonya melts, gives way to the undertow. She sinks, knowing that there is a rope tied to her waist and that Law is on the other end.

Law pulls away from her and looks down into her streaming face. He wipes away Sonya's salty tears with the wide heel of his thumb. *Things will be fine,* Sonya tells herself. *If I keep my head down. Things will be fine if I just don't look up at him.*

"Sonya," Law says, barely a whisper. This is when she feels it, the fluttering of his excitement, pressed against her stomach. "Sonya," he says again. It is a plea.

She looks up. There are his eyes—somber, wide and giving. There is his childlike face, much too young for his thirty-nine years. There is his glowing, beautiful spirit. His innocence. His protection.

It is she, not Law, who pulls forward. It is Sonya who raises her head and closes her eyes. Law pulls her up to him, lifts her from the ground. He accepts her invitation. Their lips meet, Sonya's and Law's, in a long, slow kiss.

★ ★ ★

Sonya does not know she has fallen asleep until she wakes up. Her awakening is just as passive as her slumber. She lay on the bed, still as a body in a coffin, while sleep exits, burning off her body like a mist. There is a brief moment in which Sonya forgets her life as Sonya. She thinks she is Sonya in her old Buckhead home. She thinks it is another mundane morning. She thinks she is lying in bed, reluctant to rise and face Dr. Hillman, Sami, the black girls on the train, and Crestman. She thinks her mother is in the other room, still groggy from a night of drugs. Thinking all of these things for this brief moment between sleep and consciousness makes Sonya content, happy almost. Then it comes to her, swift as a kick: Maurice Maitland. Lydia and Tandy. The pregnancy test.

Law!

For the first time in years, Sonya misses her mother. She especially misses the Doris she knew before the success and the money, before Madison and the drugs. The old Doris made corndogs and French fries and stayed up with her, watching old movies long into the night. The old Doris gave her advice about Danny Panatelas, who, after some coaxing, Sonya admitted to having a crush on. After Danny Panatelas moved away, the old Doris wrote a series of love notes to Sonya, going so far as to fake a lazy sixth-grade boy's script. The old Doris, writing under the penname Danny Panatelas, let Sonya down easy. Sonya misses her mother, the old Doris who took care of everything.

The old Doris would know exactly how Sonya should proceed with Law.

For the first time Sonya faces the hard fact that the old Doris is gone. For the first time, Sonya feels sad that her mother left.

Doris called a hundred times. Sonya ignored most of the calls. The few calls Sonya did take lasted less than five minutes. And she only took those because Doris had caught her off guard. Sonya would rush to the phone without checking the caller ID. She would be expecting a call from Kush, or, back then, Tandy. When her mother's voice came through the receiver— "Hi, sweetie"— Sonya made no effort to hide the disappointment in her voice.

"Hi, Doris," she would say dismally, like someone who had just come in fourth place.

Once, Kush nibbled on Sonya's ear while Sonya talked to her mother. Sonya squirmed and giggled while Doris described the side affects of the drugs The Specialist gave her. Doris said the worst side effect was the rectal bleeding. "Rectal bleeding," Sonya squeaked. Kush burst into laughter, which caused Sonya to laugh so hard she had to hang up the phone. She didn't even say goodbye. That was the last time she heard from her mother. For all Sonya knows, Doris could be dead.

Now Sonya must face her new, bright, horrible circumstances alone.

Sonya has told everyone she is biracial.

Sonya has abandoned her mother.

Sonya has betrayed Tandy.

Sonya has kissed Law.

Reality crowds the room, suffocates her. While Sonya slept, the hours shifted from day to night. Outside a clammy blackness covers everything. It seeps into the room, slithering across the walls and under the bed. Sonya lies on her back and stares up at the ceiling. Law's face shimmers before her like a mirage. It was only a kiss, she tells herself. But also, it was a kiss full of promises Sonya cannot keep.

Sonya does not go beyond the fact of the kiss and her mixed emotions. She does not allow herself to think of the possibilities. The territory beyond Law's kiss is too treacherous. To think of Law romantically would be futile. Sonya knows she cannot be with him. For one, Law is older, much older. Two, he deals drugs, and with Madison, a man who Sonya despises so completely she can taste it. Three, an affair with Law does not fit into her constructed life. It would be incest as far as anyone at PLD knew. She would be sleeping with her brother.

Now comes the hard part. Sonya must rise from her bed, walk out into the living room and face Law. She can hear him now, fiddling around in the kitchen. The pots and pans clang on the grill of the stove. Piano music tinkles from the speakers. Law has probably skipped his medication again (he's trying to go clean, he'd said). Still, he sounds happy. Sonya hears him hum-singing a Billie Holiday tune. His voice wafts through the air, light and melodic. He's a good singer, Sonya thinks. And then: *I have to let him down easy.* She places these two facts side by side in her head, a pencil box and a purple plum, as if one has anything to do with the other.

As a sufferer of depression, as a survivor of suicide, Sonya knows Law needs to be protected. Part of that protection is feeding him reality (one of the few things she got from her visits to Dr. Hillman). This must be done carefully, teaspoon by teaspoon. She must ease the sour, sorry mush of it into his mouth, the fact that she cannot be with him in the way he wants. She must be delicate with Law lest she hurt him, lest she provoke Law to hurt himself.

Law knocks on the door, three sharp taps of his knuckles. Sonya has no time to gather her thoughts into any cohesion. She swings her feet off the bed and pushes herself upright. Her head twirls once, twice and all is still.

"Law?" she says. There is no answer.

Sonya opens the door to find the living room ablaze with light. There are candles everywhere: in the windowsill, on the mantle, and lining the kitchen counter. A flame wiggles on the tip of a slim candle sitting in the middle of the dinning room table. The table has been set for dinner.

Law enters from behind and wraps his arms around Sonya. She is caught, momentarily, in the muscle of his grip. Suddenly, she realizes his size and strength. She thinks about the knife which no longer lives under her pillow, which rests in its casing in the kitchen all the way across the room. She thinks how, even if she had to use it, even if she got a jab at Law, she may not be strong enough to make a lethal cut. I'm not in any danger, she tells herself. It's only Law. If anything Law is in danger, of heartbreak. Suddenly, she realizes the immense power she has over Law, a power she has been wielding recklessly. Now, it has come to this.

"Wow," she says, slipping out of his arms to survey the table. Her heart runs a marathon inside her chest. "What's the occasion?"

"Hope you're hungry," Law says. He is dressed in a sleek black tux. Silk, she thinks. His skin glistens against the white shirt.

"Ravenous." Sonya swallows the tremor welling up in her voice. She sits down at the table and looks at the spread of food on the counter: a chocolate cake, a pot of beans, Cornish hens, macaroni salad, wine and cheese, apple pie. Her tongue swells in her mouth. Her throat tightens. She is not sure she can swallow.

Law brings a dish of deviled eggs to the table. "Bon appetite," he says.

Sonya picks up one of the eggs, an oval of white with a yellowish dollop in the center. Paprika, the dried blood of it, is dusted lightly over the top. Sonya slides the egg into her mouth and chews mechanically. Her stomach buckles. All she can think about are ovaries and bird semen and unborn chick fetuses mashed into mayonnaise and sprinkled with garnish.

Somehow, some way, Sonya makes it through the meal. Twice she dashes to the other side of the room and chucks handfuls of her steamed vegetables and mashed potatoes out of the window while Law is in the bathroom. She does not throw it away in the garbage for fear he will find it there. Each time Sonya sits back down, repositioning her napkin on her lap, she hears the familiar sound—the long, hard snorts. She has not heard this since Doris left. Law re-enters the living room with wide, dazzled eyes. He claps his hard hands and walks around in circles. He talks incessantly. Now he is talking about his plans to paint the house, to become a doctor, to run the New York Marathon and the Peachtree Road Race, to finish his graduate work in Physiology and walk dogs and stretch more so that he can do the splits, although he knows it's not masculine but so what, and learn every song by Donny Hathaway on the piano, no, the flute, no, the guitar and the harmonica, you can play them both at once if you're good, because no one has every done that, it's a good idea, don't you think, so Sonya you are so beautiful I love you so much I'm sorry I know I shouldn't say that but it's true I've loved you since I first met you outside that night when you were acting like a fucking cunt to me like you were some hot fucking shit just because you're yellow I'm a virgin I never told Mad Man that because he would have laughed I want you to be my first tonight I think I'm ready are you enjoying the food?

The words whiz through Sonya's head. *I'm a virgin.*

Law? A virgin? At thirty-nine!

"Law," she says. "You're talking a mile a minute." Sonya laughs high and off-key. Everything in the room seems slanted and bright and melting, surreal as a Salvador Dali painting.

"Law," Sonya says, and nothing more. She has her hands pushed out before her, a sign of surrender.

"Let's dance," Law says. Before Sonya can decline, Law snatches her up and smashes her against him. Again, she feels his excitement. It scares her to death.

"I love Billie Holiday," Law says.

"This is Miles Davis."

"You yellow bitches think you know everything," he says. His voice is chiding but he tightens his grip. Sonya can hear Law's heart thundering in his chest. She wills the phone to ring. But who would call? Tandy? Kush? Madison, who has been away in New Jersey for the two past months?

Law sighs and looks up at the ceiling reflectively. "This is perfect," he says. "Isn't this perfect? My first time, with candles and music. This is just how I pictured it."

She feels him twitching against her. She feels the deep sway of his hips, his intentional pressing. Oh God, Sonya thinks. I can't. The thought of Law on top of her, naked, with his dark, psychotic, virginal penis poised for entry pierces Sonya with terror. Taking Law's virginity would bind Sonya to him just as surely as she is bound to Kush. She imagines Law driving her to school, waiting for her outside in the parking lot. She imagines him stalking her while she is out with Kush, listening in on her phone calls, masturbating outside the door while she and Kush have sex. The kiss was too much. The kiss was wrong, Sonya is sure of it now. She cannot continue this charade, else she will be trapped with Law forever.

The CD has played its last song and died. There is no sound save the electric hiss of the empty speakers and the left-right-left pat of Law's boots on the carpet. Law falls into a sudden lull. Sonya thinks it is the cocaine wearing off—that and some other substance taking over. Who knows what all he snorted and popped and shot through his veins while in the bathroom? Either way, Sonya feels grateful for this calm. It makes her less afraid to say what she must say.

"Law?"

"I love this song," he says.

"Law." Sonya pulls back to see his face, which takes a bit of effort. Law grasps her elbows tightly. He does not want her to escape. "This isn't right."

"I know," he says. "I know. It's too bright in here." Law runs around the room blowing out candles. Sonya stands in the center with her arms folded tightly around her. Without the circle of Law's arms she feels naked and cold. Also, she feels newly freed, like an uncaged animal. Just as an animal broken of its wildness and later freed into it, Sonya's instincts are off. She does not know where to run.

Law returns, huffing from the trot around the room and the blowing out of the candles. Spittle glistens on his bottom lip. He presents himself, stands stiff as a cadet in front of Sonya. She thinks he will salute.

"No, not the light," Sonya says. "Us. We are not right. For this." He opens his mouth to speak, but she does not give him a chance to. "I'm too young. I'm in high school. You work for my mother's boyfriend. People at school think you're my bother." This last part sends a dark cloud across Law's face.

"Law." Sonya reaches for his arm. It is a plea, a plea for his understanding. His cooperation. He steps back. "Law, I like you. I really do. It's just—I'm still so confused about who I am and who I want to be. I'm the daughter of a drug addict. My father's nowhere to be found. I've just broken up with my best friend. I'm confused Law. I'm no good for you."

Even she recognizes this new version of the old line, *It's not you. It's me.* It's so obvious, so predictable Sonya feels sickened saying it. Though, of course, she does not say it, at least, she does not say those exact words. Nothing moves in the room. Sonya is hyper aware of herself, her hair which falls in matted knots on her shoulders; her skin, which glows a muted yellow; her round nose and muddy eyes. She feels faux, speaking these words, wearing this hair, feigning this look of sympathy and apology. She feels counterfeit, like a replica of something she has read about in a book but has never seen in real life.

Law is the nicest man she has ever met. And Sonya used him. She led him on. She hurt his feelings. Now, she pulls up the old story again, the tragic, confused mulatto, fatherless, friendless, daughter of a drug addict. All at once, Sonya is disgusted with herself. She wants to jump out of a window. Law will never fall for this, she thinks as she looks into Law's lineless face. He will see right through her. Sonya is afraid of course. Law could turn violent and pummel her to death. One part of Sonya fears this. But another part of her prays for it, for Law to punish her. At least then, she will have paid her penance for all the lies and deceits. At least then, she will be put out of her misery. She will have gotten what she deserves.

"I'm sorry," Sonya says. "I'm so so sorry."

The light in Law's eyes goes out. His lip falls to a stern line. Sonya's face withers too. The room goes dark, except the space in which she and Law stand. This space seems horribly brilliant. It seems spotlighted.

"In another world, yes," Sonya says. "Yes, yes, yes, we could love each other. But not here. Not now. It's just not right. We're just not meant to be."

So, Sonya has done it. She has employed every cliché in the book, as they say. She has tugged at her own heartstrings. She has cried Law a river. She has let him down. She hopes she has done it is easy enough. She hopes Law is a good sport.

Celesta's voice sounds in the recesses of Sonya's head. *Girl, this big motherfucker is about to fuck you up.*

Sonya stands with her hands crossed over her body. She narrows her eyes slightly and braces herself for the blow that is sure to come. It will be like falling, she thinks, after the first few blows.

She hopes Law does not prolong the agony, tie her up and dole out tortures. She hopes she is knocked out with the first strike.

Sonya stands and waits for her punishment, which does not come. When she opens her eyes, Law is still there, large and sullen. She can see it in his face, a pain so thick it has weighed him down.

"Oh, Law." She reaches for his wide shoulders. "Oh, Law. Oh, Law, come here."

Silently, he falls down to his knees and presses his head into her stomach. They remain that way, Sonya above, Law below, like some Catholic statue of penance and devotion. Law sighs once, twice. His sighs are deep and rough. His sighs preface the opening of the damn and his flood of tears.

part three

29

....

Peace sista

This morning, she lingers in bed a bit longer. This is the first day of her two-day suspension. It is Tuesday, five days before Festivale. She can tell by the timber of the sky outside that it will be a clean, sunny day. Perfect weather. She lingers in the bed in hopes of missing Law. Surely he has deliveries to make, business to attend to. When she doesn't hear him, she thinks the coast is clear. Sonya rises from the bed and descends the stairs. There he is, sitting at the table, eating a bowl of oatmeal.

Law's eyes are still a little puffy. He wears the tuxedo from last night. It is crumpled and stained with food. He looks as if he has been in a brawl. Other than that, he seems fine. Sonya walks to the refrigerator, stepping lightly as if Law is a sleeping baby who must not be disturbed.

"Good morning, sunshine," he says.

"Morning," Sonya responds. His cheerfulness catches her off guard. She fills a glass with milk that she is not prepared to drink.

"Isn't this your first day of your two-day sentence?" His face holds its same wide, innocent smile. Perhaps, she thinks, he has gotten over it. Or perhaps the drugs erased his memory of last night.

"Yep."

"What's on the agenda?"

"Some exhibit," she says. "Going with a friend. I don't really know."

"Kush?"

She had tried to maneuver around Kush's name for Law's sake. But here it is, another spoonful of reality for her to feed him. "Yes, Kush is taking me."

"Hey." Law looks at her directly. "I'm sorry about last night. I know it was, well, awkward. I guess the kiss had gone to my head. Both of them."

"I'm cool, dog, if you're cool."

"I'm cool, 'dog,'" he says sarcastically. They both laugh. Just like that, Sonya and Law slip back into their normal roles. A little lapse, Sonya thinks, that's all last night was. Just like that, they are both forgiven.

The exhibit is titled *REPARATIONS: An I for an Eye.* The artist stands at the door and greets her patrons with a diminutive nod of her head. She places her hand across her heart as if in mourning, as if it falters. Of course it doesn't. Her heart is supposed to be stronger, deeper, full of more meaning and grace than the average Joe because she is an artist. She has been written about in *Creative Loafing* and the *Atlanta Journal.* She's appeared on the cover of lesser magazines. In many ways, people think her heart is better. That's why they are all here, to see these pieces, whatever they will be, which are supposed to have come from her heart.

Sonya hates this woman immediately, this woman with her little nod and her superior heart. The artist makes a display of her righteousness, at least this is what Sonya thinks. But that's not why Sonya hates her. Sonya hates her because the woman is undeniably beautiful. Hard bones under milky, yellowy skin. Dark eyes. A mane of dreadlocks. Sonya hates the woman because of her name, which Sonya cannot remember now. She only has a notion of it—something complicated and Nigerian—from seeing it on the cover of one of those magazines. Something made up probably. Mostly though,

Sonya hates this woman because Kush loves her. He wants to fuck her, Sonya thinks as she watches Kush watch the artist. His eyes lick her, bite her, poke in and out of the crevices of her clothing.

Then she remembers Kush is also an artist. He may be attracted to more than her beauty. He may be attracted to her work and her inner light and all that crap. He may be in love with her *essence,* her *spirit* or some other New Age bullshit. The worst part is even Sonya can see the artist's essence, though she tries to ignore it. This essence glows around the artist, genuine, humble and hazy. The vapor of it rises from the artist's skin.

Sonya takes stock of the artist who seems more convincing and more convicted than herself. Minus the essence, the artist could be Sonya's twin. She has the same pale face, thin noise, fine hair twisted into locks, though hers are much longer, of course. Still, she is a better version of Sonya, an upgrade. The artist has all the necessary Rasta props: copper jewelry, flowing skirt, red-black-and-green crocheted cap.

Sonya hooks herself into Kush's arm and plants three rapid-fire kisses on his cheek. She snuggles into Kush and giggles for no reason at all. She knows she is being childish. She knows she is pissing on trees, but fuck it. As Sonya walks pass, taking a flyer and returning the artist's "Peace, Queen" greeting, she can feel the artist's eyes look through her. They are quick in their tabulation. And the verdict they issue is harsh: You don't deserve this King Man, the eyes say. You're not really down with the struggle.

Again, Sonya's stomach tumbles. This time it is from guilt, from the feeling of being naked under the artist's eyes. Not from the other thing. I can be this artist, Sonya thinks, with a little practice. Already, Sonya begins to plagiarize the woman's style. She will borrow the artist's nod (the bitch!) which hints of sight beyond sight, of inner meditation. She will buy more skirts and caps, one for every day of the week (she'll get money from Law). Sonya makes a vow to purchase wooden bracelets. Also, she will learn to crochet. It is not like having an exhibit, but it is something. Directly after the museum, Sonya will get a Bob Marley tattoo.

"This sista's work is going to blow your mind," Kush

whispers as they round the corner into the exhibition space. "She is on the some other shit. Her essence," Kush says. "Her spirit transcends."

Kush is captivated by this woman. He is bedazzled. Sonya can see this. He claps his hands between words and his face glows as if it has been oiled. "I'm trying to get her to talk at Festivale."

"Hmph."

"For real. This sista is the real deal. She's already had one national exhibit. And people are *buying* the shit. So you know it's got to be hot."

"Whatever you say." Sonya knows Kush wants her to be impressed. But she will not co-sign. She will not praise this woman's genius. First of all, Sonya has never seen the woman's work. So how can she attest to its genius. But also, Sonya hates this woman, hates her as thoroughly as she hates Madison. Sonya hates this woman as intensely as she hated Tandy in the brief instance Tandy tried to expose her with Lydia's pictures.

Tandy. Sonya thinks. Whatever happened to her?

"I'm telling you. Wait until you see it," Kush says.

The line to the exhibit is backed up. She and Kush rustle up behind the crowd. A large easel beside the door boasts a picture of the artist. There is no denying her beauty. Underneath the picture is her name. Ngoya Ova Komataya. So that's it, Sonya thinks. That's her fucking name.

Kush continues clapping and glowing. This annoys Sonya. Briefly, she thinks of telling Kush about this morning, about her pregnancy test. She thinks of scaring him with this information. She won't do that, though. That's not the way she wants to talk about it. She does not want Kush to resent her later.

"She's *really* good," Kush says of the artist. "No." He jerks Sonya to a halt. "She's not good. She's a prodigy. Her stuff is unlike anything I've seen before. Ever. She's going to be the next Zing."

That's what the cover of one of the magazines said, *prodigy*. They didn't preface it with *child*. The artist is nineteen, well on her way to adulthood. Still, she's young enough to attract Kush.

"We'll see," Sonya says dismissively. She feels Kush's eyes flicker over her. She almost hears it, the word *bitch* blinking like a neon sign in his head. Kush shakes it off, swallows it.

"You'll see," he says, with one final clap. "You'll see."

It is worse than she could have imagined. Much worse.

The fifteen-foot painting dwarfs Sonya. It is a tree. The tree sits on a massive trunk and rises with the canvas, exploding at its head into a thousand branches. Leaves tumble from the tree lazily. A haze of sun illuminates it from the left. At first glance, the branches of the tree seem to hold nuts of some sort, pods of peas, or overly ripe bananas. Upon closer inspection, Sonya finds that the objects dangling from the branches are not fruit at all, but black bodies. At the base of the tree is a girl. She wears a blue dress with a white apron. She is small and blue-eyed and strikingly blonde, some version of Alice from *Alice in Wonderland*. The girl in the painting sits with her legs crossed. She munches on something that may or may not be a fruit from the tree. The caption to the painting reads *Breakfast at Tiffany's*.

Sonya wants to find Kush now. She wants to jostle his arm happily and screech, "It is brilliant! It *is* brilliant!" She wants him standing beside her now so that they can discuss the images in the painting, so that they can ruminate and philosophize. But Kush is nowhere to be found. He walked away from her as soon as they entered the exhibition. Sonya pushed it too far with her surliness. Now, she will have to wait until Kush cools off and comes back to tell him that he is right. Ngoya Ova Komataya is brilliant.

Sonya walks slowly from painting to painting, luxuriating in the rich, striking images. After some time, she makes her way to the hors d'oeuvres and serves herself a cup of warm grape juice. The bio on the table tells her that Ngoya's mother is Black American and her father is Japanese. This explains the name, Sonya thinks. She learns from the bio that Ngoya is originally from Chicago. She is a student at the Savannah College of Art and Design and she has lived in London, Tokyo and Brazil.

Just as Sonya begins to relinquish her hate toward Ngoya, just as she shakes her pen and nods, placing its ball-pointed tip on the contract to co-sign with Kush on Ngoya's genius, just as Sonya is about to give Ngoya her credit (because credit is due), she spies them, Kush and Ngoya, across the room. They lean into each other while they talk. Kush's smile is obnoxiously wide. Ngoya's arm rests lightly on Kush's shoulder.

Sonya marches toward them, pushing her way through the crowd. She can see their mouths moving now. She can see the flashes of flirtation, the smiles, the wispy hand gestures, the big blinking eyes. Now, she is close enough to hear the words. "Nzinga Herman," Kush is saying now. So, Sonya thinks, this is how it works. Kush does the opposite of Tandy. He does not hide his wealth or his mother's status. He flashes it like a badge, like a pick-pocket displaying watches inside a trench coat.

"Love to see some of your stuff," Ngoya is saying now to Kush. Sonya is close enough to see the woman's pendants dangling deliciously from her thin long neck. She can see the swaft of hair on Ngoya's forearm as she pulls a card out of her oversized bag and hands it over to Kush.

"Peace, sista," Sonya says pointedly. She intercepts Ngoya's card—Kush was mid-reach—and tucks it into her brassiere like a floozy at a saloon taking a tip.

"I'm Ngoya." Ngoya extends a delicate, talented hand. Sonya looks down at it and scoffs.

"I know who you are."

"Oh," Ngoya says. "Are you an artist also?"

"No," Sonya says. "Not of any type you would recognize. I'm Nyahbinghi. Praise Jah Ras Tafari."

Ngoya slides her hands between Sonya's breasts to retrieve the card. Her movement is so slight and swift that Sonya barely notices it. Only after Ngoya has the card does Sonya feel anything. "Then you won't be needing this." Ngoya hands the card over to Kush who accepts it with a bemused smile.

"Don't worry," Ngoya says. "I'm not trying to steal your King here. I'm a...a feminist, shall we say." She winks at Sonya. "In the traditional sense of the word."

"I'll be around," Sonya says to Kush. "When you're finished entertaining yourself come find me." She tromps across the room feeling angry and disgraced. She wills Kush to trot up behind her. He doesn't.

Despite Kush's flirting with the artist, despite Ngoya's hand slithering between Sonya's breasts, despite Sonya's anger about all of these, she cannot deny the genius of Ngoya Ova Komataya's work. With a cup of grape juice in hand, Sonya stands before another canvas, equally as large as the *Breakfast at Tiffany's* piece. In this one an army of sleek black bodies march listlessly down a city street. The crowd is flanked on either side by long, gray buildings. A naked woman floats above the crowd. Her yellow-brown body shimmers limply in the sun. Her arms and legs hang at her side. Hers lips are parted and bright red. Her legs dangle. It is as if a giant, invisible hand had lifted her. The title card reads *Helga In Ecstasy*.

"One of my earlier pieces," Ngoya says. She stands beside Sonya with her hands tucked discretely behind her. "When I was struggling with my racial identity." Ngoya says this a little pointedly. At least, this is what Sonya hears. Then again, Sonya has become hypersensitive to such phrases.

"I couldn't decide what I should be. I was tormented by questions. Am I Japanese? Am I Black American? How does one decide? Men were attracted to my—are attracted to me—" here, she looks at Sonya "—because of my 'exoticness.' Because I am their yellow fantasy. Especially black men with their Patty chick fetish and their post-traumatic slavery disorder."

"Syndrome," Sonya corrects. "The term isn't post-traumatic slave *disorder*. It's *syndrome*."

"No," Ngoya says. "It's a disorder. We just like to think of it as a syndrome. Syndrome makes it more palatable."

"Hmph," is all Sonya says. She wants to walk away, but, for some reason, she feels trapped. Is it social norm or Ngoya's essence that has Sonya locked with her into this ultra-polite conversation with its subtext of spite?

"You've experienced that I'm sure. How men flock when they see any flash of yellow. You must experience that everyday, being that you are mixed and all. Aren't you?" Ngoya says. "Aren't you biracial?"

"Yes. I am."

"Really?" Ngoya says, as if she is giving Sonya a chance to re-consider a decision, which, in some sense, she is.

"Yes. Really," Sonya says.

"Kush was telling me that. About your mother and all." Ngoya sighs languidly. She is toying with Sonya. Cat and mouse. "Either way," she says. "This piece is inspired by Nella Larsen's novel *Passing*. Ever read it?"

"Nope," Sonya says. She knows what this is. Ngoya has thrown a canister of tear gas inside the bandit's house. Now she waits for Sonya to run out coughing and gasping, clawing at her eyes. She wants Sonya to turn herself in.

"What's the title of the book again? I'll put it on my list."

"The title is *Passing*. P-A-S-S-I-"

"I got it."

"It's about a woman, Helga, who pretends to be something she's not. Helga passes for white."

"Hmph."

"Helga's living a lie," Ngoya says.

"Is she? Well too bad for Helga."

"Yes, too bad. What do you think?" Ngoya says. "About the piece? Does it strike you in anyway? Does it register with you? Personally?"

Sonya taps her thumb against her chin. "What do I think?" She says this to herself, reflectively. "What do I think? I think Helga is too morbid."

"Really?" Ngoya perks up now. She is like a dog that has been whistled at. "Expound."

"Everything is so dismal and gray." Sonya swishes the cup of grape juice in her hand. She looks down into the eye of its little tornado. "It needs a splash of color, some texture."

And so Sonya gives it a splash. In one sharp toss she douses *Helga In Ecstasy* with a tide of grape juice. Next, she takes a pen from her pocket and punches holes across the bottom of the canvas. With the last hole punch, she pulls the pen upward, gashing a foot-long tear across the bottom.

"That's *much* better," Sonya says, crumpling the cup in her hand. "Don't you agree?"

Ngoya stands with her hands tucked behind her. Her face glows. Fucking righteous bitch! Sonya thinks. She braces herself for Ngoya's retaliation. Sonya can feel her heart thumping wildly in her chest.

30

....

Her f---ing essence

Silver buildings glinting in the sun. Wide, gray streets. Spurting fountains. A crowd of tourists stepping off a bus, chatting their way toward The Coca Cola Museum. The yawning pavilion of Underground Atlanta. The clutter of Five Points Flea Market. The CNN Center, its bulbous body, parked, it seems, like a waylaid spaceship—a mother ship that has returned to the earth after a hundred thousand years, returned to gather the worthy. The Righteous.

Sonya and Kush drive home in silence. Sonya's forehead rests against the passenger-side window. She watches the scenery whoosh by. This was one of Kush's early theories, about the mother ship, back in his space Rasta days. He was not so ignorant to propose real-life buildings such as the CNN Center as one of these ships. Given a little more false information, Sonya thinks, he probably would have. She looks over at him now as he drives. His chin juts out slightly. His hands sit at the prescribed forty-five degree angle. His eyes narrow to slits. Driving for Kush is not effortless. He does not lean back as he drives as Celesta does. He performs no quick cuts into roaring traffic or sharp turns with one wide swing of the wheel like Law. There are no such one-handed stunts for him. He simply drives, sitting behind the wheel like a chauffeur for hire. It is so impersonal, Kush's connection to his car. Not like a man at all.

Pussy! Sonya thinks. *Livingston!*

He laughed when he saw the mess Sonya made with the grape juice and the pen. He laughed even more when Ngoya shrugged her shoulders and flagged the security guard down, when Ngoya's voice rose from her full, beautiful Black-Japanese lips. "Sista Sonya will be taking this piece. Write her a ticket, will you. I think this one is forty-two hundred."

Sonya slapped Kush then, thinking she would pull another Maurice Maitland. Thinking, *This ought to shut you up.* But it didn't. Kush laughed harder. Ngoya stood behind Kush, grinning like an evil stepmother. Sonya stormed out in a fit of tears. The money she owed Ngoya as a result of damaging the painting was not the cause of Sonya's tears. Sonya could get that easily enough from Law. It will take some finagling, of course, but she can convince him to borrow it from Madison's stash. It wasn't even Kush's laughter that caused her to cry, though that was definitely part of it. What upset Sonya then, and what upsets her now is the level of control Ngoya Ova Komataya displayed throughout the entire ordeal. Ngoya kept herself anchored as a rock. She seemed just as indomitable.

How does a nineteen-year-old girl become so poised? Sonya thinks. What keeps her grounded? What keeps her level?

Her essence! This is the only answer Sonya can come up with. It must be her fucking essence!

Kush was not angry then. Or perhaps he was. Perhaps he laughed to mask his anger. Either way, he is angry now. Sonya can feel it, Kush's fury, radiating from his skin like heat. He has not spoken to her since they got in the car.

Kush pulls to the curb in front of Sonya's house. Looking out at the square of yard and the long, slim driveway lined with monkey grass (Law's extra touch) strikes Sonya with a loneliness so sharp she feels as if she is going to cry. She imagines Kush, at home, retelling the story to Tandy and Zing. They will listen intently. They will nod. At the part about the slap, Zing will cover her mouth, shocked. Tandy will make some biting remark. Kush and Zing and Tandy will go through the night with this story in their heads. Sonya will no longer be invited over, of course. Zing could have looked over the incident with Tandy—the lines were a bit blurred. Malice was not obvious. But slapping Kush? Her son? For this Sonya is sure to be excommunicated.

A pang of lonesomeness hits Sonya again. The other pain in her stomach, the pain signaling the growth of a new life, intensifies it. She places her hand on her navel, rests it there for a moment and then slides it down to her lap. She does not want to betray her pregnancy to Kush, especially not now when he is furious with her.

"You didn't have to slap me."

"You didn't have to laugh," Sonya says. "You didn't have to grin all up in her face like you were."

"She's a lesbian. Couldn't you tell by the way she groped your breasts?"

"Whatever, Kush."

Kush leans back in his seat and sighs. "I can't do this right now. Just…just…"

Sonya feels herself fading to black. She is like a landmark—a mountain or a waterfall—from which Kush is driving away. Soon, she will be no more than a shadow on his horizon. Sonya can hear Tandy now, "She let all that yellow go to her head."

Sonya's mind reels. Her stomach doubles up on itself, folds itself in half. She grabs for his arm. "Kush, please. Please." He snatches away.

"You slapped me. In front of everybody."

"What can I do? I said I'm—"

"You ruined Ngoya's painting. Do you know how long it took her to create that piece? Six months. Six months! And that's not counting coming up with the concept."

"Kush." Sonya's voice goes whiney with desperation. The inside of the SUV expands, becomes a wide, gaping cavern. Sonya stands on one side. Kush, on the other. Kush looks at her as if waiting for an explanation. For once, Sonya has none.

"I just don't know," Kush says. His head falls into his hands. He takes a deep breath and sighs.

Sonya stares at the back of his neck, the tender skin and tufts of crinkly black hair. She knows Kush is trying to break up with her. Just like Doris when she wanted to ask Sonya to go to Hillman for the pills, Kush doesn't know how to say what he wants. Pathetic, Sonya thinks. How fucking pathetic.

Harsh words scuttle up Sonya's throat, scratching it raw. She spits them out. "Fuck it. What would I do with a pussy like you anyway?" Sonya says. "You ain't 'bout it, niggah."

Kush looks up. His eyes are wide with disbelief.

"You talk about it but you ain't about it," Sonya says. "Not really."

"Sonya."

"With your big house and your fancy clothes. All your misin-formed-ass prophesy. You ain't no real Black Rebel. You're a motherfucking faker." Sonya recognizes the fury roiling within her. It is the same fury she felt for her mother each time she was forced to visit Dr. Hillman.

"You don't really see me," she says. "You've never really seen me. Queen Woman hell. That's bullshit. Bullshit. All you see is a yellow piece of ass."

"Don't start this," Kush says.

"You talk a good game but when it comes down to it, the yel-lowest bitch wins with you. That's why you were all up in Ngoya's face. Dog, you have a disease," she says, repeating Ngoya's words. "A syndrome."

The tears rolling down Kush's face shine in the evening's light. So! Sonya thinks. She will not be moved this time. Nor will she be hurt. She will not be subject to a man's whim. Sonya had done that before, with Madison, obliging his favors. Foregoing murder because of the fear in his eyes. She knows where listening to her emotions leads. This time, she'll cut deep. This time, she'll draw blood.

Kush reaches over her and opens the door. "Get out—"

"You're such a fucking pussy," she says. "You're so goddamn—"

"Get out of my car," Kush yells. It is the first time she has heard him raise his voice in anger.

"It ain't your car, dog. It's Zing's car. Remember?"

"Get out!" He sounds terrified, frantic and pitiful like a child cornered by a growling dog.

"Fuck you, niggah," Sonya says. "Fuck you, *Livingston!*"

Sonya slides out of the seat. Her skirt blooms beneath her. It is much too heavy for this weather. The skirt feels as if it is made of lead. Sonya gathers its folds before stepping onto the curb.

Kush closes the door and drives away. Sonya is left in the driveway, alone, under a tent of blackening sky.

31

Payback

So, Kush is gone. Standing in front of the house, Sonya feels angry and alone. She hadn't expected it to last much longer. After all, she had betrayed Tandy, Kush's sister. Even if their argument didn't happen today, Tandy would have worked on Kush at home. Eventually, Tandy would have turned him against Sonya.

Sonya will have to pay, of course. Ngoya was cold about the entire matter. Businesslike. Matter-of-fact. "Forty-two hundred," she said as if she were talking about nail polish. She handed over an invoice, which was surprisingly official. Sonya could tell by the glint of self-satisfaction in Ngoya's eyes that Ngoya thought she could not pay. *I'll show you,* Sonya thinks as she stands in the empty driveway. She says this in her head. She says this to both Kush and Ngoya. She will produce the money, quick as a pinch. Sonya's only regret is that she won't be able to see the look on Ngoya's face when she receives the check. Perhaps Sonya will deliver it personally. First, though, she has to work on getting the money.

Sonya thinks about how she will play it. She does not want a repeat of last night. Thinking about Law's eyes, blazing as they were, with infatuation sends a trill of panic along her skin. No, she doesn't want to give Law a reason to go back there. Still, Sonya knows she will have to flirt. She can't just ask for the money, forty-two hundred dollars, as if it is a loan from one friend to another. She can't just ask as if she has any means or intentions of paying it back.

As Sonya walks up the drive, she plots her plan. She won't ask immediately. And how could she? "Law, can I have forty-two hundred dollars?" That won't work. Especially after last night. Especially after she rejected him. No matter how gently she did it, in the end, Sonya let Law down. To get the money, Sonya will use more stealth. An ambush attack, she thinks. He won't even see it coming.

She will make a meal. Yes, a meal of rich, savory foods. Chocolate cake, creamed corned, dumplings. Along with this meal, Sonya will suggest a sleepover in the living room, a night of B-movies and music videos. Friendly and platonic, with a hint of flirtation lingering, like a mist in the air. Law will go for this, she thinks. If nothing else, he is a child at heart. Sonya will cook this meal and they will watch movies and videos. Law, being as astute as he is, will notice Sonya's detachment (she will have to act mildly depressed, which won't be hard considering her fight with Kush). Law will ask what's wrong. During a commercial break Sonya will recount the story. "Kush kissed her," she will add, for dramatic effect. Also, "She called me a bitch." Sonya will leave out the part about slapping Kush. She will have to tell about ruining the painting of course. But, by the time she gets to that, Law will be loaded with empathy.

Sonya stands at the front door and weaves together the last bit of her strategy. She will cook the food, watch the movies, and fake distress. Law will ask, and Sonya will retell her tale. In her version, she will have been persecuted, wronged. Victimized. She will tell all of this, even her argument with Kush, saving the part about the money until the very end. "And now I have to come up with four grand," she will say with a disheartened sigh. This will come as a side note, to top off all of the humiliation and tragedy suffered by her. This, she will say, as if the money were not the point at all.

After this, Sonya will exit to her room and leave Law's empathetic, infatuated brain to fill in the gaps. If she plays it right, Law will offer the money on his own.

Sonya opens the door and walks inside. Silence cushions the house. She treads through it lightly, on her tiptoes, like a cat burglar. She wants to get to her room and prepare her face before meeting Law. She wants to go over her lines once more.

Midway through her trek, Sonya hears her name.

"Oh." She jumps. It is Law.

He sits on the couch. He is still in his tuxedo, Sonya notices, but more casual now. Cuffs rolled up, shirt open at the neck. He looks like an ad for expensive cognac.

"Dog, you scared the shit out of me," Sonya says.

"I've been thinking about you," he says.

"Have you?" Sonya says. Already the inflection in her voice has changed. It takes on the timber of mild flirtation.

"I've been thinking about you for months," Law says. His eyes gleam in the dark. His face is pimpled with sweat. He sits stiffly, like a schoolboy under the gaze of a headmaster. Something shines in his lap. A gun, Sonya realizes. Longer than a normal gun because it has a silencer attached.

A silencer so that neighbors won't hear the shot.

"Oh," Sonya says again.

"I've been thinking about all the shit you put me through," Law says. "How you toyed with me. Fucked with my head."

"Law. No." Sonya's hand goes to her stomach as if that will protect it from Law's bullet. Already she is developing maternal instincts.

Sonya's heart rumbles. Other than that, she feels fine, perfectly in control. She is amazed at herself for being so in control in such an emergency. Then again, part of her does not believe Law will kill her. Part of her believes it is a scare tactic, something he's doing for attention, like her suicide attempt at Crestman. She nearly chuckles, "Silly, Law."

She will not scream. She will not cry out. Sonya has gotten herself into this situation and she can get herself out. Her only chance now is cunning.

Sonya summons up her old cool. "L.A. Law," she says, adding extra slack to her voice. "What's all this, man? You're sitting here—"

"Shut the fuck up," Law says. He lifts the gun from his lap.

Sonya thinks about running. Also, she thinks about the futility of running, the little kick-start to nothing. She will make slight headway, four or five steps maximum, before Law shoots her in the back of the head. Sonya imagines falling to the ground, her legs buckling behind her. She imagines reaching forward and knocking something over, the Ginsu knives on the counter.

The gun hovers between them, levitates like a ghost.

Even now, facing death, Sonya can't really believe it. Law, breathing like a dragon. Law, his eyes aflame with hate. Law lifting the gun ever so slowly as if it weighs a thousand pounds, as if it is the most fragile vase in the world.

"You used me," Law says. "You used me."

Sonya stares at the gun, its thin, gleaming barrel. She tries to make sense of it all.

Something about the inevitability of it comforts Sonya. An end, at last. Of course she could say something to Law. She could plead. But there is nothing more to say. No magic words float to the surface of her tongue. More than her heartbeat or the throbbing in her chest, more than her arms hanging limp at her sides, Sonya is aware of her ankles, exposed under the billow of her skirt. For a second, she thinks her clothing might protect her and that Law will shoot her there, in the ankles, they being the barest part of her body.

"I want you to know the pain you've caused," Law says. The gun hovers in the space between them. Not until he takes aims does Sonya feel her tears, which have been spilling down her face all this time. Law looks directly into her wet eyes. He smiles wide. She can see that her terror satisfies him.

"I want you to know the pain you've caused," he says again. "I want you to know exactly what you have done."

A quick click. A hushed boom. A spray of red against the wall. A sound not unlike the patter of rain on a slow Sunday morning. A thudded fall. A rip of pain. Or is it only her imagination? The pain?

How can she know? Either way, Sonya crashes to her knees. Her eyes slam shut.

The house falls silent.

32

....

Mad men

For nearly an hour, she lay on the ground, shocked. Paralyzed. Sweat puckers out of the pores of her back, her forehead, her thighs and her armpits. Her body trembles and curls in on itself. Explosions of lightning flare behind her eyelids, which have been closed since the sound of the fatal shot.

Sonya feels her locks of hair trembling around her face. She feels her exposed ankles tucked beneath her. She feels her pulse pumping through them, pumping up her legs, pumping through the fleshy circuits of her veins into the bloodred chambers of her alive, beating heart. In the silence of Law's death, Sonya's pulse thunders in her temples like a braggart's boast. This pulse belongs to her and her unborn child.

Sonya lifts her head to face the body. She prepares herself for a garish display. Blood and guts, as they say. Her eyes are rusty-hinged doors that open slowly.

What Sonya comes face-to-face with is not gory in the least. Law lies slumped over to his left—my right, she thinks now, as if it matters. His mouth is agape. His eyes are closed. Moonlight falls in slices through the blinds and casts swords of light over the furniture and the walls. Except for the star of red along the wall, the scene is peaceful, serene, something out of a children's book, a book titled *The Sleeping Giant,* perhaps. Law does not look dead at all. Law looks as if he has fallen to sleep while watching television. He looks as if at any moment he will begin to snore.

Sonya rises to her feet and whispers his name. "Law?" The night snatches up her voice, presses it to a pebble and flicks it away.

"Law," she calls again. He does not respond.

Sonya wrings her hands and wipes the tears streaming from her eyes. Law is dead, she tells herself. Law is dead and his dead body is in the living room. Blood on the wall. Blood on the floor. Blood on the blinds. Blood on the couch and Law is dead. What to do? Sonya looks up at the ceiling as if an answer will appear there. What to do? What to do? What should I do?

At the refrigerator, Sonya takes out a lemon and cuts it into wedges for no other reason than to do something with her hands. She runs to her room and slams the door. She cries. She tears at the pillow. She beats her hands on the mattress. She comes out and Law is still there, slumped. Dead.

The circle Sonya walks around the kitchen counter and the living room table becomes a warped figure eight. She can see her foot treads on the carpet. She can see the Ginsu knives on the counter. She can see the splash of blood floating just above Law's head like an ornament. The more she paces the living room, and the more she looks at Law's lifeless body, the less shocking it becomes.

Stealthily, Sonya creeps toward Law, as if he might awake grumbling, out of his slumber. As if she is trying to pull a prank, slather his face with shaving cream or steal his wallet. Then she burst into laughter. He won't wake. He's dead.

A singular thought pushes its way through the crowd of others: *They will think I did it.* They will think I killed Law. There will be police and sirens, interrogations. They will question her friends at PLD. Eventually, they will find Doris and question her. Kush,

Celesta, everyone will find out she's not black. Her jig will be up. Her cover will be blown. All because of Law.

Sonya has to move him. She has to get the body out of the house. She wedges her arms under his thigh and heaves. The bones in her shoulders pop, but Law does not budge. She tries pull-sliding his torso. Nothing. She tries pushing him with the bottom of her feet. He does not move. Sonya heaves and pushes with all her might and finally manages to arrange Law on the couch in a semi-fetal position.

Reaching into his back pocket, Sonya pulls out Law's wallet. She cannot do this alone. She has to call for help.

Madison works quickly. He employs his usual mixture of bleach, peroxide and ammonia to clean the splatter of blood from the wall. Madison dips the horse brush into the bucket and works the red off the walls using quick, circular motions. Dip, scour, rinse. Dip, scour, rinse. He blow-dries the washed area and then repaints the entire wall the egg-white color. Using Law's truck, Madison transports the couch to a local dump and burns it to char. Then he returns to the house where he goes over the wall again, snorts a few lines of heroin and waits until the second coat dries. The cleanup takes no more than five hours.

Summer, the wild, rabid cat of it, has pounced. Even in this early morning hour heat rises, seeping through the windowpanes, sliding beneath the crevices of the doors and climbing, spider-like, along the ceiling.

"Fuck, it's hot," Madison says. "Turn up the fucking AC."

"Down, you mean."

"What?" He marches over to the thermostat and sets it to sixty.

"You mean down." Sonya sits at the table with her head in her hands. "If you turn it up, that would increase the temperature. Make it hotter."

"Can't really get much hotter in here." Madison laughs. "One-hundred-and-ten grand in cash gone. Plus a truckload of smack. And a murder." He whistles admiringly. "This is the hottest house in town now. Whatcha gonna do, little missy?"

"I didn't *murder* him."

"That fucker," Madison says. "Can't believe I put it past him. Snorting up my shit. Stealing my money." Madison scoffs. He is like a father who has found out his teenage son has had sex with a whore. He is both angry and proud. "The little fucker. Well, the money's one thing. He probably spent that on bullshit. Or gave it away." Law's eyes stop momentarily on Sonya, considering her as the recipient of these monetary gifts. "But the smack. What could he have done with all that fucking smack?"

Madison sighs, leans back on the couch and scratches his stomach. "That fucker," he says again. It is like a savory meal he has eaten, this post-suicide cleanup. He seems fattened by it. "Glad it's all over though. I would have had to river-dump him once I found out about the money anyway. That fucker! You took care of it, though."

"I didn't—"

"He tried to touch you, didn't he? That lust got to be too much for him. He tried to mount you like a fucking—"

"I didn't murder him," Sonya yells. Tears roll down her cheeks. "How many times to I have to tell you? I did not murder Law!"

"You don't have to convince me." Madison smiles his same flat smile and laughs his same flat laugh. The murder and the cleanup have lifted his spirits. "I'm not the judge," Madison says. "And if we both keep our fucking mouths shut, there won't be a judge."

33

····················

A visitation of spirits

The sun approaches Sonya's room tentatively at first, like a child petting a horse. As the morning progresses, it gains confidence. By half-past six, it slices through her blinds, dividing her room with brackets of light.

Sonya rises from the bed, her brain foggy and slow. She has slept all Wednesday through, the last day of her suspension. Now it is Thursday morning, a school day—a day on which she is supposed to go to school. Looking at the bars of sun crossing her sheets, Sonya feels temporarily happy. Then she remembers.

Tandy.

Kush.

Law.

Madison.

Inside Sonya's head, a voice sounds. Small at first, it gains volume quickly. It comes upon her, whistling it warning like a missile dropped from a plane. "Pack your bags!" the voice says. "Hurry and pack your fucking bags!

★ ★ ★

Right under his nose, Sonya thinks as she carries the duffle bags of money out the door. Madison sits on the couch he bought yesterday—an expensive, gaudy red leather one—and nods, or sleeps, Sonya can't tell which. Last night, before Madison came over, Sonya searched the house. She was afraid Law had left a note detailing his reasons for his suicide. Sonya imagined a journal chronicling his infatuation for her, the last page of which would describe their kiss. Sonya scoured the house for any evidence that would incriminate her.

What Sonya found was money, small stacks of hundred dollar bills hidden in vases, in the toes of shoes, in her mother's document boxes. Madison was right. Law had been skimming, taking a thousand here, three grand there. Sonya also found viles with powdery residue. This had been the supplement to Law's lithium. Law wasn't as clean as he claimed to be.

Sonya gathered the money, as much of it as she could find. The bulk of the cash was downstairs with the drugs. She had no need for the heroin so she hid it behind a hollow wall in the basement. Madison would find it eventually. Or not. Either way, by the time he caught on to her theft, Sonya planned to be long gone.

Last night Sonya had not had time to count the money. Madison showed up too quickly. So she shoved it under her bed and prayed Madison would not search her room. She did not know how much she had found then. Now she knows the total, thanks to Madison. One-hundred-and-ten grand. Sonya will use part of it to pay Ngoya. With the rest, she will plan her escape.

Early this morning she called a taxi, whispering into the phone while Madison slept or nodded in the other room. Now Sonya hops inside the cab and gives the driver the address. With the bags crouched on either side of her, Sonya settles down for the short ride.

She arrives before any of the students or teachers just as she planned. The janitor allows her in when she explains she has early morning practice. She doesn't say for what and he doesn't bother to ask. Sonya walks along the hallways with the bags hanging on either side of her. She feels criminal, like an assassin carrying the components to a complicated weapon.

The dull hallways, dented lockers and cheerful posters ("Be A Star!" "Hang in there!") flood Sonya with a weary nostalgia. Tandy, Celesta, Meeka. Kush. Maurice Maitland! She had forgotten all about him. Will he be here today? What will she say, or not say, once she faces him again? Sonya will have to make it through this day of school, and then another and another and another. She will have to stay in school for at least a week until she can come up with a plan. Skipping school would seem too suspicious. Draw too much attention.

Already, she thinks like a criminal.

Monday, when she dethroned Tandy, seems forever ago. And her argument with Kush? Sonya can barely remember the anger that seethed through her like a poisonous smoke. In the wake of Law's suicide, in the wake of Madison's condescending laugh and his accusations of murder, in the wake of Sonya stealing one-hundred and-ten-thousand dollars and hiding who knows how much in heroin, in the wake of her mother's absence and Sonya's newfound longing for her, in the wake of all of this, Sonya will have to face school. She will have to face Tandy's bitter eyes. She will have to face Kush's indignation. She will have to face Celesta and Meeka scurrying at her ankles like chipper little poodles.

How can she do it? How can she go through another day at PLD? It all seems so trite now, after what she's been through. Who cares if Tandy is rich or not? Who cares if Kush ever kisses her again? Who cares about the true color of Meeka's eyes? Now, Sonya's main concern is herself and her unborn child.

But Sonya *must* care. She has to get through school with all its petty details. She has to attend for another week at least. She has to give herself time to make a plan.

Overhead lights buzz along the empty hallways. Finally, Sonya makes it to her locker and stuffs the bags inside. For a second, she thinks they will not fit. She wrestles them in, one on top of the other, and then forces the door shut.

"Sonya?"

Sonya jumps—presses her back against the locker. It's Mrs. Larsen, standing at the other end of the hallway with her hands on her hips. "Girl, what you doing up here, sneaking around and such?"

"I—I…"

"You back already?" Mrs. Larsen walks toward Sonya. In the hazy morning light, she looks both shadowy and transparent, like a cloud.

"Yes, I—" Something backs up in Sonya's throat. A stifling sorrow, loneliness so deep and dense she can feel its residue on her tongue. Madison nodding on the couch, Sonya's mother shivering in the corner of some makeshift rehab center, one-hundred-and-ten grand in her locker and here is Mrs. Larsen, asking if she is back already. Mrs. Larsen, who, for once, is early. Now, Mrs. Larsen walks toward Sonya with a lopsided grin on her face, which means she has been in the bathroom sipping gin at seven in the morning. Mrs. Larsen, who walks toward Sonya, is about to say something slight and condescending and hilarious and Sonya has just watched Law shoot himself in the head. Mrs. Larsen prepares to scold Sonya and Sonya has stolen two bags of drug money for which she may be killed.

"I thought you were suspended," Mrs. Larsen says now.

Sonya knows there is protocol to this conversation, even now at seven in the morning, before anyone else arrives. Sonya knows there is a script. Mrs. Larsen is the mean teacher and she, Sonya, is the surly student. All Sonya has to do is roll her eyes and smack her lips. All she has to do is issue a sassy retort and the day will proceed as scripted. But she can't. Sonya's face contorts. Her lips tremble.

"What's wrong, baby?" Mrs. Larsen says. She strokes Sonya's hair, a surprisingly affectionate gesture coming from Mrs. Larsen. It reminds Sonya of her mother. "What's wrong with the baby?"

Finally it gives, the fort Sonya has built to protect her castle of lies. It splits down the center and out tumbles a tide of rocks and water. Sonya feels it—a salty river of tears streaming down her cheeks. She falls to her knees and hugs Mrs. Larsen around the waist.

"Awe, the baby," Mrs. Larsen says, stroking Sonya's hair. "The baby."

Sonya gives way to her grief. She unleashes the damn. She allows the river to flow and flow and flow.

★ ★ ★

Sonya feels like a valve attached to a pipe that is swollen with pressure. Gently, Mrs. Larsen's cooing and head rubbing turns the valve. The pressure, oh the sweet release of pressure. The story escapes Sonya's lips, seeping out like steam.

She does not tell Mrs. Larsen everything. Even in Mrs. Larsen's arms, kneeling in the empty hallway as she is, Sonya is alert enough to hold back some details. For example, she does not mention Madison, or the money or her kissing Law. She does not mention the slabs of heroin hidden behind the basement walls. She does not mention her mother's drug habit—only says she is away in rehab. From previous information, Mrs. Larsen assumes it is for alcoholism. Above all else, Sonya does not mention the baby.

Sonya does tell the most wounding part of the story, which is that Law has died. "My brother killed himself last night," she says.

"Awe, the poor baby," Mrs. Larsen strokes Sonya's head. And Sonya continues to reveal parts of her story, discharging the pressure in controlled gusts. She weaves her fictitious life as a tragic mulatto into the threads of her real life as the daughter of a heroin addict and the witness to a friend's suicide.

"Poor child," Mrs. Larsen says when Sonya finishes telling her tale. Sonya's body relaxes in Mrs. Larsen's arms. The soft scent of lilies wafts from Mrs. Larsen's powdered neck, which is creased and cracked with foundation. Sonya snuggles up against her, the most spiteful of all teachers at PLD, enemy turned friend. She feels the lull of a thousand nights of sleep.

"What on earth are you doing at school after all this?" Mrs. Larsen asks. Her eyes are round with sympathy.

"My therapist thought it was best," Sonya ad-libs a lie. She can't go home to Madison. She can't face the emptiness of the house with its death drone. She can't face the absence of her mother.

"Therapist?"

"Dr. Hillman. This guy my mother sends me to." Sonya pieces it all together. She will not have to struggle to remember these lies because they are a part of the truth.

"Guess your Dr. Hillman knows more about this stuff than I

do," Mrs. Larsen says. Then she rears her head back to look Sonya in the eye. "You sure you'll be okay?"

"I can manage," Sonya says, though she is not sure she can.

There is a clamor from a distant hallway, a chorus of voices and the shuffle-squeak of shoes across floor. "Here comes the Get-Along Gang now," Mrs. Larsen says.

Sonya stands and straightens her skirt. Mrs. Larsen grabs Sonya by her shoulders and pushes her away at arm's length. She looks Sonya up and down like a mother inspecting a daughter on her wedding day. Mrs. Larsen's eyes are full of tears. "I know about tragedy. Both my siblings and my parents died in a car crash when I was near around your age. And I know about the battle against liquor that your momma's fighting," she says. "I've been fighting it for years. She'll be okay though. We'll both be okay."

This moment of raw disclosure whips around them like twine, binding them in some unspeakable way.

"Now," Mrs. Larsen sighs and wipes a dribble of tears from her eyes. She hands Sonya a key. "You best to go to the teacher's bathroom down the hall and get yourself cleaned up. If anyone gives you shit, tell them to come see Larsen."

Sonya does just that. She walks down the hallway, a little lighter, a little less strained, to the teacher's bathroom. There she splashes her face with water and prepares to play host to Tandy, to Principal Carlton, to Kush and Maurice Maitland and all the ghosts of the Monday past.

34

. . . .

A second funeral

By the time she finishes in the bathroom, homeroom is over and class has already begun. Sonya approaches Mr. Davenvort's class. For once, every locker is closed and there are no students lingering in the hallway. The silence of the hallway pushes in on her from all sides. It is the stillness of a nightmare in which she is the last person left on the Earth.

This is a dream, Sonya thinks, seizing on this feeling. *Law has not killed himself. I haven't betrayed Tandy and Kush didn't break up with me. This is a dream. And I will wake up when I open the door to Mr. Davenvort's room.*

She holds her breath and opens the door, fully prepared to rouse from a fitful sleep.

What she finds on the other side of the door is not her bedroom, but a reality so banal it is shocking: a class of students, each sitting in his or her prescribed desk, staring up at her with wide silent eyes. As she scans the room, Sonya expects to find Tandy off to one side with her arms folded across her chest. She expects a scalding look from Tandy, or no look at all. Instead, Tandy is huddled with Celesta, Meeka and Lydia Grant. They exchange spicy whispers. Why is Celesta still speaking with Tandy? And what could they be whispering about? Much has happened, Sonya realizes, in the two days she's been out of school.

Lydia sits in the center of it all, her mouth open to an O.

Sonya had forgotten about Lydia Grant.

When Sonya enters, Mr. Davenvort doesn't make his usual speech about time being of the essence. He does not recite his little poem about "being properly prompt." Nor does he lecture Sonya for reinforcing the stereotype of CP time. Instead, he bows slightly and gestures toward the one empty seat in the room, which is next to Maurice Maitland.

"Now that we are all here—" Mr. Davenvort nods to Sonya "—let's begin today's lesson by tackling the ever evasive inverse."

Mr. Davenvort dashes off a series of equations, his large hands flashing the chalk sword-quick across the board. He gives instructions about page numbers and handouts. The class follows, turning pages in books and scribbling notes on paper. Sonya can barely follow what is happening. She is somewhere else, deep down below in a canyon, beneath miles and miles of fog. She barely notices Maurice Maitland sitting in the desk to the left of her. Surely he will retaliate today, she thinks. Maurice Maitland turns to look at her every now and again—a quick, assessing glance and nothing more. Sonya takes his silence as a type of truce. Perhaps he is asking for a stalemate, a cease-fire. Fine, Sonya thinks. She does not have the energy or concern to slap him again.

Or perhaps Maurice is biding his time, waiting till lunch where he will have a larger audience for his revenge. Either way, Sonya cannot muster up the energy to care. The canyon into which she has fallen is much too deep.

The class drones on. Sonya looks up from her half-hearted notes and catches Tandy's, Celesta's, Meeka's and Lydia's eyes on her. They stare and whisper. What can it be now? Sonya asks herself. It is likely that Tandy has found out Sonya's secret. Easy enough, Sonya thinks. All anyone had to do was look on the school records her mother filled out. They would see that Caucasian/White was checked for her race. Tandy might have done this. She might have quizzed Lydia Grant and found some detail that gave Sonya away. Perhaps she called Crestman, or visited while Sonya was on suspension. Tandy's anal enough. Injured enough. Perhaps Tandy ran into Samantha Klieg, who, out of her own spite, told Tandy everything. "See," Tandy would have said to Celesta and Meeka waving the evidence before their faces. "I knew that little cunt was up to something."

The group continues to whisper and stare—Tandy, Celesta, Meeka and Lydia. Sonya looks down at her notebook. It looks back up at her. Wavering across its blue lines is a jumble of numbers, letters and symbols, all indecipherable. Mr. Davenvort explains something about tangents. He recites a formula that can be found, he says, on page one-forty-seven.

Sonya closes her notebook. Fuck it, Sonya thinks of both the lesson and Tandy's sidelong glances. She can't bring herself to care anymore, about anything. Sonya gives up on the lesson completely and stares out the window at the shiny green grass.

She will leave today, after school. After school, Sonya will go from PLD to the Greyhound station. There she will purchase a ticket and get on a bus. To where, she has yet to decide. Where doesn't matter, as long as it is far from here.

Tandy says something which sends a flurry of whispers through the group.

No.

Sonya will not leave after school.

She will leave after class.

"Page one-forty-three through one-forty-five, ladies and gentlemen. Numbers one through seventy-seven." The class groans and Mr. Davenvort holds up his hands. "Odd numbers only. Use the back off the book to get the answers. Why?"

"Answers aren't important," a few students in the class recite in unison.

"Exactly." Mr. Davenvort smiles. "What do I want to see?"

"Process," they grumble.

The bell rings. The class ends. Sonya hustles her way to the front of the crowd and out the door. She does not wait to see if Maurice Maitland will dole out his revenge in the hallway. She will not wait to find out her mistake, the detail she forgot to cover, the detail, uncovered by Tandy that will indict her in the eyes of all of PLD. She will not wait for this indictment. She will leave today, right this minute.

Sonya's heart races as she weaves through the crowded hallway. "Soul Sista," someone yells. She does turn around to meet the owner of the voice. Instead she continues her quick stride, looking over her shoulder every now and then to measure the distance between her and Tandy. Already Sonya can feel the pressure of her child in her belly. It weighs her down.

Rounding the corner, Sonya comes upon her finish line—her locker. But her path is cut short. Something engulfs her—two dark, slender arms. A face presses against hers.

"I'm sorry, I'm sorry," the face says. "Oh my god, I'm so sorry I left you. I don't know what I was thinking. I don't know, Queen Woman. I'm so so sorry."

They all want an explanation. Though no one says this, this is what they are waiting for.

Sonya's escape was interrupted by Kush. Their hurried exchange in the hallway broke Sonya's momentum. Kush's hug and kiss made leaving seem less urgent. Suddenly, Sonya was no longer sure of her plan. "We'll talk at lunch," Kush said. Sonya's heart twirled. Being so obviously loved, as Kush said he did in the hallway, halted Sonya. She could not leave just then. Not after falling back into Kush's arms. Without a new plan to guide her, Sonya had nowhere to go but class, which she somehow made it through. The fog protected her, though Kush almost lifted her out of it, almost forced her up from her canyon onto the sharp, rocky edges of reality.

Now it is lunchtime and they have all gathered around the table—Tandy, Celesta, Meeka, Kush, and Lydia Grant. Even Maurice Maitland is there. No one says anything about Tandy being rich or Maurice having been pimped slapped. An unspoken asylum has been granted, given the gravity of this new situation.

This is not exactly what Sonya had in mind when Kush said he wanted to talk. But they are all here. What else can she do but explain?

"Well," Sonya says. It comes out as a sigh. She hunches her shoulders then lets them drop.

"Well," Celesta says. All of them lean in, ignoring the trays of lunch sat before them, except Maurice Maitland who chomps his food like a horse.

"Just get to the blood," Maurice Maitland says through a mouth full of Salisbury steak.

"Shut up fool," Celesta says. "Haven't you learned your lesson already."

A chorus of *oohs* comes from the table. Sonya knows other students have their eye on them. She, Maurice and Tandy are the popular kids, at the popular table, sharing the latest gossip.

"Law, my brother, was on medication," she says, "for depression. It runs in the family. But I think I told y'all that already."

"Law?" Maurice says. "What kind of name is that?" Sonya sees her slap had short-lasting effects with Maurice. He has gotten over his embarrassment and is back to his normal, brazen self.

Tandy nudges Maurice in the ribs. "Shut up!"

"I don't know," Sonya says, "that's just what we call him. Kinda because he is always—I mean was always so anal about stuff. Like he abided by every law or something. Either way, he hadn't been taking his medication. I kind of knew it but not really. I thought he had just been skipping a dose or two. Turns out he hadn't taken it in weeks, which was really bad."

"Weeks?" Lydia Grant shrieks her disbelief. "My cousin who was on Prozac hadn't taken her medication in three days and Ohmygod she was such a basket case I mean we had to like carry her out of the house into the mini-van and haul her all the way to the psych ward which was twenty-two miles away and I'd never seen her do some of—"

"Lydia baby—" Celesta places a hand on Lydia's shoulder "—this ain't your flashback. We'll do your cousin's story on the next episode."

Lydia nods heartily. "Oh, okay. Sorry, Sonya."

"That's fine," Sonya says. She takes in all the faces, their parted lips and expectant eyes. Kush sits next to her, patting her hand every now and again.

In the bathroom, as she washed up and prepared to face the day, Sonya had regretted telling Mrs. Larsen. Sonya thought Mrs. Larsen might tell the other teachers or use the information against her later. Instead, Mrs. Larsen, tottering with her morning sip of gin, announced to the entire homeroom that Sonya's brother committed suicide. "So don't say nothing stupid when the girl get in here, or Mrs. Larsen will have to get on you," Mrs. Larsen said. "Just act normal cause she's all busted up about it." By first period, the news spread through the entire school. Now, they all know.

So Sonya too has been granted asylum. Tandy has forgotten Sonya's coup. Kush has forgiven her for her temper tantrum. Even in death, Law has found a way to help Sonya. For this she is thankful.

"He shot himself," Sonya says now. "I walked in the door right after—" she glances up at Kush "—right after you dropped me off. Law was sitting on the couch. He said…" Her voice falters, tears stream down her face. She can barely manage the words. "He said he wanted me to see it. And then…"

"Bang!" Maurice Maitland says.

Celesta mushes his face. "Niggah damn. Shut up!"

"It's okay. It's okay," Sonya says, sniffling. Kush wipes the tears from her face. Tandy takes Sonya's other hand.

"You are so damn insensitive," Celesta say.

"Yes, dog," Lydia Grant says. "Chill out." Her voice is bright and airy and completely off-key. The gathering bursts into laughter.

"What?" Lydia says.

"We're going to have to give you some sister girl lessons," Celesta says.

Sonya laughs through her tears.

"You cool?" Meeka asks.

"I'm okay," Sonya says. "Really."

More than the fact of Law's death, it is her friends' empathy that harnesses Sonya's tears. She had been so caught up with leaving she had forgotten how good it feels to belong. Now she is not sure if she will stay or go.

"What about your mom?" Lydia asks.

"She's still away," Sonya says, "at rehab. My therapist thought it was best if we didn't tell her. He didn't want to interrupt her process. We've already taken care of the funeral stuff. It was quick. Private."

"We?" Kush asks.

"My uncle," she says to Kush. "He's back again." No one questions this.

"Is there anything we can do?" Tandy asks.

"No, I guess I'll just have to get through."

"You have to release him," Kush says, "the spirit of your brother."

"Yeah," Celesta says, "my granny taught me about that. You got to release them spirits, girl."

The circle closes in on her, growing warm with body heat. These are my friends, Sonya thinks of the group around her. These are my friends. How could I ever leave them? Still, Sonya is aware that tragedy has formed this moment. They have come to her out of pity. Like anything else, bereavement is temporary. A week later, maybe two, they will have forgotten about Law's death. Perhaps then Tandy will remember the betrayal, Maurice the slap, Kush the episode at the gallery.

The old yearning roils in Sonya, the yearning to belong, to be accepted, to be a part of the group. She must have these friends around her. They are the only true friends she has ever known. They are her family. Sonya can't leave now, just when things are turning around, almost back to normal. Sonya must seize this moment; she must bind them to her. She must offer them something. She must make it all right.

"I wanted to put together a second funeral," she says, improvising an idea.

"Somebody else died?" Maurice says.

"A second funeral for my brother," Sonya explains, "to celebrate his passage." Yes, a party funeral. With all her friends, and Zing and even Ngoya to show there are no hard feelings. Sonya will gather them all in her living room. At the stroke of midnight Sonya will announce her pregnancy.

"Ohmygod," Lydia says. "How totally weird. Celebrating someone's death. That's kind of freaky."

Kush pats Sonya's hand. "Like what slaves did in the old days," he explains to the others. "Slaves had to have a second funeral for the relatives who didn't have time to travel to the first one."

Sonya looks into his eyes. King Man, she thinks. Father-to-be.

"Not just slaves," Tandy says. "The Ashanti, the Xhosa and a lot of other African cultures practice second funerals. Death is seen as a rite of passage in these cultures. It's not only mourned. It's also celebrated."

Sonya's heart swells and her eyes, once again, fill with tears. Here, then, are her friends, surrounding her, supporting her. Here is Tandy, the black girl from the train, the one Sonya betrayed, back by her side. And here is Kush, Tandy's brother, Sonya's King Man. He smiles at her now and plants a kiss on her teary cheek. Both Tandy and Kush have pardoned Sonya for her earlier transgressions. If she can pull off this second funeral, fill their spirits with good times and cheer, then Sonya will be restored to her former glory and all will be forgotten.

Of course there is still Madison to deal with, and the money, and the blocks of heroin stashed behind the wall in the basement.

"I don't get it," Meeka says.

"Me either," Celesta says. "I mean, if you already had one funeral, why have another?"

"Once you've mourned," Tandy says, "you celebrate. Traditionally, you dress in red and white. There is food, a drumming circle and a—"

"You mean a party," Meeka says.

"Well," Kush says. "Basically."

Maurice Maitland looks up from his now empty tray. "A party!" he squeaks. His mouth is stained with ketchup. "I'm down."

35

Pity party

They zoom across the city from one venue to another. They hire drummers from the West End section of town. They buy ganja in College Park and pipes in Little Five Points. They procure decorations at a variety of boutiques in the East Atlanta Village. With each purchase, Sonya and Kush hurry back to her house and unload the car. They kiss excitedly. They are giggly and frantic.

Madison left early that morning. "I'm going on a little trip," he said, grinning slyly. "I'll be back early tomorrow morning with a little surprise for you." Madison's timing could not be worse. Sonya did not know what the surprise would be, though she had some idea. More than likely, Madison will bring in a new housemate, one of his partners from Tennessee or Alabama. He mentioned it the day after Law's death. "I got to get a new man in here," he said, "to tend my business. The show must go on."

As she and Kush unload the last of the party favors, Sonya thinks about this new roommate, whoever he might be. She'd gotten lucky with Law, for the most part. He respected her space and he didn't force himself on her. Had Sonya not manipulated him, flirted to get her way, she and Law could have lived in the house peacefully. Sonya ruined it. She knows this now. More than likely, Madison will bring in some scruffy, bearded, leather-clad hoodlum. Once again, Sonya will have to retreat to her room.

No matter. By the time of the new roommate, Sonya will have made her announcement. She will be spending her days at Tandy's house, surrounded by Zing and Kush and the NARC. In the traditional way of African births, Zing will pamper Sonya with sweet teas and soothing salves. Perhaps Kush will propose. Perhaps they will throw a rope over the house and pull it together like slaves did when they got married. Perhaps they will jump the broom.

Kush grunts under the effort of the heaviest box. Sonya moves to help him. He leans over the box and kisses her quickly on the check.

"I got it," he says.

Sonya knows other women have thought such things when they were pregnant. Other women have held similar wishes only to have them dashed by the father of the child. But Kush is different. He understands the sanctity of family. He will appreciate the gift of life growing inside of her. After all, he is her King Man.

Shortly after 9 p.m. the guests arrive in clumps, cooing and giggling as if they were attending a baby shower. Many bring gifts of bereavement and celebration, huge loaves of homemade bread, fruit baskets, ankhs and urns and baskets studded with tiger's eye and cowry shells. Sonya has seen many of the faces in the halls of PLD or in Nyahbinghi circle, but she has no names to connect to them. She plays the graceful hostess floating around in her blood red skirt, kissing guests on the cheek as they arrive.

A deliciously sly feeling curls itself in Sonya's throat, makes her chuckle every now and again. One-hundred-and-ten-thousand dollars in her locker at school, three slabs of heroin in the basement, a newly forming baby in her belly, unbeknownst to anyone in the room, and here she is having a party. She feels like a devious child, sneaking cookies from a high-up jar. She feels like a prankster placing a whoopee cushion on the teacher's seat.

Also, Sonya feels invincible. In the face of death and the absence of her mother, in the face of Madison leering words, "a surprise for you," he'd said, in the face of all these threats Sonya is having a party. A successful party at that. The guests have been served, the gifts have been stowed away. All that is left to do is to make the announcement.

From corner to corner, the house is filled with people. Her guests laugh and dance and eat heartily. Tandy and Celesta wave to her from the red couch.

"This African shit is good," Celesta yells and then forks up another piece of ox tail.

"That's Caribbean food girl," Tandy chuckles. Then, to Sonya, "It's going great."

"Thanks," Sonya says.

Kush produces a chalice and passes it around. Zing pours the ceremonial wine. The drummers beat their instruments. Sonya feels the reverberations in her chest, the raw, tribal beauty of the music. Tandy squishes between Kush and Sonya. She holds the ganja pipe to her lips and takes two quick puffs. The smoke escapes her mouth in a hacking cough.

"If you can't beat 'em," she says to Sonya between coughs, "join 'em."

Madison is on his way back with her new roommate. Slabs of heroin lay behind the basement walls. Thousands of dollars in stolen drug money sit in Sonya's locker at PLD. Tandy and Celesta unknowingly lean their heads at the very spot of Law's suicide. A baby, Kush's unborn child, grows in Sonya's belly. And here, now, around Sonya are all of her friends. Her family. Here is her second funeral.

Other attendees produce pipes and bottles and joints. Soon a cloud of marijuana smoke looms over the gathering. The sweet aroma of incense and the pounding of the drums, the dancing and singing, the eating and drinking fill Sonya with euphoria. Everything is perfect, right on cue. She moves to the center of the crowd. It is time to make her announcement.

36

....

Busted

Candlelight flickers over the walls. Incense fumes in intricately carved holders. The second funeral attendees settle down on couches, chairs and windowsills. Many sit on the floor. They form a circle three-rows deep, fifty-plus people. Lulled by food and wine, fatigued from singing and dancing, mellow with ganja smoke, they look to Sonya, who stands in the center. Their eyes are soft and eager.

The clock on the back wall reads half-past eleven. Sonya wanted to make her announcement at midnight, the transition from night to day. She thinks about waiting but decides against it. She wants to have this done before Madison arrives with her new roommate.

The blank space in Sonya's head does not bother her. She has felt this emptiness of mind before. Zing calls it a clearing, like a treeless space in a forest. This is how Sonya thinks of the blankness in her mind now. It becomes a clearing circled by trees. A place to build a speech, word by word.

The gist of the message is simple: I am pregnant with Kush's child. But Sonya wants to lead up to it with simile and metaphor.

She wants to build a cathedral of language, a space in which she and her attendees can adequately praise this gift of new life growing inside her.

Kush looks up to her with a wide grin. To the left of him is Zing. Just behind her is the crew: Tandy, Celesta, Meeka and Lydia Grant. Maurice Maitland sits on the arm of the couch occupied by Tandy. Even he is serious and attentive. Sonya stands in the center, closes her eyes and looks up to the ceiling. "All praises be to Jah," she says, her standard beginning.

Suddenly, she can see the words forming behind her eyelids, in her mind's eye. She can see the electrons of thought flitting and flickering, arranging into a pattern of speech. The light brightens. Sonya smiles.

"Where's that light coming from?" Maurice Maitland asks.

At first Sonya thinks Maurice is up to his usually prankstering. Then she opens her eyes to the gathering. Everyone rouses and murmurs. The living room is punctuated with flashing lights.

It happens quickly. The squeal of car tires on the street. Footfall as heavy a cinder blocks. Pounding. Boom! Boom! Boom! And the door caves in. A squad of men clad in black storm the room. Sirens blare. The gathering scatters. Women scream. Men push and shove. Platters of ox tail, plaintans, curried goat and black-eyed peas crash to the ground. The coffee table overturns, and then the dinning room table. A candle catches a curtain and the far left wall is ablaze. Sirens, bullhorns, fire and smoke. Sonya spies Tandy pressed against the wall by an officer. The officer snatches Tandy's hands behind her and slings cuffs around her wrists. Maurice, Zing and Lydia are on the floor, held at gunpoint. They lay face down with their hands behind their head. Celesta attempts to climb out of a window. An officer snatches her back. "Niggah, you better chill," she says, as he cuffs her.

Scuffling, grunts, cries, smoke and fire and chaos and Sonya stands in the center of it all. Celesta yelling. Lydia crying. Tandy as silent as death. Then the unthinkable, gunfire from the back room. A woman's wail. A horrible fall and a scream so loud it blinds.

Sonya searches the crowd frantically. Kush is nowhere to be found.

"Just keep it calm, Miss," an officer says to Sonya as he guides her hands behind her back. "Just keep it calm." Having run out of handcuffs, the policewoman zip-ties Sonya's wrists together.

37

. . . .

Surprise! Surprise!

The wagons shuttle them to the police station, two trucks and four carloads of Second Funeral attendees. At the station they are placed in holding cells. Some officers question Kush briefly about the packages he and Sonya unloaded in the house this morning, the packages for the party. But Sonya is the main culprit. It's Sonya they want to talk to.

"We've been detailing the house for some time now," Captain Henderson says. Henderson's heavy southern accent puts a twang in his voice. He is old, painfully so. He is almost as old as Dr. Hillman. Captain Henderson's face is pale and deeply lined like crumpled paper. "We know about Frank Blueport, the guy you call Madison. We know about Cecil Knox, his partner. Law, you call that fellow, though I don't know why. That guy's the furthest thing from lawful. He's committed more hits than the Braves."

"That's not saying much," says the rookie officer who sits in the corner chair behind Henderson. His eyes sparkle and his hair crowns his head in a bushel of blonde curls. The rookie winks at Sonya. He is twentysomething and obnoxiously attractive. A toothpick dangles from his mouth. Sonya is sure he placed it there just before she entered for dramatic effect. "Cecil Knox is one bad motherfucker."

"Cecil," Sonya says, touching her hands to her lips. "Cecil?" She conjures up Law's face from the recesses of her memory and places it in front of this name. It fits.

"Funny thing is, we haven't been able to locate Mr. Cecil Knox. Now how is that?" Henderson asks.

Henderson is stringing Sonya along, baiting her. That much is clear. So how much do they know? Do they know about the money? Her mother? Law's death? She imagines Henderson and the rookie cop watching in a car parked across the street as she loads the bags of money into the cab, snapping pictures as Madison disposes of Law's body.

Another question burrows deep in Sonya's gut: *Will I be tried for murder?*

Sonya's stomach lurches. "I'm going to…"

Henderson hands her a wastebasket. "Go ahead," he says. "Take your time. We have all night."

Sonya retches embarrassingly into the basket until her stomach is empty and settled. From outside the room it must sound like torture.

"What we don't know is your part in all of this," Henderson continues. "For all we know you could be the main man, the key distributor."

"Woman," the other rookie says.

They both laugh. They are surprisingly causal, Sonya thinks, given the gravity of the situation. Perhaps this is a part of their strategy.

"Man. Woman. You know what I mean. The minor stuff alone could land you in juvy. Possession of marijuana. Under-aged drinking. Noise pollution. Your neighbor called by the way. The drums were driving her two-month old crazy."

"Thanks for the party," the rookie says. "We wouldn't have had reason to enter otherwise."

Sonya touches her belly. Kush, she thinks. The new baby. She never got to make her announcement.

The other officer leans back and pats his own stomach. "Let's not forget the heroin."

"Ee-you-moe-jay," Henderson reads the name from a sheet of paper.

"Is that an alias?" the rookie asks.

"No," Sonya says. "It's Swahili."

"Like African?" the rookie says. "You African? I never met a white African before. What do they call y'all? Af-free-can-ers or something, right?"

Sonya feels the heat of anger rising in her face. Her eyes narrow. She's seen enough police dramas on television. She must keep her cool if she wants to get out of here without a hitch.

"Rupert, let me handle this," Henderson says to the rookie cop. But Rupert ignores him.

"We have a real live white African on our hands." He beats his chest and makes monkey noises, then laughs at his own joke. "You from that So-way-toe place over there?"

"I'm not African, jackass." Anger sizzles under Sonya's skin.

"Tough girl. Grrrr!" Rupert smiles. The toothpick falls from his mouth. He winks again. He thinks this is playtime. He thinks this is cute.

If the Ginsu knives were before her now, Sonya would carve out Rupert's eyes.

"Can it, Rupert," Henderson says.

"Grrr," he says once more then settles back in his chair.

"As far as we're concerned," Henderson says to Sonya, "you've been caught with enough heroin in your possession to make this a felony."

"It's not mine," Sonya says. "It's not mine."

"You're seventeen now," he glances down at the file, her file, Sonya realizes. She has a file with the police. "Sonya Crane, is it? Mother Doris Millbrook-Crane. Father, Michael Crane." He nods and closes the file as if satisfied. "You're seventeen now."

"One year in juvy and then it's straight to the pen." Rupert makes a locking sound. "The motherfucking slammer. Woo-wee!" He slaps his thigh. "A pretty young girl like you, fresh from the suburbs."

"Rupert," Henderson says.

"Patty chick," Rupert continues. "That what they call white girls like you. You'd be some muscle dyke's bitch. Serving her food, washing her feet. That's the big thing now, washing your bitch's feet."

"Rupert." Henderson waggles his finger. "I'm warning you."

"They even have a welcoming song. Sweet sweet patty meat," Rupert sings. "They'd eat you alive. Literally."

"Rupert," Henderson twangs, "I said can it!"

Sonya knows this is an act. They are double teaming her. The old good cop, bad cop routine. Despite it, she feels fear quaking through her bones. Sonya has heard stories of women having babies in prison. She does not want to be one of them. She does not want to go to jail. Her eyes sting out tears. Her stomach retches, but nothing comes up.

Henderson rubs her back as Sonya dry-heaves over the wastebasket. She looks down into her spittle, which covers a wad of Starburst wrappers. Lemon was Doris's favorite.

It is all over now, Sonya thinks. Kush, Tandy, Zing, Lydia. They wait in the holding cell but soon they will fade into the distance. Zing will get her family out by morning. She talked to her lawyer, one of the top in Atlanta. Most of the others have already been released. "I was just there for the party," they said. After questioning, after Henderson and Rupert were satisfied, they were allowed to go.

In the end, Sonya will stand alone.

"We see that you're a little shaken now," Henderson says. "So we're going to send you back to the holding cell. Give you time to think. I'll come for you in a couple of hours. Rupert here will be long gone by then," Henderson whispers. "I promise."

The holding cell is nearly empty now. Zing, Tandy, Celesta, Meeka sit on a bench against a far wall. Kush is on the floor next to them. Maurice Maitland leans against a back wall with his hands tucked deep into his pockets. A few NARC members lounge on benches. There are two or three other students from

PLD awaiting the arrival of their parents. When Sonya enters they rush to her.

Kush engulfs Sonya in his arms. "Are you okay?"

"No," Sonya says. "Not really."

"Girl, they kept you in that room forever," Celesta says. "I was scared you'd come out black and blue." Despite the raid and the handcuffs, they are all pretty calm. In the two hours Sonya was in questioning, they have had time to unruffle.

"My lawyer's on his way," Zing says. "He'll clear up this mess."

"I might be in for a while," Sonya says. She takes in the holding cell with its dull overhead light and pale green walls. Sonya shudders with the thought of spending ten or twenty years in a room just like this, a room an eighth of the size of the holding cell's size. "I think they have more questions for me."

"They can't hold you without probable cause," Tandy says.

"Unfortunately, they have that," Sonya says, "and more."

"You mean them drugs were yours?" Meeka says. "I swore they were crazy when they asked me about that."

"No," Sonya says. "The drugs don't belong to me. But I live in the house so..."

"What about the black thing tomorrow?" Celesta says.

"It's today," Tandy says looking down at her watch. "In about ten hours actually."

In all the turmoil, Sonya had forgotten about Festivale. There is no chance of her making her speech tomorrow. She'd probably still be in this cell staring about the puke-colored walls. Anyway, after all that has happened, what would she have to say.

"Guess y'all will have to cancel," Meeka says.

"Cancel," Kush says. "King didn't let imprisonment hold up his marches. That's just what The Man wants. That's probably why this whole thing went down. They probably planted those drugs. They are probably just waiting for a false confession."

"We won't have to cancel," Sonya says flatly. "Everything's already in place. The auditorium's been paid for. The food's coming. Only thing that will be missing is me." She sighs and realizes how fatigued she is. "Just tell me how it goes."

"This is kind of cool," Maurice says. "Now I have a record, like Tupac and Biggie."

"And they're both dead," Celesta says.

"We'll see what my lawyer can do," Zing says. "He's on his way."

Sonya knows Zing's lawyer won't be able to save her, especially if Henderson and Rupert find out about Law's death. She should have made her escape earlier, right after the blaze of Law's suicide. Instead she acted like a rich miser, running back into the flames of her mansion to save priceless works of art—her priceless friends. Sonya acted out of greed. With the money she stole from Madison, Sonya could have run to Mexico and made a new life for herself. She could have been free of her mother's habit and Madison's evil ways. But Sonya wanted more. In a way, she was just as bad as Doris, just as addicted. What Sonya craved was attention, friendship and popularity. The money wasn't enough. Freedom wasn't enough. Sonya wanted Kush, Tandy, Zing *and* the baby—a new family. Sonya wanted a huge party. She wanted recognition and belonging. Sonya wanted it all.

Sonya does not know how Madison disposed of Law's body, but surely Henderson and his cronies will find it. She'll be blamed. If not directly, they will convict her as an accomplice. After all, she did watch Madison scrub the blood off the wall. She watched Madison wrap Law's body in tarp and drag him down to the basement by his ankles. She doesn't know what Madison did from there, but he hid the body and Sonya consented. Sonya did not murder Law. Neither did Madison. But after the clean up and the disposal, and after Sonya failed to call the police the night of Law's suicide, who will believe her?

Jail, Sonya thinks. Prison. Rupert is right. She'll be raped and humiliated in jail. The other inmates will smell her weakness, the pungent, dried sweat of it. They will prey on her. Like a mangy mutt, Sonya will be housebroken.

There is, of course, another escape, one Sonya has not considered since Crestman. The scars of her first attempt still trace her wrist, however faint. Given a sharp edge, Sonya can reopen the old wounds. Not here, of course. Not now with Zing and the others in the cell. But if she is tried and convicted, Sonya will do it. She will take a sharp object to her wrists. She will cut herself open and slip out the back door into the oblivion of death.

An officer comes down the hallway, jangling and clacking with his keys and handcuffs. He casts stern eyes on the motley crew and nods to no one in particular. "Your mother's here," he says and then jangles back down the hall.

The remaining PLD students look up expectantly. Meeka walks to the front of the crowd and presses her face to the bars. Each of them expects his or her mother to round the corner.

From down the hallway comes a woman's voice intermingled with that of the officer's. Sonya can't make out the words, but the timber of the voice is familiar. The tap tap tap of footsteps brings the voices closer. As soon as she hears the sprightly click of heels Sonya knows the person wearing those heels is Doris.

Sonya's mother is here.

38
....

Strangers in the night

Downtown Atlanta passes swiftly outside the window. Skyscrapers loom like sentinels in the heavy blue night. It is three in the morning. In less than eight hours, members from every major black grassroots political organization will gather for Festivale. Sonya remembers this with a distant fondness. It is like recalling a coveted childhood toy lost to a house fire. From some recess of her brain, the theme of Festivale floats up: *Finding Self in a World That Others: The State of Race Relations in Black and White.* Sonya helped shape this theme with Kush, Zing and other NARC members. Tomorrow, at Festivale, she would have given a rousing, fiery, political speech, a speech that incited, a speech that motivated and moved. After bearing witness to the display Doris put on in the holding cell, after all that has happened tonight, Sonya cannot think of speaking at Festivale. What would she have to say?

Doris drives silently. Her clean, pink hands rest on the steering wheel. All that is left of her track marks are shadowy scars along her upper arm. There are rings on her fingers again. They glint in the moonlight. Every now and then Sonya glances over at her mother. It feels surreal sitting beside Doris. It is as if Doris is a mermaid who has swum up from the bottom of the sea to hand Sonya a pearl. Doris is back to her beautiful self. Her skin glows and her hair shines in its new short, asymmetrical cut.

On the way home from the police station, neither Doris nor Sonya mentions what happened in the holding cell. Like a fresh wound, that moment between them is too raw to touch.

She is back, Sonya thinks to herself, *my smart, confident mother.* She has survived her time with The Specialist. She is now drug-free. Since they exited the police station, Doris and Sonya have said nothing to each other. A silence as thick as soup spreads between them.

"I like the new hair," Sonya says now, puncturing the quiet. She hands over the compliment like an offering. It is the least she can do after what Doris did for her at the police station. Sonya reaches over to touch Doris's hair and then thinks twice. She remembers how much she hated it when Doris touched her hair.

"Thanks." Doris runs her hand over her head. "I pulled most of it out. Had to cut the rest." Doris says this not as a pitch for pity, but as a matter of fact.

"It suits you," Sonya says.

"Mmm," Doris says, and nothing more.

In the place where Sonya punctured it, the soupy silence bubbles and thickens. Doris doesn't speak about her time at The Specialist. She doesn't mention Sonya's new name or anything she's learned about Sonya's carryings-on while she was away. Instead she drives home flipping through the channels of the radio just as casually as if she were driving Sonya to school at Crestman.

From her purse Doris produces a pack of Marlboro Ultra Lights. She taps the pack, zips it opens and lights a cigarette, inhaling deeply. She closes her eyes briefly, drinking in the smoke of the cigarette.

Doris and Sonya sit beside each other, awkward and unspeaking, like uncles from opposite sides of the family. They have become strangers to each other. There is no sound in the car save the hum of the engine and the crackle of Doris's Marlboro.

"When'd you start that?" Sonya says about the smoking. She is relieved to have something to say.

"During treatment." Doris sucks down the last of her cigarette. She flicks it out of the window and then lights another.

"Why?" Sonya fans the smoke away from her face.

"The Specialist recommended it. You know, to curb my craving."

"Some treatment," Sonya says. She falls back on her usual surly devices. It is the only way she knows how to communicate with her mother. "Trade one habit for another," Sonya says. She intends to sound bratty. Instead she sounds condescending and judgmental.

Doris looks at Sonya. Her eyes are a hard clear blue. "Would you rather I go back to pumping my veins with smack?" she says with a Madison-like flatness. "Or can you bear the smell of a cigarette every now and again?"

Inside, Sonya winces. This is not the response she was expecting. She thought Doris would pout and give in, stub out the cigarette with a sigh. So, Sonya thinks, this is how The Specialist does it. Along with excising you of your addiction, he extracts a little of your soul.

Sonya was wrong when she thought she'd gotten her old mother back, minus the heroin. This woman sitting behind the steering wheel is not the mother she knows. Even the old Doris, the Doris prior to heroin, would have given some thought to Sonya's complaint. Sonya realizes she and Doris cannot simply take up their former roles. So much has changed since Crestman, since Doris went away and Sonya recreated herself. The script has been rewritten.

In the holding cell, Sonya listened to the clacking of Doris's heels on the cement floor. Each step seemed gunshot loud and just as fatal. Looking around the room, Sonya considered her possible escapes. She could hang herself if the window weren't so high, and if Zing, Tandy, Celesta, Meeka and Maurice were not there to stop her. There was no other door, save the bars in front, where Doris would appear at any moment. There was nowhere to run. If she bit hard enough she could gnaw her wrist open and hopefully black out from blood loss. Someone would patch her up before she was all the way gone. There were no pills or no bleach to drink, nothing that would work fast enough, before Doris finished the ten or so steps she had to the holding cell. Sonya could fling herself against a wall, knock herself unconscious.

The bars cranked open and Sonya stood face-to-face with a white woman in a crisp black business suit, a woman who looked so much like a paler version of herself there was no denying she was Sonya's mother.

"Oh baby," Doris folded Sonya into her arms. "Oh, Sonya are you okay?"

Sonya's body went cold with dread. Icy tears skidded down her cheek. To anyone else, they looked like tears of relief.

This is the end, Sonya thought. This is the end.

Over Doris's shoulder Sonya watched everyone watch her.

The first thing Sonya noticed about Doris was the voice. It was not her mother's normal voice at all. Even stoned, Doris never sounded as she sounded now. This new voice was high and light and false with worry. It was the voice of someone pretending. The second thing Sonya noticed was the name. To Doris, her name had always been Sonya? But Doris said *Sonya*. How could Doris know her as Sonya?

"You uncle Maddy told me *everything,*" Doris said. "Everything."

"You're Sonya's mother?" Zing asked.

Sonya opened her mouth to speak, but Doris interrupted.

"No, no." Doris waved her hands. "I get that all the time. I'm her aunt." Doris shakes Zing's hand.

"Sonya's mother…" Doris's lips trembled but she reined in the tears. "Sonya's mother hasn't been well for some time now." Doris looked at Sonya, "Though I hear she's getting better."

Doris shot Sonya a quick look. Sonya understood the message in Doris's eyes. In the last two years Doris had neglected Sonya. She had wrecked both their lives with her drug addiction. She had allowed Madison to molest Sonya, allowed him to traffic drugs in the basement, to move Law in who proved to be just as unstable as Madison himself. Now, Doris said with her eyes: this is my fault. Let me make this sacrifice.

One by one, Sonya snapped the pieces together in her head.

This was Madison's surprise, bringing Doris home. Doris was the new roommate Madison spoke of. Madison must have told Doris about Sonya's new life during their long ride from The Specialist. When Doris found the police at their home, she came here.

Vertigo grabs hold of Sonya's insides and flings them about. Everything in the room warps and bends. It has all happened so fast. One minute, Sonya stood in the center of a gathering to announce her pregnancy, the next minute, she was in jail facing a mother she had chalked up for dead.

"Are you okay?" Doris asked again.

Panic pulled the cords in Sonya's throat. She could barely speak or breathe. It took Sonya a second to find her voice, and several more to will her mouth to open. When she did finally manage—"I'm okay," Sonya said—she found her voice just as high and false and Doris's.

Doris guided Sonya by the shoulder. "I guess we better get out of here. Is everyone else okay?" Doris asked Zing. "Do I need to make phone calls or anything?"

"We'll be fine," Zing said.

Maurice flopped down on the bench and folded his arms. "Speak for yourself. I'm hungry and tired."

"Don't mind him," Zing said. "We'll make it. My lawyer's on his way with bail. Just be sure to take that one home so she can rest up for tomorrow's Festivale. She's the star of the show."

Doris opens the front door of the house wide like a ruffian busting into a saloon. The living room is wrecked with food and bottles, with shattered glass, with smashed lamps and overturned chairs. Sonya and Doris stand just inside the door surveying the disaster. A bubble of guilt rises in Sonya's throat. She had not planned on her mother returning from rehab to find the house like this. The chaos is an expanse, a desert or an ocean, into which both Doris and Sonya stare.

"Well," Doris says. Fatigue plays a sad song in her voice. Between her last day of rehab, riding home with Madison, and finding her daughter in jail, Sonya realizes it must have been a long day for Doris also.

"Sorry," Sonya mutters. She knows her apology cannot compare to the magnitude of the mayhem, but it is the only thing she can think to say.

"I've been stoned for three years straight." Doris shrugs her shoulders. "If you told me I left it this way I wouldn't know the difference."

A beat of silence passes and then they both laugh. It is the first time Sonya has seen her mother smile in two years.

Doris throws her arm over Sonya's shoulder. "I'll get some people in tomorrow to clean this up." Then she sighs. "This is my life," she says this more to herself than to Sonya. "This is my life and there is so much to do."

Sonya turns and falls into her mother's arms. "I'm sorry. I'm sorry," she says. "I'm sorry. I'm sorry. I'm sorry."

"Yes," Doris strokes Sonya's hair. "Yes. I'm sorry too."

39

....

The final cut

Downstairs Doris makes breakfast, scrambled eggs and toast, while Sonya dresses. Her hair shoots from her head in a thousand different directions. Last night she attempted to comb the twists out only to realize that many of them had locked beyond the point of combing. She has no idea what to do with it. For now, Sonya pulls her hair back into a ponytail. It is the only thing she can do.

Sonya slides into her distressed jeans and a plain white tee-shirt. Her Soul Sister skirts lay in a mound at the foot of her bed. When she purchased them, each one felt sacred. Symbolic. Now they appear to be exactly what they were for her: a costume, a pile of rags a child would use for dress-up. Sonya dumps the skirts into a plastic bag and carries them out to the trash.

Outside, Sonya helps her mother tap the *For Sale* sign into the front yard.

"It'll be gone by next week," Doris says of the house.

"Is that a brag?" Sonya asks.

"Not really," Doris says. "If there's no offer in a week,

Madison will buy it." She runs her hand along her arm. "It's the least he can do."

A brilliant sun dominates the morning sky. Trees offer up armloads of leaves, bouquets of deep, luscious green. All around the air is heavy with the sap of summer. Doris and Sonya whiz along the streets in the hushed interior of their car. Sonya squints her eyes against the sun. She feels like a blind person recently granted the gift of sight. Everything seems too bright, too crystal clear. It all seems fake: the sleek cars, the black asphalt, the gray concrete and blue sky, the bushes and trees and candy-colored houses with their perfects squares of green grass. Sonya knows it is real, just as the waking person can distinguish the nightmare from which they roused from reality. The haze Sonya has been living in for the past six months has been lifted. Today is the first day she has looked at the world, unflinching, through her own eyes.

California, Doris had said this morning. That would be their destination. Doris wanted to get started in real estate again, but in a place where no one knew her, a place far away from Madison and all of his temptation.

California. Sonya turns the idea of their imminent move over in her head. The only thing she remembers about California is an episode of *Moesha* when Brandy won a trip but her mother refused to let him go. Or was that *The Cosby Show* and Denise? Sonya laughs to herself. After watching all of those tapes of black television shows she still doesn't have her facts straight.

"Nervous?" Doris asks.

"I'm not sure what I am," Sonya says.

Doris places a hand on Sonya's knee. "We'll be moved in less than a month," she says. "You don't have to do this."

"Yes," Sonya says, "I do."

The auditorium is packed. In the end, NARC managed to sell eight hundred tickets. Vendors set up booths in the lobby. Sonya can hear a voice over the microphone inside. The program has already begun. Walking through the crowd of black people who are dressed in various shades of red, black and green, Sonya feels her old self-consciousness return. She is hyper aware of her pseudo-dreadlocked hair and her thin, olive skin. She looks at the dreadlocks of a vendor assembling an assortment of knitted caps. The woman's hair flows in dark tassels down her back. Sonya realizes even if she had continued to twist and wax her hair, she could never have pulled off dreadlocks. At most, Sonya's brown tresses would have produced a cheap knockoff of this woman's cords of hair.

Sonya directs Doris to an empty chair in the front row. Tandy, Celesta and the others have taken seats near the center. Sonya walks down the aisle of the auditorium toward the backstage area. Kush and Zing waiting for her there.

"There she is," Kush says. He grabs Sonya by the face and kisses her hard on the forehead. Sonya smiles tightly.

"We put Sergeant on the microphone to warm up the crowd," Zing says. "He's doing a horrible job."

"Ol' Sergeant," Sonya says absently. She had forgotten he even existed.

Kush looks down at Sonya's jeans and tee-shirt. "Don't tell me," he says. "You're trying to make a point? This must be a part of the speech."

"Something like that," Sonya says. She looks at Zing and Kush, two people who think they love her. The wet sponge of guilt sloshes in her chest. All at once, Sonya realizes the magnitude of her lie, the grand and shameful thievery of it.

Zing beams down on her. "Well," she says.

"Well." Kush breathes deeply and kisses Sonya once more on the forehead.

"You should take your seats," Sonya says.

Kush looks deep into her eyes. "You okay?"

"No," Sonya says and then taps her head with her finger. "But I've finally got my facts straight up here."

One final kiss on the cheek from Kush and Zing and then they exit. Sonya is alone in the greenroom. Just beyond the door is the stage on which she must stand and face a crowd of black rebels. In that crowd is Tandy, the black girl on the bus, the best friend she undermined for the sake of popularity. Also in that crowd is Zing, who hosted Sonya, acted as a friend and surrogate mother; and Kush, her King Man, the man who taught her most of what she knows about black culture and black consciousness. Doris is there too, Sonya's mother, who relinquished that title to rescue Sonya from disgrace. Sonya has lied to all these people, in one way or another. She has pilfered from a culture, she has stolen a race and an identity. She owes so many people so much. How can she ever repay them?

Sonya spots the pair of scissors on a nearby desk. She picks them up. They are paper scissors, the old kind, made entirely of metal. They feel cool and heavy in Sonya's hand. She touches the blade to the inside of her wrist. Not razor sharp, she thinks. But sharp enough for the task.

She paces the floor of the greenroom and slaps the scissors against her thighs. She could continue with her charade or she could use the scissors, end it all right now. Nervousness, like a bag of bones, rattles in her stomach. The exit sign over the fire door gleams bright red, inviting as a siren's song. Sonya ignores it. She has the scissors. They are all she needs.

At the mirror, she holds up a lock of tangled hair. With hands a steady as a surgeon, she cuts. Her hair falls away from her head as silent as snow. With each snip Sonya feels lighter, more liberated. Phrases from her previous speeches dash through her head. *Retribution,* she had said once. *Emancipation. Gentrification. White privilege. Fuck The Man!* The words dash through her brain and then vanish, leaving an empty vessel, a hollow chalice from which she will finally speak the truth.